UNDER THE DOME OF MARS

It was the biggest dome ever built, large enough to cover all of Marsport before the slums sprawled out beyond it. The dome covered half the city, making breathing possible inside without a helmet.

But it wasn't designed to stand stray bullets, and having firearms inside—except for a few chosen men—was a crime punishable by death!

Suddenly Gordon heard a noise . . . someone was shooting at him!

POLICE YOUR PLANET

LESTER DEL REY

A Del Rey Book

BALLANTINE BOOKS • NEW YORK

A Del Rey Book
Published by Ballantine Books

ISBN 0-345-29858-6

Manufactured in the United States of America

First Ballantine Books Edition: May 1975
Second Printing: November 1981

Cover art by David B. Mattingly

To JAMES BLISH
*Who understood the intent
despite the content.*

There were ten passengers in the little pressurized cabin of the electric bus that shuttled between the rocket field and Marsport. Ten men, the driver—and Bruce Gordon!

He sat apart from the others, as he had kept to himself on the ten-day trip between Earth and Mars, with the yellow stub of his ticket still defiantly in the band of his hat, proclaiming that Earth had paid his passage without his permission being asked. His big, lean body was slumped slightly in the seat. Gray eyes stared out from under black brows without seeing the reddish-yellow sand dunes slipping by. There was no expression on his face. Even the hint of bitterness at the corners of his mouth was gone now.

He listened to the driver explaining to a couple of firsters that they were actually on what appeared to be one of the mysterious canals when viewed from Earth. Every book on Mars gave the fact that the canals were either an illusion or something which could not be detected on the surface of the planet. Gordon lost interest in the subject, almost at once.

He glanced back toward the rocket that still pointed skyward back on the field, and then forward toward the city of Marsport, sprawling out in a mass of slums beyond the edges of the dome that had been built to hold air over the central part. And at last he stirred and reached for the yellow stub.

He grimaced at the ONE WAY stamped on it, then tore it into bits and let the pieces scatter over the floor. He counted them as they fell; thirty pieces, one for each year of his life. Little ones for the two years he'd wasted as a cop. Shreds for the four years as a kid in the ring before that—he'd never made the top, though it had taken enough time getting rid of the scars from it. Bigger bits for two years also wasted in trying his hand at professional gambling; they hadn't made him a fortune, but they'd been fun at the time. And the six final pieces that spelled his rise from a special reporter helping out with a police shake-up coverage through a regular leg-man turning up rackets, and on up like a meteor until he was the paper's youngest top man, and a growing thorn in the side of the government. He'd made his big scoop, all right. He'd dug up enough about the Mercury scandals to double circulation.

And the government had explained what a fool he'd been for printing half of a story that was never supposed to be printed until it could all be revealed. They'd given him his final assignment, escorted him to the rocket, and explained just how many grounds for treason they could use against him if he ever tried to come back without their invitation.

He shrugged. He'd bought a suit of airtight coveralls and a helmet at the field. He had enough to get by on for perhaps two weeks. And he had a set of reader cards in his pocket, in a pattern which the supply house Earthside had assured him had never been exported to Mars. With them and the knife he'd selected, he might get by.

The Solar Security office had given him the knife practice to make sure he could use it, just as they'd made sure he hadn't taken extra money with him beyond the regulation amount.

"You're a traitor, and we'd like nothing better than seeing your guts spilled," the Security man had told him. "That paper you swiped was marked top secret. When we're trying to build a Solar Federation from a world that isn't fully united, we have to be rough. But we don't get many men with your background—cop, tin-horn, fighter—who have brains enough for our work. So you're bound for Mars, rather than the Mercury mines. If . . ."

It was a big if, and a vague one. They needed men

on Mars who could act as links in their information bureau, and be ready to work on their side when the trouble they expected came. They could see what went on, from the top. But they wanted men planted in all walks, where they could get information when they asked for it. Trouble was due—overdue, they felt—and they wanted men who could serve them loyally, even without orders. If he did them enough service, they might let him back to Earth. If he caused trouble enough to bother them, they could still help him to Mercury.

"And suppose nothing happens?" he asked.

"Then who cares? You're just lucky enough to be alive," the agent told him flatly.

"And what makes you think I'm going to be a spy for Security?"

The other had shrugged. "Why not, Gordon? You've been a spy for six years now—against the crooked cops and tin-horns who were your friends, and against the men who've tried to make something out of man's conquest of space. You've been a spy for a yellow scandal sheet. Why not for us?"

It had been a nasty fight, while it lasted. And maybe he was here only because the other guy had proved a little faster with the dirtiest punches. Or maybe because Gordon had been smart enough to realize that Security was right—his background might be useful on Mars. Useful to himself, at least.

They were in the slums around the city now. Marsport had been settled faster than it was ready to receive colonists. Temporary buildings had been thrown up and then had remained, decaying into death-traps, where the men whose dreams had gone seethed and died in crowded filth. It wasn't a pretty view that visitors got as they first reached Mars. But nobody except the romantic fools had ever thought frontiers were pretty.

The drummer who had watched Gordon tear up his yellow stub moved forward now, his desire to make an impression stronger than his dislike of the other. "First

3

time?" he asked, settling his fat little carcass into the seat beside the larger man.

Gordon nodded, mentally cataloguing the drummer as to social, business, and personal life. The cockroach type, midway between the small-businessman slug and the petty-crook spider types that weren't worth bothering with. He could get along without the last-minute pomposity.

But the other took it as interest. "Been here dozens of times myself. Risking your life, just to go into Marsport. Why Congress doesn't clean it up, *I'll* never know! But business is business, I always say. It's better under the dome than out here, though. Last time I was here, they found a whole gang outside the dome selling human meat. Absolutely. And cheaper than real meat."

Gordon grunted. It was the usual untrained fool's garbled account. He'd heard about it on the paper. Some poor devil had taken home a corpse to a starving family out of sheer desperation. Something about the man having come out to Mars because one of his kids had been too weak for Earth gravity, to open a cobbling shop here. Then he'd fallen behind in his protection payments and had tried one of the cheap gambling halls to make good. The paper's account hadn't indicated what happened to the family after they hung him, but a couple of the girls had been almost pretty. Maybe they'd been able to live.

Gordon's mind switched from gambling to the readers in his bag. He had no intention of starving here— nor staying, for that matter. The cards were plastic, and should be good for a week or so of use before they showed wear. During that time, by playing it carefully, he should have his stake. Then, if the gaming tables here were as crudely run as an old-timer he'd known on Earth had said, he could try a coup. If it worked, he'd have enough to open a cheap-john joint of his own, maybe. At least, that's what he'd indicated to the Security men.

But the price of bribing a ship to take him back to Earth without a card came to about the same figure,

4

and there were plenty of ways of concealing himself, once he got back . . .

". . . be at Mother Corey's soon," the fat little drummer babbled on. "Notorious—worst place on Mars. Take it from me, brother, that's something! Even the cops are afraid to go in there. Seven hundred to a thousand of the worst sort—See it? There, to your left!"

The name was vaguely familiar as one of the sore spots of Marsport. Gordon looked, and spotted the ragged building, half a mile outside the dome. It had been a rocket maintenance hangar once, then had been turned into a temporary dwelling for the first deportees when Earth began flooding Mars. Now, seeming to stand by habit alone, it radiated desolation and decay.

Sudden determination crystalized in Gordon's mind. He'd been vaguely curious as to whether the Security boys would have a spotter on his movements. Now he knew what to do about it—and this was as good a spot to start as any.

He stood up, grabbing for his bag, and spinning the fat thighs of the suddenly squealing drummer aside with a contemptuous shove. He jerked forward, and caught the driver's shoulder. "Getting off!" he announced.

The driver shrugged his hand away. "Don't be crazy, mister! They . . ." He turned and saw it was Gordon. His face turned blank, even though there was no yellow card for his eyes to study now. "It's your life, buster," he said, and reached for the brake. "I'll give you five minutes to get into coveralls and helmet and out through the airlock."

Gordon needed less than that. He'd practiced all the way from Earth, knowing there might be times when speed in getting into the airtight clothing would count. The transparent plastic of the coveralls went on easily enough, and his hands found the seals quickly. He slipped his few possessions into a bag at his belt, slid the knife into a spring holster above his wrist, and picked up the bowl-shaped helmet. It seated on a plastic seal and the little air-compressor at his back began to hum, ready to turn the thin wisp of Mars' atmosphere into a barely breathable pressure. He tested the Marspeaker—an amplifier and speaker in another pouch, designed to raise the volume of his voice to a level where it would carry through even the air of Mars.

The driver swore at the lash of sound, and grabbed for the airlock switch. Gordon barely had time to jerk through the form-hugging plastic orifice before it snapped shut behind him. Then the bus left him. He didn't look back, but headed for the wreck of a building that was Mother Corey's.

He moved down unpaved streets that zig-zagged along, thick with the filth of garbage and poverty—the part of Mars never seen in the newsreels, outside the shock movies. Thin kids with big eyes and sullen mouths crowded the streets in their airsuits, shouting profanity. Around a corner, he heard yelling, and swung over to see a man beating a coarsely fat woman who was obviously his wife. The street was filled with people watching with a numbed hunger for any kind of excitement.

It was late afternoon, obviously. Men were coming from the few bus routes, lugging tools and lunch baskets, slumped and beaten from labor in the atomic plants, the Martian conversion farms, and the industries that had come inevitably where inefficiency was better than the high prices of imports. They were sick men, sick down inside themselves, going home to the whining of wives and the squabbling of their unwanted children; they were sicker because they knew themselves for failures, and could not deny the truth of the nagging accusations of their families.

The saloons were doing well enough, apparently, judging by the number that streamed in through their airlock entrances. But Gordon saw one of the barkeepers paying money to a thick-set rat with an arrogant sneer, and he knew that the few profits from the cheap beer were never going home with the owner. Storekeepers in the cheap little shops had the same lines on their faces as they saw on the faces of their customers.

Poverty and misery were the keynotes here, rather than the vicious evil half-world the drummer had babbled about. But to Gordon's trained eyes, there was plenty of outright rottenness, too. There were the young punks on the corners, eyeing him as he passed, and the furtive glances of women coming out early to begin their emotionless rounds. Here and there, men with the ugly smirks of professional tough guys lounged in front of taverns or barber-shops. Gordon passed a rickety old building where a group inside were shooting craps or working on their knives and bludgeons. If it was a gang hideout, there was no hiding involved. He saw two policemen, in what seemed like normal police clothes except for their bowl-helmets; the aspirators and speakers were somehow built in, and unnoticeable. But they passed the hideout without a look, and stalked down the street while sullen eyes followed them.

He grimaced, grateful that the supercharger on his airsuit filtered out some of the smell which the thin air carried. He had thought he was familiar with human misery from his own Earth slum background. But there was no attempt to disguise it here—no vain flowers withering in windows, no bravado from anyone who was growing up to leave all this behind. This was dead end.

It grew quiet then, until he could hear the hissing of the compressor in his suit. Life here would depend on that sound. Great atomic machines had been digging through the Martian deserts for nearly a century, cracking oxygen out of the red sands. But the air was still too thin to breathe without compression.

The crowded streets thinned out now, and the buildings were older—so battered and weathered that not even the most abject wage-earner could stand them. A few diseased beggars lounged about, and a scattering of too-purposeful men moved along. But it was a quiet section, where toughness was taken for granted, and no smirk was necessary to prove a man's rise to degradation.

Ahead, Mother Corey's reared up—a huge, ugly half cylinder of pitted metal and native bricks, showing the patchwork of decades, before repairs had been abandoned. There were no windows, though there had once been. And the front was covered with a big sign that spelled out *condemned*, in mockery of the tattered shreds that had once been an official notice. The airseal was filthy, and there was no bell.

Gordon kicked against the side, waited, and kicked again. A slit opened and closed. He waited, then drew his knife and began prying at the worn cement around the airseal, looking for the lock that had once been there.

The seal suddenly quivered, indicating the metal inside had been withdrawn. Gordon grinned tautly, stepped through, and pushed the blade against the inner plastic.

"All right, all right," a voice whined out of the darkness. "You don't have to puncture my seal. You're in."

"Then call them off!"

A wheezing chuckle answered him, and a phosphor bulb glowed weakly, shedding some light on a filthy hall that led to rickety steps, where four men stood ready to jump downward on the intruder. "Okay, boys," the voice said. "Come on down. He's alone, anyhow. What's pushing, stranger?"

"A yellow ticket," Gordon told him. "A yellow ticket and a Government allotment that'll last me two weeks in the dome. I figure on making it last six here, until I can shake down and case the lay. And don't let my being a firster give you hot palms. My brother was Lanny Gordon!"

That happened to be true, though he hadn't seen his brother from the time the man had left the family as a young punk to the day they finally convicted him on his tenth murder and gave him the warming bench for a twenty-first birthday present. But here, if it was like places he'd known on Earth, even second-hand contact with "muscle" was useful.

It seemed to work. A fat hulk of a man oozed out of the shadows, his gray face contorting its doughy fat into a yellow-toothed grin, and a filthy hand waved back the other men. There were a few wisps of long,

8

gray hair on the head and face, and they quivered as he moved forward.

"Looking for a room?" he whined.

"I'm looking for Mother Corey."

"Then you're looking at him, cobber," the grotesque lump of flesh answered. "Sleep on the floor, want a bunk, squat with four, or room and duchess to yourself?"

There was a period of haggling then, followed by a wait as Mother Corey kicked four grumbling men out of a four-by-seven hole on the second floor. Gordon's money had carried more weight than his brother's reputation, and for that Corey was willing to humor his insane wish to be completely by himself, even. He spread a hand out coarsely. "All yours, cobber, while your crackle's blue."

It was a filthy, dark place. In one corner was an unsheeted bed. Marks on the floor showed where another had been beside it, to house another couple before. There was a rusty bucket for water, a filthy sink, with a can on the floor for waste water, and a disposal pail that had apparently been used only as a chair, from the looks and smell of the place. Plumbing and such luxuries hadn't existed for years, except for the small cistern and worn water recovery plant in the basement, beside the tired-looking weeds in the hydroponic tanks that tried unsuccessfully to keep the air breathable.

"What about a lock on the door?" Gordon asked.

"What good would it do you? Got a different way here, we have. One credit a week, and you get Mother Corey's word nobody busts in. And it sticks, cobber—one way or the other."

Gordon paid, and tossed his pouch on the filthy bed. With a little work, the place could be cleaned enough, and he had a strong stomach. Eating was another matter—there was a section in the back where thermocapsules could be used to heat food, but . . .

He pulled the cards out of his pouch, trying to be casual. Mother Corey stood staring at the pack while Gordon changed out of his airsuit, retching faintly as the full effluvium of the place hit him. "Where does a man eat around here?" he asked.

Mother Corey pried his eyes off the cards and ran a thick tongue over heavy lips. "Eh? Oh. Eat. There's a place about ten blocks back. Cobber, stop teasing me! With elections coming up and the boys loaded with vote money back in town—with a deck of cheaters like that—you want to *eat?*"

He picked the deck up and studied the box fondly, while a faraway look came into his clouded eyes. "Same ones—same identical ones I wore out nigh thirty years ago. Smuggled two decks up here. Set to clean up—and I did, for a while." He shook his head sadly, making the thin hairs wave wildly around his jellied jowls and head, and handed the deck back to Gordon. "Come on down. For the sight of these, I'll give you the lay for your pitch. And when your luck's made or broken, remember Mother Corey was your friend first, and your old Mother can get longer use from them than you can."

He waddled off, trailing a cloud of garbage odors and telling of his plans to take Mars for a cleaning, once long ago. Gordon followed him, staring at the filth around him. Corey's plans had been about the same as his present ones, and this was the result: landlord of a crumbling pile of decay, living beyond the law, and growing old among crooks and riff-raff.

He grimaced. Ten days! He wouldn't make the mistake of being too greedy. Ten days, and then he'd make his big pitch.

His thoughts were churning so busily that he didn't see the blond girl until she had forced her way past them on the stairs. Then he turned back, but she had vanished into one of the rooms. Anyhow, this was Mars, and Gordon had no time for by-paths now. Mars! He spat into the moldy dust on the floor and hurried after Mother Corey.

II

A lot could be done in ten days, when a man knew what he was after and hated to go back to the place he called home. It was exactly ten days later when Gordon stood in the motley crowd inside the barnlike room where Fats ran a bar along one wall and filled the rest of the space with assorted tables, all worn. Gordon was sweating slightly as he stood at the roulette table where both zero and double-zero were reserved for the house.

The croupier was a little wizened man wanted on Earth for murder, but not important enough to track down to Mars. Now it seemed as if he'd soon be wanted here for more of the same, from the looks he was giving the big, dark man who faced him. His eyes darted down to the point of the knife that showed under Gordon's sleeve, and he licked his lips, showing snaggle teeth. The wheel hesitated and came to a halt, with the ball trembling in a pocket.

"Twenty-One wins again," he mouthed, and pushed chips across toward Gordon, as if every one of them came out of his own pay. "Place your bets." The words were automatic, now no more than a conditioned reflex.

Two others around the table watched narrowly as Gordon left his chips where they were; they reached for their own chips, then exchanged looks and shook their heads. In a Martian roulette game, numbers with that much riding just didn't turn up. Some of the others licked eager lips, but the croupier gave them no time. It was bad enough without more riding on it. Sweat stood out on his head, and he shifted his weight, then caught the wheel and spun it savagely.

Gordon's leg ached from his strained position, but he

shifted his weight onto it more heavily, and new spots of sweat popped out on the croupier's face. His eyes darted down, to where the full weight of Gordon seemed to rest on the heel that was grinding into his instep. His eyes flicked to the knife point. But there was some degree of loyalty in him toward Fats Eller. He tried to pull his foot off the button that was concealed in the floor.

The heel ground harder, bringing a groan from him. And the ball hovered over Twenty-One and came to rest there once more.

Slowly, painfully, the little man counted stacks of chips and moved them across the table toward Gordon, his hands trembling. The sweat began to dry now, and his tongue darted across his broken teeth in a frenzy.

Gordon straightened from his awkward position, drawing his foot back, and reached out for the pile of chips. For a second, he hesitated, watching the little man fidget, while he let the knife blade slide out another quarter inch from his sleeve. Then he scooped it up and nodded. "Okay," he decided. "I'm not greedy."

The strain of watching the games until he could spot the fix and then holding the croupier down had left him momentarily weak, but he still could feel the tensing of the crowd. Now he let his eyes run over them—the night citizens of Marsport, lower dome section. Spacemen who'd missed their ships, men who'd come here with dreams, and stayed without them—the shopkeepers who couldn't meet their graft and were here to try to win it on a last chance, street women and petty grifters —those who believed that a rude interior meant a more honest wheel and those who no longer cared, until their last cent was gone. The air was thick with the smell of their unwashed bodies—all Mars stank, since water was still too rare for frequent bathing—and their cheap perfume, while the air was clouded with Marsweed cigarettes. But thicker than that was a hunger over them—something demanding excitement, and now about to be fed.

Gordon swung where their eyes pointed, until he saw Fats Eller sidling through the groups. The sour-faced, pudgy man wasn't happy about the turn of events. His face showed that, together with determination to do something.

Gordon let the knife slip into the palm of his hand as the crowd seemed to hold its breath. Fats stared at it with a half-contemptuous sneer, but made no move to come closer. He plucked a sheaf of Martian banknotes from his pocket and tossed them to the croupier.

"Cash in his chips," he ordered harshly. Then his pouchy eyes turned to Gordon. "Get your money, punk, and get out! And stay out!"

For a moment, as he began pocketing the bills, Gordon thought he was going to get away that easily. Fats watched him dourly, then swung on his heel, just as a shrill, strangled cry went up from someone in the crowd.

The deportee let his glance jerk to it, then froze. His eyes caught the sight of a hand pointing behind him, and he knew it was too crude a trick to bother with. But he paused, shocked to see the girl he'd seen on Mother Corey's stairs, gazing at him in well-feigned warning. She looked like a blond angel who had been out in the rain just long enough to begin tarnishing. But on her, the brassiness of her hair and the too-experienced pout of her lips looked almost good. Or it could have been the contrast with the blowsy women around her. Her figure ... In spite of his better judgment, it caught his eyes and drew them down over curves and swells that might be too ripe for Earth fashion, but would always be right for arousing a man's passion.

Then he ripped his eyes back to Fats, who had started to turn again. Gordon took a step backward, preparing to duck. And again the girl's finger motioned behind him. He disregarded it—and realized suddenly that his action was a mistake.

It was the faintest swish in the air that caught his ear, and he brought his shoulders up and his head down, just as the sap struck. Fast as his reaction was, it was almost too late. The weapon crunched against his shoulder and slammed over the back of his neck, almost knocking him out. But he held his grip on himself.

His heel lashed back and caught the shin of the man behind him. His other leg spun him around, still crouching, and the knife in his hand started coming up, sharp edge leading, and aimed for the belly of the bruiser who confronted him. The pug-ugly saw the blade, and a thick animal sound gurgled from his mouth, while he tried to check his lunge.

Gordon felt the blade strike, but he was already pulling his swing, and it only sank half an inch, gashing a long streak that crimsoned behind it. The thug shrieked hoarsely and fell over. That left the way clear to the door, where the bouncer had been stationed. Gordon was through it and into the night in two soaring leaps. After only a few days on Mars, his legs were still hardened to Earth gravity, so he had more than a double advantage over the others.

Outside, it was the usual Martian night in the poorer section of the dome, which meant it was nearly dark. Most of the street lights had never been installed—graft had eaten up the appropriations, instead—and the nearest one was around the corner, leaving the side of Fats' Place in the shadow. Gordon checked his speed, threw himself flat, and rolled back against the building, just beyond the steps that led to the street.

Feet pounded out of the door above as Fats and the bouncer broke through. Gordon's hand had already knotted a couple of coins in his kerchief. He waited until the two turned uncertainly up the street and tossed it. It struck the wall near the corner, sailed on, and struck again at the edge of the unpaved street with a muffled sound.

Fats and the other swung, just in time to see a bit of dust where it had hit. "Around the corner!" Fats yelled. "After him, and shoot!"

In the shadows, Gordon jerked sharply. It was rare enough to have a gun here. But to use one inside the dome was unthinkable. His eyes shot up, where the few dim lights were reflected off the great plastic sheet that was held up by the air pressure and reinforced with heavy webbing. It was the biggest dome ever built, large enough to cover all of Marsport before the slums sprawled out beyond it; it still covered half the city, making breathing possible here without a helmet. But it wasn't designed to stand stray bullets, and having firearms inside it, except for a few chosen men, was a crime punishable by death.

Fats had swung back and was now herding the crowd inside his place. He might have been only a small gambling-house owner, but within his own circle his words carried weight. They stayed inside, and the door shut behind them, sealing tightly as doors always sealed, even under the dome.

Gordon got to his hands and knees and began crawling away from the corner. He came to a dark alley, smelling of decay where garbage had piled up without being carted away. He turned into it, stumbling over a woman busy rolling a drunk. She darted to the end of the alley, and he moved after her more slowly. Beyond lay a lighted street, and a sign that announced *Mooney's Amusement Palace—Drinks Free to Patrons!* He snapped a look up and down the street, and walked briskly toward the somewhat plusher gambling hall there. Fats couldn't touch him in a competitor's place.

For a second, he thought he heard steps behind him, but a quick glance back showed nothing. Then he was inside Mooney's, and heading quickly for the dice table.

He lost steadily on small bets for half an hour, admiring the skilled palming of the "odds" cubes. The loss was only a tiny dent in his new pile, but he bemoaned it properly, as if he were broke, and moved over to the bar. This one had seats. The bartender had a consolation boilermaker waiting for him, and he gulped half of it down before he realized the beer had been needled with ether. The tastes here were on the rugged side.

Beside him, a cop was drinking the same, slowly, watching another policeman at a Canfield game. He was obviously winning, and now he got up and came over to cash in his chips.

"You'd think they'd lose count once in a while," he complained to his companion. "But nope—fifty even a night, no more . . . Well, come on, Pete, we'd better get back to Fats and tell him the swindler got away."

Gordon followed them out and turned south, down the street toward the edge of the dome and the entrance where he'd parked his airsuit and helmet. He kept glancing back whenever he was in the thicker shadows, but there seemed to be no one following him, in spite of the itching at the back of his neck.

At the gate of the dome, he glanced back again, then ducked into the locker building. The money in his pockets seemed heavier now—something that kept worrying him with every step. For a minute, he debated going back to register at one of the better hotels in Marsport Center. But too many stories came into his head. He wasn't clothed for it, and the odor of bathless living in Mother Corey's still clung to him. He'd be immediately suspected there, and it wasn't too hard to bribe one's way into a room. A bum with money had more chances in a place like Mother Corey's—where the grotesque hulk that ruled the roost apparently lived up rigidly to the one ethic of his given word.

He threaded through the maze of the lockers with his knife ready in his hand, trying not to attract suspicion. At this hour, though, most of the place was empty. The crowds of foremen and delivery men who'd be going in and out through the day were lacking, and there were only a few who crossed the line from the dome to the slums.

He found his suit and helmet and clamped them on quickly, transferring the knife to its spring sheath outside the suit. He checked the little batteries that were recharged by tiny generators in the soles of the boots with every step. Then he paid his toll for the opening of the private slit and went through, into the darkness outside the dome.

Lights bobbed about—police in pairs patrolling in the better streets, walking as far from the houses as they could; a few groups, depending on numbers for safety; some of the very poor, stumbling about and

16

hoping for a drink somehow, sure they had nothing to lose; and probably hoods from the gangs that ruled the nights here.

Gordon left his torch unlighted, and moved along; there was a little light from the phosphorescent markers at some of the corners, and from the stars. He could just make his way without marking himself with a light. And he'd be better able to see any light following him.

Damn it, he should have hired a few of the younger bums from Mother Corey's—though that might have been inviting robbery instead of preventing it.

Here he couldn't hear footsteps, he realized. He located a pair of patrolling cops and followed them down one street, until they swung off. Then he was on his own again.

"Gov'nor!" The word barely reached him, and he jerked around, the knife twitching into his hand. It was a thin kid of perhaps twenty years behind him, carrying a torch that was filtered to bare visibility. It swung up, and he saw a pock-marked face that was twisted in a smile meant to be ingratiating.

"You've got a pad on your tail," the kid said, again as low as his amplifier would permit. "Need a convoy?"

Gordon studied him briefly, and grinned. Then his grin wiped out as the kid's arm flashed to his shoulder and back, a series of quick jerks that seemed almost a blur. Four knives stood buried in the ground at Gordon's feet, forming a square—and a fifth was in the kid's hand.

"How much?" Gordon asked, as the kid scooped up the blades and shoved them expertly back into shoulder sheaths. The kid's hand shaped a C quickly, and Gordon slipped his arm through a self-sealing slit in the airsuit and brought out two hundred-credit bills.

"Thanks, gov'nor," the kid said, stowing them away. "You won't regret it." He swung his dim light down, and Gordon started to turn. Then the kid's voice rose sharply to a yell.

"Okay, honey, he's the Joe!"

Out of the darkness, ten to a dozen figures loomed up. The kid had jumped aside with a lithe leap, and now stood between Gordon and the group moving in for the kill. Gordon turned to run, and found himself surrounded. His eyes flickered around, trying to spot something in the darkness that would give him shelter.

A bludgeon was suddenly hurtling toward him, and he ducked it, his blood thick in his throat and his ears ringing with the same pressure of fear he'd always known just before he was kayoed in the ring. But pacifism would do him no good. He selected what he hoped was the thinnest section of the attackers and leaped forward. With luck, he might jump over them, using his Earth strength.

There was a flicker of dawn-light in the sky, now, however; and he made out others behind, ready for just such a move. He changed his lunge in mid-stride, and brought his arm back with the knife. It met a small round shield on the arm of the man he had chosen, and was deflected at once.

"Give 'em hell, gov'nor," the kid's voice yelled, and the little figure was beside him, a shower of blades seeming to leap from his hand in the glare of his now bare torch. Shields caught them frantically, and then the kid was in with a heavy club he'd torn from someone's hand.

Gordon had no time to consider his sudden traitor-ally. He bent to the ground seizing the first rocks he could find, and threw them. One of the hoods dropped his club in ducking, and Gordon caught it up and swung in a single motion that stretched the other out.

Then it was a mêlée. The kid's open torch, stuck on his helmet, gave them light enough, until Gordon could switch on his own. Then the kid dropped behind him, fighting back-to-back. Something hit his arm, and Gordon switched the club to his left, awkwardly. He caught a blow on the shoulder, and kicked out savagely as someone lunged for his feet. Here, in close quarters, the attackers were no longer using knives. One might be turned on its owner, and a slit suit meant death by asphyxiation.

Gordon saw the blond girl on the outskirts, her face

taut and glowing. He tried to reach her with a thrown club wrested from another man, but she leaped nimbly aside, shouting commands. Nobody paid any attention, and she began moving in cautiously, half-eager and half-afraid.

Two burly goons were suddenly working together. Gordon swung at one, ducked a blow from the other, and then saw the first swinging again. He tried to bring his club up—but he knew it was too late. A dull weight hit the side of his head, and he felt himself falling. This was it, he thought. They'd strip him or slash his suit—and he'd be dead without knowing he had died. He tried to claw his way to his feet, hearing a ghost-voice from his past counting seconds. Then he passed out.

It took only minutes for dawn to become day on Mars, and the sun was lighting up the messy section of back street when Gordon's eyes opened and the pain of sight struck his aching head. He groaned, then looked frantically for the puff of escaping air. But his suit was still sealed. Ahead of him, the kid lay sprawled out, blood trickling from the broken section of an ugly bruise along his jaw.

Then Gordon felt something on his suit, and his eyes darted to hands just finishing an emergency patch. His eyes darted up and met those of the blond vixen!

Amazement kept him motionless for a second. There were tears in the eyes of the girl, and a sniffling sound reached him through her Marspeaker. Apparently, she hadn't noticed that he had revived, though her eyes were on him. She finished the patch, and ran perma-sealer over it. Then she began putting her supplies away, tucking them into a bag that held notes that could only have been stolen from his pockets—her share of the loot, apparently.

He was still thinking clumsily as she rose to her feet and turned to leave. She cast a glance back, hesitated, and then began to move off.

He got his feet under him slowly, but he was reviving enough to stand the pain in his head. He came to his feet, and leaped after her. In the thin air, his lunge was silent, and he was grabbing her before she knew he was up.

She swung with a single gasp, and her hand darted down for her knife, sweeping it up and toward him. He barely caught the wrist sweeping forward. Then he had her firmly, bringing her arm back and up until the knife fell from her fingers.

She screamed and began writhing, twisting her hard young body like a boa constrictor in his hands. But he was stronger. He bent her back over his knee, until a mangled moan was coming from her speaker. Then his foot kicked out, knocking her feet out from under her. He let her hit the ground, caught both her wrists in his, and brought his knee down on her throat, applying more pressure until she lay still. Then he reached for the pouch.

"Damn you!" Her cry was more in anguish than it had been when he was threatening to break her back. "You damned firster, I'll kill you if it's the last thing I do. And after I saved your miserable life . . ."

"Thanks for that," he grunted. "Next time don't be a fool. When you kill a man for his money, he doesn't feel very grateful for your reviving him."

He started to count the money. About a tenth of what he had won—not even enough to open a cheap poker den, let alone bribe his way back to Earth.

The girl was out from under his knee at the first relaxation of pressure. Her hand scooped up the knife, and she came charging toward him, her mouth a taut slit across half-bared teeth. Gordon rolled out of her swing, and brought his foot up. It caught her squarely under the chin, and she went down and out.

He picked up the scattered money and her knife, then made sure she was still breathing. He ran his hands over her, looking for a hiding place for more money. It produced no sign of that, though he felt other results inside himself. The witch was exciting enough, even when out cold. For a moment, he debated reviving her, and then shrugged. She'd come to soon enough. If he bothered with her, it would only lead to more trouble. He'd had enough.

"Good work, gov'nor," the kid's thin voice approved, and he swung to see the other getting up painfully. The kid grinned, rubbing his bruise. "No hard feelings, gov'nor, now! They paid me to stall you, so I did. You bonussed me to protect you, and I bloody well tried. Honest Izzy, that's me. Gonna buy me a job as a cop now, why I needed the scratch. Okay, gov'nor?"

Gordon hauled back his hand to knock the other from his feet, and then dropped it. A grin writhed onto his face, and broke into sudden grudging laughter.

"Okay, Izzy," he admitted. "For this stinking planet, I guess you're something of a saint. Come on along, and we'll both apply for that job—after I get my stuff."

He might as well join the law. He'd tried gambling—and the cheaters were gone, while he'd be watched for at every gambling house crude enough to use such a fix on the wheel. He'd had his try at fighting, and found that one man wasn't an army. Reporting was closed to him permanently, on all the worlds. And that left only his experience as a cop.

Anyhow, it looked as if Security had him trapped on Mars. They wanted him to police their damned planet for them—and he might as well do it officially.

He tossed the girl's knife down beside her, motioned to Izzy, and began heading for Mother Corey's.

III

Izzy seemed surprised when he found Gordon was turning in to the quasi-secret entrance to Mother Corey's. "Coming here myself," he explained. "Mother got ahold of a load of snow, and sent me out to contact a big pusher. Coming back, the goons picked me up and gave me the job on you. Hey, Mother!"

Gordon didn't ask how Mother Corey had acquired the dope. Probably someone had been foolish enough not to pay for the proprietor's guarantee of protection and had regretted it briefly. When the Government had deported all addicts to Mars two decades before, it had practically begged for dope smuggling—and had gotten it.

The gross hulk of Mother Corey appeared almost at once. "Izzy and Bruce. Didn't know you'd met, cobbers. Contact, Izzy?"

"Ninety percent for uncut," Izzy answered, and the puttylike old man nodded, beaming and rubbing filthy hands together.

They went up to Gordon's hole-in-the-wall, with Mother Corey wheezing behind, while the rotten wood of the stairs groaned under his grotesque bulk. At his questions, Gordon told the story tersely.

Mother Corey nodded. "Same old angles, eh? Get enough to do the job, they mug you. Stop halfway, and the halls are closed to you. Pretty soon, they'll be trick-proof, anyhow. In my day, the wheels had hand brakes, and a croop had to be slick about it to stop right. Now they're changing over to electric eyes. Eh, you haven't forgotten me, cobber?"

Gordon hadn't. The old wreck had demanded five percent of his winnings for tipping him off. And even if it meant cutting his small stake to half now, he still had to pay it. Mother Corey had too many cheap hoods among his friends to be fooled with. He counted out the money reluctantly, while Izzy explained that they were going to be cops.

The old man shook his head, estimating what was left to Gordon. "Enough to buy a corporal's job, pay for your suit, and maybe get by," he decided, his eyes seeming to clutch the money and caress it. Then he tore them away. "Don't do it, cobber. You're the wrong kind. You take what you're doing serious. When you set out to tin-horn a living, you're a crook. Get you in a cop's outfit, and you turn honest. No place here for an honest cop—not with elections coming up, cobber. Well, I guess you gotta find out for yourself. Want a good room?"

Gordon dropped his eyes to the hole he'd called home for over a week, and his lips twitched. "Thanks, Mother. But I'll be staying inside the dome, I guess."

"So'll I," the old man gloated. "Setting in a chair all day, being an honest citizen. Cobber, I already own a joint there—a nice one, they tell me. Lights. Two sanitary closets. Big rooms, six by ten—fifty of them, big enough for whole families. And strictly on the level, cobber. It's no hideout, like this. But the gee running it is knocking down till it won't more than pay its way. Now . . ."

He rolled the money in his greasy fingers. "Now, with what I get from the pusher, I can buy off that hot spot on the police blotter. I can go in the dome and walk around, just like you, cobber." His eyes watered slowly, and a tear went dripping down his nose, to hang pendulously. He rubbed it off with the back of his hand.

Gordon had already heard some of the story of the man's exile. In some earlier, more respectable period of his life, Mother Corey had incurred the wrath of the mayor of Marsport and a trumped-up charge of carrying a rifle inside the dome had been lodged against him. He retreated out here where the police were weak.

The mayor had been killed soon after, and the charge could have been fixed easily then; Corey had enough money to take care of it. But he'd stubbornly determined that he would use only funds obtained somehow from looting the graft taken by the police. The dope Izzy was to unload must have been some of that graft.

Mother Corey sighed gustily. "I'm getting old. They'll be calling me Grandmother pretty soon. And some day, some punk will come and collect me. So I'm turning my Chicken House over to my granddaughter—damned wench will probably steal the lodgers blind, too—and I'm going honest. Want a room?"

Gordon grinned and nodded. It was worth standing

the smell of Mother Corey to have someone around who knew the ropes and who could be trusted within some limits. "Didn't know you had a granddaughter," he said.

Izzy snorted, and Mother Corey grinned wolfishly "You met her, cobber," the old man said. "The blond who shook you down! Came up from Earth eight years ago, looking for me. Romance of the planets, long-lost grandfather, all that slush. She needed a lesson, so I sold her to the head of the East Point gang. Eventually, she killed him, and since then she's been getting on pretty well on her own. Mostly. Except when she makes a fool of herself, like her patching your suit up. But she'll come around to where I'm proud of her yet. If you two want to carry in the snow, collect, and turn it over to Commissioner Arliss for me—I can't pass the dome till he gets it, and you two are the only ones fool enough not to steal me blind—I'll give you both rooms for six months free. Except for the lights and water, of course."

Izzy nodded, and Gordon shrugged. On Mars, it didn't seem half so crazy to begin applying for a police job by carrying in narcotics. He was only curious about how they'd go about contacting the commissioner.

But that turned out to be simple enough. After collecting, Izzy led the way into a section marked *Special Taxes* and whispered a few casual words. The man at the desk went into an office marked private, and came back a few minutes later.

"Your friend has no record with us," he said in a routine voice. "I've checked through his forms, and they're all in order. We'll confirm officially, of course."

He must have been one of the idealists once. His face was bitter as he delivered the lines, and he looked seedy, unlike most of the men around the police office.

In the Applications section of the big Municipal Building at the center of the dome, the uniformed men looked even better fed. Izzy and Gordon waited outside on a plastic bench for an hour, and then went in. There was a long form to fill out at the desk, but the captain there had already had answers typed in.

"Save time, boys," he said genially. "And time's valuable, ain't it? Ah, yes." He took the sums they had ready—there was a standard price, unless the examiner thought the applicant not suitable, in which case it went up—and stamped their forms. "And you'll want suits. Isaacs? Good, here's your receipt. And you, Corporal Gordon. Right. Get your suits one floor down, end of the hall. And report in at eight tomorrow morning!"

It was as simple as that. Gordon was lucky enough to get a fair fit in his suit. He'd almost forgotten what it felt like to be in uniform, and was surprised to find he stood straighter.

Izzy was more businesslike. "Hope they don't give us too bad a territory, gov'nor," he remarked. "Pickings are always a little lean on the first few beats, but you can work some fairly well."

Gordon's chest fell. He suddenly realized again that this was Mars!

The first week taught him that, though it wasn't too bad. The room at the new Mother Corey's—an unkempt old building near the edge of the dome—proved to be livable, though it was a shock to see Mother Corey himself in a decent suit, using perfume to cover his stench. He'd even washed his hands, though his face was still the same. And the routine of reporting for work was something that became familiar almost at once.

He should have known the pattern. He'd seen it when he was on the Force on Earth, though not quite the same. He'd turned up enough evidence when he was a beginning reporter. But it had always been at least one step removed from his own experience.

The beat was in a shabby section where clerks and skilled laborers worked, with the few small shops that catered to their needs. It wasn't poor enough to offer the universal desperation that gave the gang hoodlums protective coloring, nor rich enough to have major rackets of its own. But it was going down-hill rapidly, and the teenagers showed it. They loitered about, the boys near

25

a poolhall, the girls hanging around a bedraggled school-yard that took up half of one block.

Izzy was disgusted. "Cripes! You can't shake a school down. Hope they've got a few cheap pushers around it, that don't pay protection direct to the captain. You take that store, I'll go in this one!"

The proprietor was a druggist, who ran his own fountain where the synthetics that replaced honest Earth foods were compounded into sweet and sticky messes for the neighborhood kids. He looked up as Gordon went in, his worried face starting to brighten. Then it fell. "New cop, eh? No wonder Gable collected yesterday ahead of time. All right, you can look at my books. I've been paying fifty, but I haven't got it now. You'll have to wait until Friday."

Gordon nodded and swung on his heel, surprised to find that his stomach was turning. The man obviously couldn't afford fifty credits a week. But it was the same all along the street. Even Izzy admitted finally that they'd have to wait.

"That damned cop before us!" he groaned. "He really tapped them! And we can't take less, so I guess we gotta wait until Friday."

The next day, Gordon made his first arrest. It was near the end of his shift, just as darkness was falling and the few lights were going on. He turned a corner and came upon a short, heavy hoodlum backing out of a small liquor store with a knife in throwing position. The crook grunted as he started to turn and stumbled onto Gordon. His knife flashed up.

Without the need to worry about an airsuit, Gordon moved in, his arm jerking forward. He clipped the crook on the inside of the elbow while grabbing the wrist with his other hand. A pained grunt was driven out of the man. Then he went sailing over Gordon's head to crash into the side of the building. He let out a yell.

And across the street, two loafers looked up, and echoed his cry. Gordon rifled the hood's pockets, and located a roll of bills stuffed inside. He dragged them out, before snapping cuffs on the man. Then he pulled the crook inside the store.

A woman stood there, moaning over a pale man who was lying on the floor with blood gushing from a welt on the back of his head. There was both gratitude and resentment as she looked up at Gordon.

"You'd better call the hospital," he told her sharply. "He may have a concussion. I've got the man who held you up."

"Hospital?" Her voice broke into another wail. "And who can afford hospitals? All week we work, all hours. He's old, he can't handle the cases. I do that. Me! And then you come, and you get your money. And he comes for his protection. Papa is sick. Sick, do you hear? He sees a doctor; he buys medicine. Then Gable comes. This man comes. We can't pay him! So what do we get—we get knives in the face, saps on the head—a concussion, you tell me! And all the money—the money we had to pay to get stocks to sell to pay off from the profits we don't make—all of it, he wants! Hospitals! You think they give away at the hospitals free?"

She fell to her knees, crying over the injured man. "Papa, you hear? Papa! God, you hear me, please! Don't let Papa have concussions, don't let them take him to the hospital!"

Gordon tossed the roll of bills onto the floor beside her, and looked at the man's head. But the injury seemed only a scalp wound, and the old man was already beginning to groan. He opened his eyes and saw the bills in front of him, at which the woman was staring unbelievingly. His hand darted out, clutching it. "God!" he moaned softly, echoing the woman's prayer, and his eyes turned up slowly to Gordon, filled with something that should never have been seen outside of an archaic slave pen.

"In there!" It was a shout from outside. Gordon had just time to straighten up before the doorway was filled with two knife-men and a heavier man behind them.

His hands dropped to the handcuffed man on the floor, and he caught him up with a jerk, slapping his body back against the counter. He took a step forward, jerking his hands up and putting his Earth-adapted shoulders behind it. The hood sailed up like a sack of meal being thrown on a wagon and struck the two knife-men squarely.

There was a scream as their automatic attempts to save themselves buried both knives in the body of their friend. Then they went crashing down under the dying body, and Gordon was over the top of them, his fist crashing into the chin of the leader.

When the paddy wagon came, the driver scowled and seemed surprised. But Gordon hustled his prisoners and the dead man inside. He wanted to get away from the soft crying gratitude of the woman and the look in the storekeeper's eyes.

The desk captain at the precinct house groaned as they came in, then shook his head. "Damn it," he said. "I suppose it can't be helped, though. You're new, Gordon. Hennessy, get the corpse to the morgue, and mark it down as a robbery attempt. I'm going to have to book you and your men, Mr. Jurgens!"

The heavy leader of the two angry knife-men nodded and grinned, though his look toward Gordon was nasty. "Okay, Captain. But it's going to slow down the work I'm doing on the mayor's campaign for reelection! Damn that Maxie—I told him to be discreet. Hey, you know what you've got, though—a real considerate man! He gave the old guy the money back."

They took Gordon's testimony, and sent him home, since his time was up.

Jurgens set him straight the next day. The man was waiting for him when he came on the beat. From his look of having slept well, he must have been out almost as soon as he was booked. Two other men stood behind Gordon, while Jurgens explained that he didn't like being interrupted on business calls "about the mayor's campaign or about anything else," and that next time there'd be real hard feeling—real hard. Gordon was surprised when he wasn't beaten, but he wasn't surprised when the racketeer issued a final suggestion that any money found at a crime was evidence and should go to the police. The captain had told him the same.

By Friday, he had learned enough. He made his collections early, without taking excuses. Gable had sold him the list of what was expected, and he used it, though he cut down the figures in a few cases. There was no sense in killing the geese that laid the eggs, and business wasn't good enough to afford both kinds of protection at that rate.

The couple at the liquor store had their payment waiting for him, and they handed it over without a word, looking embarrassed. It wasn't until he was gone that he found a small bottle of fairly good whiskey tucked into his pouch. He started to throw it away, and then lifted it to his lips and drank it without taking the bottle away. Maybe they'd known how he felt better than he had. Mother Corey's words about his change of attitude came back. Damn it, he'd given up his ideals before he left the slums of his birth! He had a job to do—he had to dig up enough money to get back to Earth, somehow, unless he wanted to play patsy for the Security boys.

He collected, down to the last account. It was a nice haul. At that rate, he'd have to stand it for only a few months. Then his lips twisted, as he realized it wasn't all gravy. There were angles, or the price of a corporalcy would have been higher. And he could guess what they were.

One of the older men answered his questions, a gray-haired, stout corporal with sadism showing all over his face. "Fifty per cent of the take to the Orphan and Widow's fund, of course. Better make it a little more than Gable turned in, if you want to get a better beat. You can squeeze 'em tighter than he did. He was a softie!"

The envelopes were lying on a table marked "Voluntary Donations," and Gordon filled his out, with a figure a trifle higher than half of Gable's take, and dropped it in the box. The captain, who had been watching him carefully, settled back and smiled.

"Widows and Orphans sure appreciate a good man,"

29

he said, ponderously humorous. "I was kind of worried about you, Gordon. But you got a nice touch. One of my new boys—Isaacs, you know him—was out checking up after you, and the dopes seem to like you."

Gordon had wondered why Izzy had been pulled off the beat. He was obviously making good. But he grinned, and nodded silently. As he turned to leave, the captain held up a hand.

"Special meeting, tomorrow," he said. "We gotta see what we can do about getting out a good vote. Election only three weeks away."

Gordon went home, forgetting the conversation until the next night. He'd learned by now that the Native Martians—the men who'd been here for at least thirty years, or had been born here—were backing a reform candidate and new ticket, hoping to get a businessman by the name of Murphy elected. But Mayor Wayne had all of the rest of the town in his hand. He'd been elected twice, and had lifted the graft take by a truly remarkable figure. From where Gordon stood, it looked like a clear victory for the reformer, Murphy. But that should have worried the police, and there was no sign of it. He didn't give a darn, though. Even with the take-out that left him only about thirty percent of his collection, he should be able to get off Mars before the new administration came into power.

He went into the meeting willing to agree to anything. And he clapped dutifully at all the speeches about how much Mayor Wayne had done for them, and signed the pledge expressing his confidence, along with nodding at the implied duty he had to make his beat vote right. Wayne might get two votes from his beat, he thought wryly. Then he stopped, as the captain stood up.

"We gotta be neutral, boys," he boomed. "But it don't mean we can't show how well we like the mayor. Just remember, he got us our jobs! Now I figure we can all kick in a little to help his campaign. Nothing much—a little now and a pledge for the rest of the election. I'm going to start it off with five thousand credits, two thousand of them right now."

They fell in line, though there was no cheering. The price might have been fixed in advance. A thousand for a plain cop, fifteen hundred for a corporal, and so on, each contributing a third of it now. Gordon grimaced. He had six hundred left—and that would take nearly all of it, leaving him just enough to get by on, if he didn't eat too well, at Martian prices. And without the free room, he couldn't have done it at all. He wondered how often such donations were required.

A man named Fell shook his head. "Can't do a thing now," he said, and there was fear in his voice. "My wife had a baby and an operation, and . . ."

"Okay, Fell," the captain said, without a sign of disapproval. "Freitag, what about you? Fine, fine!"

Gordon's name came, and he shook his head. "I'm new—I haven't any real idea of how much I can give, and I'm strapped now. I'd like . . ."

"Quite all right, Gordon," the captain boomed. "Harwick!"

He finished the roll, and settled back, smiling. "I guess that's all, boys. Thanks from the mayor. And go on home . . . Oh, Fell, Gordon, Lativsky—stick around. I've got some overtime for you, since you need extra money. Boys out in Ward Three are shorthanded. Afraid I'll have to order you out there!"

Ward Three was the hangout of the Scurvy Boys—a cheap gang of hoodlums, numbering some four hundred, who went in for small crimes mostly. They averaged too young to be used for goon squads or for beating down strikes by infiltrating and replacing. But they had recently declared war on the cops, who'd come under local pressure severe enough to force the closing of their headquarters.

After eight hours of overtime, Gordon reported in with every bone sore from small missiles and his suit filthy from assorted muck. He had a beautiful shiner where a stone had clipped him. But he grinned a little, as he remembered the satisfying sound of two heads thunking together before a third member had joined and given the hoodlums a chance to get away.

The captain smiled. "Rough, eh? But I hear robbery

31

went down on your beat last night. Fine work, Gordon. We need men like you. Hate to do it, but I'm afraid you'll have to take the next shift at Main and Broad, directing traffic. The usual man is sick, and you're the only one I can trust with the job!"

"But . . ."

"Can't be helped. Oh, I know you've been on duty two shifts, but that's the way it goes. Better report to duty!"

He hadn't handled traffic before, and it was rough, even with the minor traffic snarls here in Marsport. In two hours of standing absolutely still, his feet were killing him. In four, his head was swimming.

He stuck it out, somehow. But it wasn't worth it. He reported back to the precinct with the five hundred in his hand and his pen itching for the donation agreement.

The captain took it, and nodded. "I wasn't kidding about your being a good man, Gordon. Go home and get some sleep, take the next day off. After that, we've got a new job for you!"

His smile was still nasty, but Gordon had learned his lesson.

IV

The new assignment was to what had been the old Nineteenth Precinct, the roughest section in all Marsport—the slum area beyond the dome, out near the rocket field. Here all the riff-raff that had been unable to establish itself in better quarters had found some sort of a haven. At one time, there had been a small dome and a tiny city devoted to the rocket field. But Marsport had flourished enough to kill off lesser centers.

The dome had failed from neglect, and the buildings once inside it had grown shabbier. Men had looted the worst of them and built crude shelters, some with only a single room that would hold air, many over a mile from the nearest official water store.

Somehow, the people eked out a living. Most of them worked in the shops where the stringy vines of native Mars plants were beaten into a sort of felt, glued together with adhesive from other plants, and built up to form a substitute for the wood and plastic of Earth. The work was ill paid and unhealthy. Slivers from the vines worked into the skin of anyone coming in contact with them, carrying with them the slow poison of the glue. But despite the known risk, both adults and children formed long waiting lines for the jobs.

It was a miserable section for everyone, including the police, but Gordon was trapped, and there was nothing he could do about it. He couldn't quit his job with the police; to do so would brand him as a criminal. Some of Mars' laws were rough, dating back to the time when law enforcement had been hampered by the lack of men, rather than by the type of men attracted to it. Until he had enough money to buy off his police contract, he was stuck with it for the full three year—Martian years, nearly double those of Earth. No matter where they chose to assign him—or to punish him—he had to sweat it out, much as he hated being stuck out there.

The people there had been complaining for years about the Stonewall gang. It was made up of the lowest level of hoodlums, and numbered perhaps five hundred. They made their chief living by hiring out members to other gangs during the frequent wars between gangs. But between times, they picked up what they could by mugging and theft, with a reasonable amount of murder thrown in at a modest price.

Even derelicts and failures had to eat. And that meant that there were stores and shops throughout the district which eked out some kind of a marginal living. They were safe from protection racketeers there—none bothered to come so far out—except for the disorganized work of the Stonewall gang. And police had been taken off the beats there for years, after it grew unsafe for even men in pairs to patrol the area.

The shopkeepers and some of the less unfortunate people there had finally raised enough of a protest to reach clear back to Earth, and Marsport had hired a man from Earth to come in and act as captain of the section. No one from the city would take the job, and none of the regular captains could have coped with it. Captain Whaler was an unknown factor. He'd sat tight for two months, and now was asking for more men. And the pressure from the petty merchants and the itinerant crop prospectors was enough to get them for him.

Gordon reported for work with a sense of the bottom falling out, mixed with a vague relief. There was little chance for graft here. And Whaler discouraged even what there was.

"You're going to be busy," he announced shortly in the dilapidated building that had been hastily converted to a precinct house. "Damn it, you're men, not sharks. I've got a free hand, and we're going to run this the way we would on Earth. Your job is to protect the citizens here—and that means everyone not breaking the laws—whether you feel like it or not. No graft. The first man making a shakedown will get the same treatment we're going to use on the Stonewall boys. You'll get double pay here, and you can live on it!"

He opened up a box on his desk and pulled out six heavy wooden sticks, each thirty inches long and nearly two inches in diameter. There was a shaped grip on each, with a thong of leather to hold it over the wrist.

He picked out five of the men, including Gordon. "You five will come with me. I'm going to show how we'll operate. The rest of you can team up any way you want tonight, pick any route that's open. With six patrolling you should be safe, and I'll expect no great action until you're broken in. Okay, men, let's go."

Gordon grinned slowly as he swung the stick, and Whaler's eyes fell on him. "Earth cop!" he guessed.

"Two years," Gordon admitted.

"Then you should be ashamed to be in this mess,"

the Captain told him. "But whatever your reasons, you'll be useful. Take those two and give them some lessons, while I do the same with these."

For a second, Gordon cursed himself. He had fixed it so he would be a squad leader, even without his corporal's paid-for stripes. And that meant he'd be unable to step out of line if he wanted to. At double standard pay, with normal Mars expenses, he might be able to pay for passage back to Earth in three years—if Security let him, which it wouldn't. Otherwise, it would take thirty.

He began wondering about Security, then. Nobody had tried to get in touch with him. He'd come here and vanished. The first ten days, while staying at the old Mother Corey's, that had been natural. But since joining the force, they'd have no trouble locating him. Nobody had mentioned it, and nobody had asked him questions that were suspicious:

If they were waiting for him to get on a soap box, they were wrong. But it worried him, suddenly, all the same.

There was a crude lighting system here, put up by the citizens. At the front of each building, a dim phosphor bulb glowed. It was still light outside, but darkness would fall in another half hour, and they would have nothing else to see by.

Whaler bunched them together. "A good clubbing beats hanging," he told them. "But it has to be good. Go in for business, and don't stop just because the other guy quits. Give them hell!"

Moving in two groups of threes, at opposite sides of the street, they began their beat. They were covering an area of six blocks one way and two the other, which seemed ridiculous to Gordon. The gang would simply hold off for a few days to see what happened.

But he was wrong about that. They had traveled the six blocks and were turning down a side street when they found their first case, out in broad daylight. Two of the Stonewall boys, by the gray of their sweaters under the airsuits, were working over a tall man in regular clothes and a newer airsuit. As the police swung around, one of the thugs casually ripped the airsuit open with his knife and reached for a pocket.

A thin screech like a whistle came from Whaler's Marspeaker, and the captain went forward, with Gordon at his heels. The hoodlums tossed the man aside easily, and let out a yell. From the buildings around, an assortment of toughs came at the double, swinging knives, picks, and bludgeons.

There was no chance to save the citizen who was dying from lack of air. Gordon felt the solid pleasure of the finely turned club in his hands. It was light enough for speed, but heavy enough to break bones where it hit. A skilled man could knock a knife or even a heavy club out of another's hand with a single flick of the wrist. And he'd had practice.

He saw Whaler's club dart in and take out two of the gang, one on the forward swing, one on the recover. Gordon's eyes popped at that. The man was totally unlike a Martian captain. And a knot of homesickness for Earth ran through his stomach. They were tough by necessity here. But only old Earth could produce the solid toughness of a man who had a job to do, instead of merely responding to desperation.

He swallowed the sentimental nonsense, knowing it was true for him because he'd seen only one side of Mars. His own club was moving now. Standing beside Whaler, they were moving forward. The other four cops had come in reluctantly, but were now thoroughly involved.

"Knock them out and kick them down!" Whaler yelled. "And don't let them get away!"

He was after a thug who was attempting to run, and brought him to the ground with a single blow across the kidneys.

The fight was soon over. They rounded up the men of the gang, and one of the cops started off. Whaler called him back. "Where are you going?"

"To find a phone and call the wagon," the man said, his voice surprised at the stupidity of the question.

"We're not using wagons on the Stonewall gang," Whaler told him. "Line them up."

It was sheer brutality. When the men came to, they found themselves helpless, and facing police with clubs. If they tried to run, they were hit from behind, with little regard for how much danger the blow meant. If they stood still, they were clubbed carefully to bruise them all over. If they fought back, the pugnaciousness was knocked out of them at once.

Whaler indicated one who stood with his shoulders shaking and tears running down his cheeks. The expression on the captain's face was as sick as Gordon felt, but Whaler went on methodically, while he gave his orders. "Take him aside. Names."

Gordon found a section away from the others. It was just turning dark now, but he needed less light than there was to see the fear in the gangster's face. "I want the name of every man in the gang you can remember," he told the man.

Horror shot over the other's bruised features. "I ain't no rat! My God, Colonel, they'd kill me. They'd stick a knife in me! No! *No!* I don't know, Goddammit I *don't* know!"

His screams were almost worse than the beating. But Gordon kept his face straight, and moved in again. The other cracked, dropping to the ground and bawling. Between the other noises, names began to come. Gordon took them down, and then returned with the man to the others.

Whaler took his nod as evidence enough, and turned to the wretched toughs. "He squealed," he announced. "If he should turn up dead, I'll know you boys are responsible, and I'll go looking for you. Now get out of this district or get honest jobs. Because every time one of my men sees one of you, this happens all over again. And you can pass the word along that the Stonewall gang is dead!"

He turned his back and moved off down the street, with the other police at his side. Gordon nodded slowly. "I've heard the theory, but never saw it in practice. Suppose the whole gang jumps us at once?"

Whaler shrugged. "Then we're taken. The old book I got the idea from didn't mention that."

Trouble began brewing shortly after, though. Men stood outside studying the cops on their beat. Whaler sent one of the men to pick up a second squad of six, and then a third. After that, the watchers began to melt away, as if uncertain of how many the police could summon.

"We'd better shift to another territory," Whaler decided and Gordon realized that the gang had fooled itself. They'd figured that concentrating the police here meant other territories would be safe, and they hadn't been able to resist the chance to loot—even to bring about a quick warfare in which they might win.

There were two more muggings spotted, and two more groups were given the same treatment. In the third one, Gordon spotted one of the men who'd been beaten before. He was a sick-looking spectacle, and he'd been limping before they caught him.

Whaler nodded. "Object lesson!"

The one good thing about the captain, Gordon decided, was that he believed in doing his own dirtiest work. When he was finished, he turned to two of the other captives, and motioned to the second offender.

"Get a stretcher, and take him wherever he belongs," he ordered. "I'm leaving you two able to walk for that. But if you get caught again, you'll get worse than he got."

The police went in, tired and sore. There wasn't a man in the squad who hadn't taken a severe beating in the brawls. But the grumbling was less than Gordon had expected, and he saw grudging admiration in their eyes for Whaler, who had taken more of a beating then they had.

Gordon rode back in the official car with Whaler, and both were silent most of the way. But the captain stirred finally, sighing. "Poor devils!"

Gordon jerked up in surprise. "The gang?"

"No, the cops they're giving me. We're covered, Gordon. But the Stonewall gang is backing Wayne for the election, of course. He's let me come in because he

38

figures it will prove to Marsport that he's progressive and will get him more votes than he can win in the whole district out there. But afterwards, he'll have me out, and then the boys with me will be marks for the gang when it comes back. Besides, it'll show on the books that they didn't kick into his fund. I can always go back to Earth, and I'll try to take you along—I guess we can chisel your fare. But it's going to be tough on them."

Gordon grimaced. "I've got a yellow ticket, and it's from Security," he said flatly.

Whaler blinked. He dropped his eyes slowly. "So you're *that* Gordon? Sorry, I should have sent you back to your own precinct, I guess. But you're still a good cop."

They rode on further in silence, until Gordon broke the ice to ease the tension. He found himself liking the other.

"What makes you think Wayne will be reelected?" he asked. "Nobody wants him, except a gang of crooks and those in power."

Whaler grinned bitterly. "Ever see a Martian election? No, you're a firster. He can't lose! And then hell is going to pop, and this whole planet may be blown wide open!"

It fitted with the dire predictions of Security, and with the spying Gordon was going to do, according to them. It also left things in a fine mess. With Wayne out and an honest mayor in, there would be small chance to get the fare he needed. With Wayne in, he'd be about as popular as a dead herring—and as defunct, probably. He'd been a fool not to take the Mercury mines!

But curiously, he had no desire to back out and leave Whaler in the lurch, even if he'd had the power to do so. He discussed it with Mother Corey, who agreed that Wayne would be reelected.

"Can't lose," the old man said. He was getting even fatter, now that he was eating better food from the fair restaurant around the corner. Gordon noticed that he'd apparently washed his face and had trimmed the wisps of hair. The widow in the small restaurant might have had something to do with that, though he couldn't imagine any woman showing interest in the monstrous hulk.

"He'll win," Corey repeated. "And you'll turn honest all over, now you're in uniform. Take me, cobber. I figured on laying low for awhile, then opening up a few rooms for a good pusher or two, maybe a high-class duchess. Cost 'em more, but they'd be respectable. Only now that I'm respectable myself, they don't look so good. Anyhow, I do all right. No protection from me—I know too much! But this honesty stuff, it's like dope. You start out on a little, and you have to go all the way."

"It didn't affect Honest Izzy," Gordon pointed out.

"Nope. Because Izzy was always honest, according to how he sees it. But you got Earth ideas of the stuff, like I had once. Too bad." He sighed ponderously, letting his chins move sorrowfully, and squeezed up from his huge chair to go inside. Gordon went to his own room and worried.

The week moved on. The groups grew more experienced, and Whaler was training a new squad every night. Gordon's own squad was equipped with shields now, since he'd remembered the ones on the blond vixen's gang, and they were doing better. The number of muggings and hold-ups in the section was going down. They seldom saw a man after he'd been treated.

One of the squads was jumped by a gang of about forty, and two of the men were killed before the nearest squad could pull a rear attack. That day the whole force worked overtime, hunting for the men who had escaped, and by evening the Stonewall boys had received proof that it didn't pay to go against the police in large numbers. Kidneys and other organs were harder to replace than bruised flesh or broken bones.

After that, the police began to go hunting for the members of the gang. By then they had the names of nearly all of them, and some pretty good ideas of their hideouts.

It wasn't exactly legal, of course. But nothing was,

here. Gordon's conscience was almost easy, on that—whenever he had time to think about it. If a doctor's job was to prevent illness instead of merely curing it, then why shouldn't it be a policeman's job to prevent crime? Here, that was best done by wiping out the Stonewall gang to the last member.

It could lead to abuses, in time, as he'd seen on Earth. But there probably wouldn't be time for it, if Mayor Wayne was reelected, as even the Native Martians seemed to feel he would be.

The gang had begun to break up and move, but the nucleus would be the last to go. The police had orders to beat up a member of the gang now, even if he were merely found walking down the dirty street for a pack of Marsweed. Citizens were appearing on the streets until it was fully dark for the first time in years. And here, in this one section of Marsport, there were smiles —hungry, beaten smiles, but still genuine ones—at the cops.

A storekeeper approached Gordon timidly at the end of the second week, offering a drink of cheap native whiskey to break the ice. He took it, forcing it down. The other man hemmed and hawed, pulling at his dirty gray mustache—a mannerism that seemed completely out of place when done through the thickness of an airsuit.

Then he got down to business. "Hear there's a new gang set to move in. Likely figure you won't stop 'em, being so busy with the Stonewallers. Hear as there's a gal running this one." The man was both scared and a bit ashamed to pass information to the police, but he was worried.

Gordon's mind swept back to the blond granddaughter of Mother Corey, without prodding, and he straightened. If the vixen was deliberately needling him—as it seemed, if the man's story was true—she had a debt to collect, all right—but not the one she expected. "Where?"

"Cain's warehouse. Know where it is?"

Gordon nodded, and handed back the bottle. "Thanks, citizen," he said. He must have sounded as if he meant it, for reassurance and some measure of pride suddenly flashed onto the man's face. He shoved the bottle through the slit in his airsuit, drained it, and nodded.

Gordon considered getting a squad and going in for a mopping-up operation. By a little bit of manipulation, it could seem that he was stumbling on her while looking for Stonewall members. But then he remembered her crying over him as she patched his slit airsuit, and her apparently honest warning to him in Fats' Place.

Besides, while he knew she could be as dangerous as a man, he somehow couldn't get over the idea that she was only a girl. He started back to the precinct headquarters, then swung on his heel. It wouldn't do any harm to spy out the situation.

He made his way to the old warehouse building from the back, taking what cover he could. It was still two hours until sundown, and the gang would probably be holed up. But he could at least find out whether the building had been airproofed.

He found no evidence at first, until the sun glinted on a spot that seemed to glisten. It could be airproof cement, put on too heavily, and spilling through. He slid around nearer to the street, where the view was better, and began inching forward, using a heap of ruined foundation as cover.

He hugged it, moving around it, and started forward.

Something scraped against his suit.

He turned, but with the slowness of caution this time. It was a good thing. The blonde stood there, a grin stretching her mouth into a thin line, and pure murder in her eyes. A knife was in her left hand, almost touching the plastic of his uniform's airproofing. In her right hand was one of the forbidden guns—probably legal out here, but so rare on Mars that he hadn't actually seen one until now. But she looked as if she could use it.

"Drop the stick!" she ordered him. Her voice was low with some obscure passion. He had no way of knowing it wasn't fear—but it was more probably sheer desire to kill him.

The stick hit the ground. Her knife flashed, and he stepped back. "Looking for something—or someone?" she asked.

He shook his head, trying to estimate his chances. They didn't look good. "For you," he told her, forcing his voice to hold steady. "I couldn't get you off my mind. When you wouldn't come to visit your poor old grandfather, I had to hunt you down. And now . . ."

Fury lifted her voice an octave. "Damn you, Gordon. Get down on your knees and crawl like a dog! Crawl, damn you! When I save the life of a piece of scum, I want to see gratitude."

"You've seen it, beautiful," he told her. "Your own kind. Or don't you remember the love tap, and the little present we exchanged?"

For a second, he thought she was going to pull the trigger. Then she shook her head. "When they let the air out of your suit, you should have died. I fixed that. But I can unfix it. Take off your helmet—and don't think I'm kidding this time. Take it off, you yellow first-er, or I'll puncture your belly—and then seal up your suit again, so you'll die slowly! Well?"

"Is that the way you killed your—ah—husband?" he asked her. He could feel the first trickle of sweat on his forehead, and there was a cold lump in his stomach, but he held his grin. "I heard you settled that out of court."

She had gone white at the first words, and the gun in her hand jerked and trembled tautly. She tried to speak, choked, and then bit out a single sentence, her eyes pin-points of hate.

"Take-it-*off!*"

He could feel the false amusement slip from his face, and a chill of fear wash over him. This time, she meant it.

A man could live for a couple of minutes without a helmet . . . In that time . . .

He reached for it, loosing the seal, and beginning to lift it off. The air went out of it, spurting in little clouds of frost as the expansion cooled it off, and froze the water vapor in it.

43

. . . In that time, the precious two minutes, he could do nothing. He'd been a fool. The effort of holding his breath was too great, and his vision was already growing unfocussed.

"So long, baby," he said, and hurled the helmet at her. The air exploded from his lungs with the words, and for a minute everything began to turn black.

V

His nose had been bleeding from the change in pressure, and there was a taste of blood in his mouth. Gordon licked his lips, and opened his eyes slowly, while the fuzziness gradually moved out of his mind. He was lying on his back, staring at a grimy ceiling, and the air had a musty quality. By turning his eyes, he could see that he was in a small, dimly lighted room, and that the hasty work of making it air-tight had changed none of the ravages of time; the rottenness had simply been covered up with patches of permaseal plastic, glued down to hold in the air.

The girl was squatting on her heels beside him, and the gun was in one of her hands, a knife in the other. Her face was sullen now. But it firmed up as she saw that his eyes were open, and the knife twisted pointing toward him. She opened her mouth, but he beat her to it.

"So you're still soft underneath it all?" he challenged her. The words were thick on his tongue, and his head had a thousand devils beating tom-toms inside it, but he ignored them ruthlessly. "Just because I don't cry and whimper, you can't let me die. You had to lug me inside here to find out why, eh?"

Her face had frozen at the sound of his voice, but

she seemed to pay no attention to his words. "Why'd you laugh? Damn you, Gordon, why did you laugh when you threw that helmet?"

"Because I knew you'd have to find out why," he told her. The surprising thing about it was that he suddenly realized it had been true. He'd operated on a last-second hunch, and it had paid off. "I knew you couldn't let me die without finding out why I didn't do what you expected. You're still soft, Cuddles."

"Damn you! I'll show you . . ." The knife whipped back in an overhand that no skilled fighter would use, and then dropped as he managed to grin at her. "The name's Sheila—Sheila Corey, and no cracks about that!"

She stood up and began packing, keeping her eyes on him. She swung back to face him as he shoved himself into sitting position. "You look like a human being. You bleed like one. But inside, you're a rotten, stinking machine!"

He grimaced at that. He'd been told that before. Compensation, he'd been told by the psychiatrist in the Security office—a fear of being hurt that had begun in the slums as a kid and frozen him, until he thought he couldn't be hurt. He'd walled in the softness he should have had, until it couldn't be reached. He'd hidden his own feelings, and learned to disregard those of others. And the professions he'd chosen—fighter, gambler, cop, reporter—had proved it.

"You're just the sort that grandfather of mine *would* admire!" she finished hotly.

He laughed again, then, and her actions slipped into a slot he could understand. Before, she had been a random factor. There'd been no reason why she should pick him out as her target. But he could remember her passing them that first day, with Mother Corey so enraptured at the sight of the new deck of reader cards that had reminded him of his own beginnings. To an outsider, it probably would have looked as if Mother Corey had been taking the newcomer to his enormous bosom.

"And he doesn't admire you, eh?" Gordon guessed.

45

"He laughed at your romantic nonsense, didn't he? He sent you out to toughen up—and *that* must have been an experience! Too bad your—ah—husband couldn't control . . ."

A shrill whisper of a scream came from her lips, barely giving him warning as she charged. The gun dropped from her fingers, and the knife lifted. She leaped for him, her knees striking the floor where his stomach had been, and her clawed hand groping for his throat. The knife went all the way back and began to come forward.

He got one hand up to her wrist, barely in time. The inertia of the blow carried the point of the knife to the fabric of his suit. He forced it back, while his other hand jerked her fingers away from his neck. Then she was a screaming, clawing madwoman, her lips snarled back to expose her teeth, while her sharp canines snapped at his throat, slashed his wrist, and drove forward again and again. Her fingers were raking at his face, tearing at his hair. And her whole body was a writhing knot of fury, as she tried to swarm over him, beating at him with her knees and feet. She seemed to have at least a score of wild limbs, and the governor on her internal motor had long since cut out.

His knowledge of the ring was useless—as useless as the dirty fighting he'd learned elsewhere. His mind snapped all the way back to his slum childhood, and his body reacted as it had done when the neighborhood tomboys had ganged up on him. He drove a sharp elbow against her breasts, slapped the edge of his hand against the small of her back, and then grabbed for her legs and twisted. Her furious snarling changed to a gasp, but before she could catch herself, he'd rolled out from under her. He brought a knee up against the place where a sensitive gland in the groin lay between abdomen and leg. His hands caught her arms, and he forced them back by sheer superiority of muscle, while his other knee found the second tender gland. He let his weight rest there, changing his hold on her wrists from two hands to one, and jerked her head back with the other.

46

He thumped the back of her head against the hard floor, and her agonized groans cut off. For a scant second, she was out. He found the zipper on her Mars suit, jerked it down, and caught the shoulders of the suit in his hands, bringing it down over her arms and pinioning them at the elbows.

Briefly, then, he hesitated. Her thin blouse had snapped partly open, exposing the upper part of her chest. On it were lines and small scars, telling their own story of a captivity where the thug had clawed and mauled her into temporary submission. No wonder she'd killed the devil! And the soiled edges of her underclothing told their own story of a girl who must have been neat once, but who was now forced to live where even a change of clothing was too great a luxury, and where water was available only for drinking.

He reached forward to straighten her blouse. She jerked to an abrupt steely stiffness, and gray horror hit her face, while her eyes threatened to leap out of their sockets.

"No!"

It tore out of her lips like a board being ripped from a sawmill.

There was a sickness in him—the same sickness he'd felt when his first and only girl-friend had been found killed at the hands of a maniac the parole board had decided was cured. He stood up, shaking his head, and located the knife and the gun.

"Button your blouse, Sheila," he told her. "And the next time don't let a man goad you into going crazy. All I wanted was your weapons—and I've got them."

There was a total lack of comprehension in her eyes as she sat up and reached for the buttons. He studied her, unsure of what to do next. Then, as she reached for the zipper on her suit, he shook his head.

"Take it off," he told her sharply. Without a suit, she would have to stay inside the hovel here until he could make up his mind, at least.

Her face blanched, but she reached for the zipper, and began unfastening it. Her hands shook, but she drew it down, and started to shrug her way out of the suit.

He stopped her, and again there was the sickness inside him. The few pitiful rags inside the suit were totally incapable of covering her decently. It was a hell of a life for a woman—any kind of woman. He wondered abruptly how many others he saw going about in their suits were in the same desperate fix—and how many had sat futilely trying to patch what they had while the police and the gangs came regularly for their graft.

He reached for the zipper himself, and drew it up. "Forget it. I guess your helmet's all I need."

Then she broke. Her legs seemed to buckle slowly under her, until she was sitting on the floor. Her hands dropped to her sides, and her head slumped forward. She made no sound, but her shoulders shook, and tears began to drop slowly to the dirty floor, leaving muddy splotches where they fell.

Gordon found his helmet and put it back on, cutting out the musty smell of the place. He picked up her smaller plastic bowl and strapped it to his belt. Then he swung to look at her.

The tears were gone now, and she was on her feet, staring at him. "You damned human machine!" she said, and her voice was flat and harsh. "I should have known. You wouldn't even know what to do with a woman if she didn't care. You're not even human enough for *that!* You—you *robot!*"

It hurt, inside him. But he sealed off the hurt of it almost at once. His lips twisted bitterly. "Your gratitude's appreciated, Cuddles. But I like my women feminine—and clean!"

Her hand hit the side of his helmet with a sharp splat. The red spots on her cheeks spread outward to cover her face as she realized the stupidity of the gesture. Then she shrugged. "Go on, then, kill me and get it over with. You might as well."

"I'll leave the killing to you," he answered her. "You'll be all right here, until I can send someone to take you off in the paddy wagon." He threw back the helmet, sniffing the air again, but there was enough ox-

48

ygen in it for several hours for her. Yet there was genuine fear in her eyes. He puzzled over it for a second, before her glance at the knife he held triggered his mind.

In a way, she was probably right. He could imagine the type of gutter-sweepings she must have recruited in her desperate attempt to set up a gang out here. If one of them came back and found her without a weapon . . .

He broke the gun and removed the bullets from it, dropping them into a pocket of his suit. For a second, he hesitated. Maybe he should take her with him. But that would mean turning her over to Captain Whaler, who would see no difference between the men of the Stonewall gang and a woman trying to set up another gang. Maybe there was no difference, but he still owed her a vague kind of obligation because of her silly attempt to save his life the other time—and he preferred to fight his own battles. This came under the heading of a personal feud. Anyhow, even if her men came back, they would have no helmet to fit her. She'd keep, until he could come back—and a little waiting and worry would be good for her.

He tossed her the gun, and started to go out through the dilapidated entrance port. Then he grinned, and turned back.

"They'll be as scared of it without bullets as with, if they don't know," he told her. "But this time, if I let you keep it, I want to see some gratitude. Come here! And if you bite, I'll knock your head off!"

Surprisingly, after a single instant of fury, she came quietly enough, even lifting her head toward him. He dragged her shoulders around, and pulled her to him, bending down to lips that neither resisted nor responded. Then he felt the beginnings of a response, and his hand dropped sharply to his knife, pressing it down into its sheath before she could reach it.

He drew his head up, and the grin came back to his lips. "Naughty, naughty," he told her.

She stamped her foot against the floor and jerked her head away. "Damn you! You stinking . . ."

But her head came up again, and her eyes met his. She fought back for a second as he pulled her to him. This time, there was life and fire in her lips, and even through the suit he could feel her sway toward him.

He straightened, snapped down the helmet, and was heading out through the entrance without a backward look. It was night outside, and the phosphor bulbs at the corners were glowing dimly, giving him barely enough light by which to locate the way back to the extemporized precinct house. He shook the fuzz out of his head, grimacing at his own reactions. Well, the vixen had needed taming.

He reached the outskirts of the miserable business section, noticing that a couple of the shops were still open. It had probably been years since one had dared risk it after the sun went down. And the slow, doubtful respect on the faces of the citizens as they nodded to him was even more proof that Whaler's system was working, however drastic it might be. Gordon nodded to a couple, and they grinned faintly at him. Damn it, Mars could be cleaned up . . .

He grinned at himself. Maybe Mother Corey was right; put a cop's uniform on him, and he started thinking like a cop. All this was fine, but it didn't help him get back to Earth. Even at double pay, he still wasn't getting anywhere. The best place for him was still back under the central dome, where the pickings were good.

Then something needled at his mind, until he swung back. The man was carrying a lunch basket, and wearing the coveralls of one of the crop prospector crews, but the expression on his face had been wrong. Gordon had noticed it from the corner of his eye, and now he saw the sullen scowl slip from the man's face abruptly and turn into a mixture of hate and fear.

Red hair, too heavily built, a lighter section where a mustache had been shaved and the skin not quite perfectly powdered . . . Gordon moved forward quickly, until he could make out the thin scar showing through the make-up over the man's eyes. He'd been right—it was O'Neill, head of the Stonewall gang, and the man they'd been trying hardest to find.

Gordon hit the signal switch, and the Marspeaker let out a shrill whistle. O'Neill had turned to run, and then seemed to think better of it. His hand darted down to his belt, just as Gordon reached him.

The heavy locust stick met the man's wrist before the weapon was half drawn—another gun! Guns, suddenly, seemed to be flourishing everywhere. It dropped from the hand as the wrist snapped, and O'Neill let out a high-pitched cry of pain. Then another cop came around a corner at a run.

"You can't do it to me! I'm reformed. I'm going straight! You damned cops can't . . ."

O'Neill was blubbering. The small crowd that was collecting was all to the good, Gordon knew, and he let the man go on. Nothing could help break up the gangs more than having a leader break down in public.

The other cop had yanked out O'Neill's wallet, and now tossed it to Gordon. One look was enough—the work papers had the tell-tale overthickening of the signature that had showed up on other papers, and they were obviously forgeries. The cops had been accepting the others in the hope of finding one of the leaders, and luck had been with them.

Some of the citizens turned away as Gordon and the other cop went to work, but most of them had old hatreds that left them no room for squeamishness. When it was over, the two picked up their whimpering captive. Gordon pocketed the revolver with his free hand. "Walk, O'Neill!" he ordered. "Your legs are still whole. Use them!"

The man staggered between them, whimpering as each step jolted his wrecked body. If any of the gang were around, they made no attempt to rescue him as he moved down the four blocks to the precinct house. This was probably the most respectable section of Marsport, at the moment.

Jenkins, the other cop, had been holding the wallet. Now he held it out toward Gordon. "The gee was heeled, Corporal. Must of been making a big contact in something. Fifty-fifty?"

"Turn it in to Whaler," Gordon said, and then

cursed himself for being a fool. There must have been over two thousand credits in the wallet, a nice start toward his pile. He was hoping that Jenkins would argue him out of his unreasoned honesty, but the other merely shrugged and stuffed it back into O'Neill's belt-pocket. It didn't make sense, but the money was still there when they dumped the crook onto a bench before Whaler.

The captain's face had been buried in a pile of papers, but now he came around to stare at the gang leader. He inspected the forged work papers, and jerked his thumb toward one of the hastily built cells, where a doctor would look O'Neill over—eventually. When Gordon and Jenkins came back, Whaler tossed the money to them. "Split it. You guys earned it by keeping your hands off it. Anyhow, you're as entitled to it as he was—or the grafters back at Police Headquarters. I never saw it . . . Gordon, you've got a visitor!"

His voice was bitter, but he made no opening for them to question him as he picked up the papers and began going through them again. Gordon went down the passage to the end of the hall, in the direction Whaler had indicated. Waiting for him was the lean, cynical little figure of Honest Izzy, complete with uniform and sergeant's stripes.

"Hi, gov'nor," the little man greeted him. "Long time no see. With you out here and me busy nights doing a bit of convoy work on the side, we might as well not both live at the Mother's."

Gordon nodded, grinning in spite of himself. "Convoy duty, Izzy? Or dope running?"

"Whatever comes to hand, gov'nor. The Force pays for my time during the day, and I figure my time's my own at night. Of course, if I ever catch myself doing anything shady during the day, I'll have to turn myself in. But it ain't likely." He grinned in satisfaction. "Now that I've dug up the scratch to buy these stripes and get made sergeant—and that takes the real crackle—I'm figuring on taking it easy."

"Like this social call?" Gordon asked him.

The little man shook his head, his ancient twenty-

52

year-old face turning sober. "Nope, I've been meaning to see you, so I volunteered to run out some red tape for your captain. You owe me some bills, gov'nor. Eleven hundred credits. You didn't pay up your pledge to the campaign fund, so I hadda fill in. A thousand, interest at ten percent a week, standard. Right?"

Gordon had heard of the friendly interest charged on the side here, but he shook his head. "Wrong, Izzy. If they want to collect that dratted pledge of theirs, let them put me where I can make it. There's no graft out here!"

"Huh?" Izzy turned it over, and shook his head. Finally he shrugged. "Don't matter, gov'nor. Nothing about that in the pledge, and when you sign something, you gotta pay it. You *gotta*."

"All right," Gordon admitted. He was suddenly in no mood to quibble with Izzy's personal code. "So you paid it. Now show me where I signed any agreement saying I'd pay you back!"

For a second, Izzy's face went blank. Then he chuckled, and the grin flashed back impishly. "Jet me! You're right, gov'nor. I sure asked for that one. Okay, I'm bloody well suckered. So forget it."

Gordon shrugged and gave up. He pulled out the bills and handed them over, noticing that he was left with less than a hundred credits. It seemed that nothing he did would increase his bank-roll over that here. "Thanks, Izzy."

"Thanks, yourself." The kid pocketed the money cheerfully, nodding. "Buy you a beer. Anyhow, you won't miss it. I came out to tell you I got the sweetest beat in Marsport—over a dozen gambling joints on it—and I need a right gee to work it with me. So you're it!"

For a moment, Gordon wondered what Izzy had done to earn that beat, but he could guess. The little guy knew Mars as few others did, apparently, from all sides. And if any of the other cops had private rackets of their own, Izzy was undoubtedly the man to find it out, and use the information. With a beat like that, even going halves, and with all the graft to the upper

53

brackets, he'd still be able to make his pile in a matter of months.

But he shook his head. "I'm assigned here, Izzy, at least for another week, until after elections . . ."

"Better take him up, Gordon," Whaler's voice told him bitterly. The captain looked completely beaten as he came into the room and dropped onto the bench. "Go on, accept, damn it. You're not assigned here any more. None of us are. Mayor Wayne found an old clause in the charter and got a rigged decision, pulling me back under his authority. I thought I had full responsibility to Earth, but he's got me. Wearing their uniform makes me a temporary citizen! So we're being smothered back into the Force, and they'll have their patsies out here, setting things up for the Stonewall boys to come back by election time. Grab while the grabbing's good, because by tomorrow morning I'll have this all closed down!"

He shook off Gordon's hand, and stood up roughly, to head back up the hallway. Then he stopped and looked back. "One thing, Gordon. I've still enough authority to make you a sergeant. It's been a pleasure working with you, Sergeant Gordon!"

He swung out of view abruptly, leaving Gordon with a heavy weight in his stomach. Izzy whistled, and began picking up his helmet, preparing to go outside. "So that's the dope I brought out, eh? Takes it kind of hard, doesn't he?"

"Yeah," Gordon answered. There was no use trying to explain it to Izzy. "Yeah, we do. Come on."

Outside, Gordon saw other cops moving from house to house, and he realized that Whaler must be sending out warnings to the citizens that things would be rough again. For a second, he started to go back to help, until he realized that he'd completely forgotten about freeing Sheila. That would have to be done first. "Come on," he said, and headed toward the abandoned section. Izzy shrugged, but followed.

But there was no need to free her. A bullet within inches of his head told him that, when they were still three hundred feet from the old ruin.

He dropped to his face, cursing himself for not checking her clothing for more bullets. In the dim light, he could just see her, with some odd thing around her head. Apparently, she'd yanked the permaseal sheets off the wall and glued them into a substitute helmet. He should have thought of that, too.

"The Mother's babe?" Izzy asked.

He nodded, and reached for the gun he had taken from O'Neill, just as another shot sounded faintly in the thin air.

Izzy's hand darted back and appeared with a knife in it. "Easy, gov'nor! Don't try anything! She gave me a retainer for protection against you, and it's good till after elections!"

"She'll kill both of us!"

"Can't be helped," Izzy said flatly. "She's a bad shot. Never had much chance to practice—I hope!"

She apparently had only one reload for the gun, but two of the bullets came painfully close before she stopped firing. Then she abruptly turned and ran back into darkness. Izzy put the knife back, and got to his feet, holding out a hand to help Gordon. "Wheew! Let's get a beer, gov'nor—on me!"

It was as good an idea as any he had, Gordon decided. He might as well enjoy what life he still had while he could, on this stinking planet. The prospect for the future didn't look too rosy.

Sheila was loose and planning vengeance. The Stonewall gang—what was left of it—and all its friends would be gunning for him now. The Force wouldn't have been fooled when Izzy paid his pledge, and they would mark him down as disloyal—if they didn't automatically mark down all who had served under Whaler. He'd be a sergeant on a good beat until after elections. Then they'd get him. And if the reform ticket should win, he'd be out cold.

It was a lovely future. And meantime, he didn't have the ghost of an idea as to what Security wanted of him, or where they were hiding themselves.

"Make it two beers, Izzy," he said. "Needled!"

VI

In the few days at the short-lived Nineteenth Precinct, Gordon had begun to feel like a cop again, but the feeling disappeared as he reported in at Captain Isiah Trench's Seventh Precinct. Trench had once been a colonel in the Marines, before a court-martial and sundry unpleasantness had driven him off Earth. His dark, scowling face and lean body still bore a military air, and there was none of the usual false subtlety currently in fashion among his fellow captains.

He looked Gordon over sourly, and shook his head. "I've been reading your record, Gordon, and it stinks. Making trouble for Jurgens—could have been charged as false arrest. No cooperation with your captain until he forced it. Out in the sticks beating up helpless men. Now you come crawling back to your only friend Isaacs. Well, if he wants you, I'll give it a try. But step out of line, and I'll have you cleaning streets with your bare hands. All right, *Corporal* Gordon. Dismissed. Get to your beat."

Gordon grinned wryly at the emphasis on his title. No need to ask what had happened to Whaler's recommendation that he be made a sergeant. He joined Izzy in the locker room, summing up the situation.

"Yeah." Izzy looked worried, his thin face pinched in. "Maybe I didn't do you a favor, gov'nor, pulling you here. I dunno. I got some pics of Trench from a gee I know. That's how I got my beat so fast in the Seventh. But Trench ain't married, and I guess I've used up the touch. Maybe I could try it, though."

"Forget it," Gordon told him.

He had his private doubts. Trench would probably

take out on him the resentment at Izzy's blackmailing. They moved out to the little car that would take them to their beat for the day in silence.

The beat was a gold-mine. It ran through the gambling section where Gordon had first tried his luck on Mars. There were a dozen or so gambling joints, half a dozen cheap saloons, and a fair number of places listed as rooming-houses, though they made no bones about the fact that all their permanent inhabitants were female. Since men outnumbered women here by six to one, it was a thriving business. Then the beat swung off the main stem, past a row of small businesses and cheap genuine rooming-houses, before turning back to the main section.

They began in the poorer section. It wasn't the day to collect the "tips" for good service that had once been an honest attempt to promote good police coverage, before it became a racket. But they were met everywhere by sullen faces, and Gordon noticed that two of the little shops had apparently gone out of business in the last few days. Izzy explained it. The city had passed a new poll tax to pay for election booths, supposedly, and made the police collect it. Whaler must have disregarded the order, but the rest of the force had been busy helping the administration kill the egg-laying goose in its drive for election funds.

But once they hit the main stem, things were mere routine. The gambling joints took it for granted that beat-cops had to be paid, and considered it part of their operating expense. The only problem was that Fats' Place was the first one on the list. Gordon remembered the bouncer with the gun and the ugly temper. He didn't expect to be too welcome there. But Izzy was heading across the street, and it might as well be faced now as later.

There was no sign of the thug, but Fats came out of his back office, just as Gordon reached the little bar. He came over, nodded, and picked up a cup and dice, to begin shaking them.

"High man for sixty," he said automatically, and expertly rolled bullseyes for a two. "Izzy said you'd be

57

around. Sorry my man drew that *knife* on you the last time, Corporal."

Gordon rolled an eight and pocketed the bills. He suspected that more of the normal fatalism of a gambler lay behind Fats' acceptance than any fear that he might report the illegal gun inside the dome. He shrugged. "Accidents will happen, Fats."

"Yeah." The other picked up the dice and began rolling sevens absently. "How come you're walking beat, anyhow? With what you pulled here, you should have bought a captaincy."

Gordon told him briefly. The man chuckled grimly. "Well, that's Mars," he said, and turned back to his private quarters.

Mostly, it was routine work. They came on a drunk later, collapsed in an alley, and pretty badly mauled. But the muggers had apparently given up before Izzy and Gordon arrived, since the man had his wallet clutched in his hand. Gordon reached for it, twisting his lips. Make hay while the sun shines, he thought bitterly.

Izzy stopped him, surprisingly. "It ain't honest, gov'nor. If the gees in the wagon clean him, or the desk man gets it, that's their business. But I'm bloody well going to run a straight beat, or else!"

That was followed by a call to remove a berserk spaceman from one of the so-called rooming houses. Gordon noticed that workmen were busy setting up a heavy wooden gate in front of the entrance to the place. There were a lot of such preparations going on for the forthcoming elections.

Then the shift was over. Gordon wasn't too surprised when his relief showed up two hours late. He'd half-expected some such nastiness from Trench. He sent a muttering Izzy back when the little man's relief came and walked his beat grimly. But he was surprised at the look on his tardy relief's face.

The man seemed to avoid facing him, as if he had the plague. "Captain says report in person at once," the cop muttered, and swung out of the scooter and onto his beat without further words. Gordon shouted after

58

him, then shrugged, and began steering the scooter back to the precinct house.

He was met there by blank faces and averted looks, but someone jerked a thumb toward Trench's office, and he went inside. Trench sat chewing on a cigar, and nodded curtly. His voice was hoarse. "Gordon, what does Security want with you?"

"Security?" It hit him like a sap, after the weeks of waiting without a sign. Some of it must have shown in his voice, because Trench looked up sharply from something on the desk. Gordon tried to cover, knowing it was probably too late. "Not a damned thing, if I can help it. They kicked me off Earth on a yellow ticket, if that's what you mean."

"Yeah." Trench wasn't convinced. He tossed a letter toward Gordon, bearing the *official business* seal of Solar Security. It was addressed to Corporal Bruce Gordon, Nineteenth Police Precinct, Marsport. Trench kept his eyes on it, his face filled with suspicion and the vague fear most men had for Security.

"Yeah," he said again. "Okay, probably routine. Only next time, Gordon, put the *facts* on your record with the Force. If you're a deportee, it should show up. That's all!"

Gordon went out, holding the envelope. The warning in Trench's voice wasn't for any omission on his record, he knew. He studied the seal on the envelope, and nodded. They'd been careful, but a close inspection showed it had been opened. He shoved it into his belt pocket and waited until he was in his own room before opening it.

It was terse, and unsigned. "Report expected, overdue. Failure to observe duty will result in permanent resettlement to Mercury."

He swore, coldly and methodically, while his stomach dug knots in itself. The damned, stupid, blundering fools! That was all Trench and the police gang had to see. Sure, report at once. Drop a letter in the mailbox, and the next day it would be turned over to Commissioner Arliss' office. Any gang as well settled as Wayne and Arliss would have ways and means of taking care of a spy for Security. Report or be kicked off to a planet that Security felt enough worse than Mars to use as punishment! Report *and* find Mars a worse place than Mercury could ever be. They'd fixed him up—it was almost as if they wanted him given the works. And for all he knew, that might be the case.

He felt sick as he stood up to find paper and pen and write a terse, factual account of his own personal doings—minus any hint of anything wrong with the system here. Security might think it was enough for the moment, and the local men might possibly decide it was all that was meant by Security—a mere required formality. At least it would stall things off for a while, he hoped.

But he knew now that he could never hope to get back to Earth legally. That vague promise by Security was so much hogwash, as he should have known all along. Yet it was surprising how much he had counted on it. Somewhere in the back of his head, he'd felt that even if he failed to get his stake to pay for smuggling him back, eventually Security might reprieve him. Now, while his chances looked slimmer with every passing day and every extra mark against him, the responsibility for leaving Mars was squarely on his own shoulders—with speed a lot more important than scruples.

He tore the envelope from Security into tiny shreds, too small for Mother Corey to make sense of, and went out to send the space cable, feeling the few bills in his pocket. Less than a hundred credits, after paying for the message—and it took thousands to pay for even a *legal* passage!

He passed a sound truck, blatting out a campaign speech by candidate Murphy, filled with too-obvious facts about the present administration, together with hints that Wayne had paid to have Murphy assassinated. Gordon saw a crowd around the truck and was surprised, until he recognized them as Rafters—men from the biggest of the gangs supporting Wayne. The few citizens on the street who drifted toward the truck took a good look at them and moved on hastily.

It seemed incredible that Wayne could be reelected, though, even with the power of the gangs. Murphy was probably a grafter, too, but he'd at least provide a change, and certainly the citizens were aching for that. If he won, of course, Gordon would be out on his ear. If he lost, however, it wouldn't help much; once the Wayne gang was back in solidly, they'd be prepared to take care of anyone whom they suspected. Yet there seemed nothing to do but play it straight for the few days left.

The next day his relief arrived later. Gordon waited, trying to swallow these petty punishments, but it went against the grain. Finally, he began making the rounds, acting as his own night man. The owners of the joints didn't care whether they paid the second daily dole to the same man or to another. But they wouldn't pay it again that same night. He'd managed to tap most of the places before his relief showed. He made no comment, but dutifully filled out the proper portion of both takes for the Voluntary Donation box. It wouldn't do his record any good with Trench, but it should put an end to the overtime.

Trench, however, had other ideas. He sent the relief man out promptly, but left a message under the special emergency heading. Somehow, they'd overlooked sending one of the destitutes over to the Employment Bureau, and it was up to Gordon to take the trip.

Gordon knew a little about the system used to save the city any cost from keeping the hopelessly poor who had given up or the drug addicts who had reached the end of their rope. In former days, it had been known as indentured servitude, but slavery of any kind was theoretically illegal here, so they called it employment procurement. And, as usual, when the honest word was avoided, the deed itself was worse.

He watched them bring out a pitifully slim girl with an old, sullen face and the body of a sixteen-year-old. He signed the papers, snapped the cuffs about her wrist and his own, and got into the back of the wagon with her. The papers he carried told the story, roughly. Hilda's father had been killed "accidentally" when he refused to meet his racket protection payments. Her brother had joined one of the petty gangs and been killed in a feud. Her mother had kept food in the girl's mouth for two years in the only way an unskilled woman could earn money on Mars, until she was picked up and fined for having no permit. Then, in default of money to pay the fine, the city had sold her services for five years to the operator of a sweat-shop, where she probably would have died of tuberculosis by now. The girl had run away to the slums beyond the dome, joined a gang, and made out for a while. But things must have gone wrong, because the police had found her dying with run-down batteries for her aspirator.

Her sullen eyes were on him as he filled in from the glib expressions on the records. "I hope you're satisfied!" she said, finally.

"Why me?"

"Because it's all your fault. I was doin' all right. Sheila and me was like *that*—see? Just like that. Gave me her second slip, she did, when I didn't have none. And she was building her a good gang. Boy, did she keep them respectful, too! And to me, even! Then she come back one night an' they told her either she got them bigger jobs or she was out. So she got them one. You! You, see? Said she'd find a sucker, and we waited, and she highsigns us it was gonna be outside the dome, and safe. And we took you, too. 'N she sent us ahead . . ."

Her voice trailed off, and Gordon waited. Sheila Corey, it seemed, had to be mixed up in everything. The girl caught her breath, and her eyes were hot now. "When they went back, they found her all beaten up. Naturally, they didn't want a gang leader that'd let things like that happen. 'N they had a big fight, and they all quit her, except me. You just try not having a gang, Mr. Cop! I run away when I seen she din't have enough for even herself to eat. Now she's probably . . ."

"She's doing all right," Gordon told her. "At least she was a couple days ago. Well enough to buy a gun, pay a retainer against me, and start operating, at least."

The girl's eyes dropped then. She sighed, almost contentedly. "Gee, I'm glad. Sheila's a queen—a real queen ... Mr. Cop, what they gonna do to me? I mean, it ain't gonna be ..."

"Somebody'll probably want you to keep house and maybe marry in a couple years," Gordon answered. He knew that it could happen—but he doubted it. The papers had carried a note that the city was putting in a bid of five hundred credits for her five years of service. It was doubtful that anyone would offer more for her, or even bother to bid against the city-owned houses.

They had reached the barnlike Employment Bureau then, and he turned her over to one of the attendants. Bidding was almost over for the day, and only a few bidders remained, while the auctioneer was proceeding in an automatic sing-song. He finished on a blowsy, elderly woman who kept protesting that she was a seamstress, she was. Then he signaled the clerk.

There was only one more up for auction, other than Hilda. The man had obviously been beaten by the drug habit, and had hit the final skids. He'd been given shots preparatory to the bidding, but his eyes still showed the agony of the final bout with the habit. The clerk glanced at his papers, and gobbled into the microphone.

"Williams, garage-mechanic. Petty theft, caught trying to trade off the proceeds. Went crazy and attacked the arresting officers. Now agrees to work willingly in return for basic needs. The employer will get a legal prescription for his drugs, and it's a five-year contract with no penalty clause!"

In spite of the fact that normal protections for Williams had been revoked, there was only one bid, from a man who wanted a new helper in a small atomic-waste refinery. The last man, he admitted, had died of radioactive poisoning in less than two years, and he protested against raising his bid of a hundred credits when he couldn't count on the full five years. The auctioneer finally agreed that the price was satisfactory.

Gordon got out, before the bidding on the girl could begin. He'd had enough. But he wondered whether

Sheila would hold this against him, too, if she heard he'd been the one to deliver the girl. Probably, he supposed. She was good at blaming her own failures on him, and then declaring war, to find something else to hold against him.

Izzy came in when he got back to Mother Corey's, fuming at Trench's campaign to keep Gordon on long hours. But Gordon was too tired to care. He chased the other out, rolled over, and was almost instantly asleep.

The overtime continued, but it was dull after that—which made it even more tiring. And the time he took the special release out to the spaceport was the worst. Seeing the big ship readying for take-off back to Earth and the people getting on board did nothing to make Gordon happier about the situation.

Then it was the day before election. The street was already bristling with barricades around the entrances, and everything ran with a last desperate restlessness, as if there would be no tomorrow. The operators all swore Wayne would be elected, but they seemed to fear a miracle. And on the poorer section of the beat, there was a spiritless hope that Murphy might come in with his reform program. Men who would normally have been punctilious about their payments were avoiding him, as if hoping that by putting it off a day or so they could run into a period where no such payment would ever be asked—or a smaller one, at least. And he was too tired to chase down the ones who could be reached. His collections had been falling off already, and he knew that he would be on the carpet for that, if he didn't do better. It was a rich territory, and required careful mining; even as the week had gone, he still had more money in his wallet than he had expected.

But it had to be still more before night.

In that, he was lucky. At the last hour, he came on a pusher working one of the better houses in the section—long after his collections should have been over. He knew by the man's face that no protection had been paid higher up. And the pusher was well-heeled, either from a good morning or a draw made to buy more supplies that were necessary to twenty percent of Mars

64

population. Gordon confiscated the money, realizing it would make up for any shorts in the rest of his collection.

This time, Izzy came up without protests. Lifting the roll of anyone outside the enforced part of Mars' laws was apparently honest, in his eyes. He nodded, and pointed to the man's belt. "Pick up the snow, too," he suggested.

The pusher's face paled. He must have had his total capital with him, because stark ruin shone in his eyes. "Good God, Sergeant," he pleaded. "Leave me something! I'll make it right. I'll cut you in. I gotta have some of that for myself!"

Gordon grimaced. He couldn't work up any great sympathy for anyone who made a living out of drugs. The end product he had seen at the Employment Bureau wasn't pleasant. And the addict wasn't just bedeviled by eventual spasms when his supply was gone—he was constantly haunted by a fear of it, long before.

They cleaned the pusher, and left him sitting on the steps, a picture of slumped misery. Izzy nodded approval. "Let him feel it awhile. No sense jailing him yet. Bloody fool had no business starting without lining the groove. Anyhow, we'll get a bunch of credits for the stuff when we turn it in."

"Credits?" Gordon asked.

"Sure." Izzy patted the little package. "We get a quarter value. Captain probably gets fifty percent from one of the pushers who's lined with him. Everybody's happy."

"Why not push it ourselves?" Gordon asked in disgust.

Izzy shook his head. "Wouldn't be honest, gov'nor. Cops are supposed to turn it in."

Trench was almost jovial when he weighed the package and examined it to find how much it had been cut. He issued them slips, which they added as part of the contributions. "Good work—you, too, Gordon. Best week in the territory for a couple of months. I guess the citizens like you, the way they treat you." He laughed at his own stale joke, and Gordon was willing to laugh with him. The credit on the dope had paid for most of the contributions. For once, he had money to show for the week.

Then Trench motioned forward, and dismissed Izzy with a nod of his head. "Something to discuss, Gordon. Isaacs, we're holding a little meeting, so wait around. You're a sergeant already. But Gordon, I'm offering you a chance. There aren't enough openings for all the good men, but . . . Oh, bother the soft-soap. We're still short on election funds. So there's a raffle. Two men holding winning tickets get bucked up to sergeants. A hundred credits a ticket. How many?"

He frowned suddenly as Gordon counted out three bills. "You have a better chance with more tickets. Gordon. A *much* better chance!"

The hint was hardly veiled. Gordon stuck a batch of tickets into his wallet, along with the inevitable near-hundred-credits that seemed to be his maximum. It was a fine planet for picking up easy money, but holding it was another matter.

Trench counted the money and put it away. "Thanks, Gordon. That fills my quota. Look, you've been on overtime all week. Why not skip the meeting? Isaacs can brief you, later. Go out and get drunk, or something."

The comparative friendliness of the peace offering was probably the ultimate in graciousness from Trench. Idly, Gordon wondered what kind of pressure the captains were under; it must be pretty stiff, judging by the relief the man was showing at making quota.

"Thanks," Gordon acknowledged, but his voice was bitter in his ears. "I'll go home and rest. Drinking costs too much for what I make. It's a good thing you don't have income tax here."

"We do," Trench said flatly. "Forty percent. Better make out a form next week, and start paying it regularly. But you can deduct your contributions here."

Gordon got out before he learned more good news. At least, though, at the present rate he wouldn't have too much tax to pay.

VII

As Gordon came out from the precinct house, he noticed the sounds first. Under the huge dome that enclosed the main part of the city, the heavier air-pressure permitted normal travel of sound, and he'd become sensitive to the voice of the city after the relative quiet of the Nineteenth Precinct. But now the normal noise was different. There was an undertone of hushed waiting, with the sharp bursts of hammering and last-minute work standing out sharply through it.

Voting booths were being finished here and there, and at one a small truck was delivering ballots. Voting by machine had never been established here. Wherever the booths were being thrown up, the nearby establishments were rushing gates and barricades in front of the buildings.

Most of the shops were already closed—even some of the saloons. To make up for it, stands were being placed along the streets, carrying banners that proclaimed free beer for all loyal administration friends. The few bars that were still open had been blessed with the sign of some mob, and they obviously were well staffed with hoodlums ready to protect the proprietor. Private houses were boarded up. The scattering of last-minute shoppers along the streets showed that most of the citizens were laying in supplies to last until after election, apparently planning to regard it as a siege.

Gordon passed the First Marsport Bank and saw that it was surrounded by barbed wire with more strands still being strung, and with a sign proclaiming that there was high voltage in the wires. Watching the operation was the flashy figure of Jurgens. From the way the men doing the work looked at him, it was obvious that his hoodlums had been hired for the job.

Toward the edge of the dome where Mother Corey's place was, the narrower streets were filling with the gangs, already half-drunk and marching about with their banners and printed signs. The parades would be starting just after sundown, and would go on until fighting and rioting finally dispelled the last paraders. Curiously enough, all the gangs weren't working for Wayne's reelection. The big Star Point gang had apparently grown tired of the increasing cost of protection from the government, and was actively compaigning for Murphy. Their home territory reached nearly to Mother Corey's, before it ran into the no-man's-land separating it from the gang of Nick the Croop. The Croopsters were loyal to Wayne.

Gordon turned into his usual short-cut past a rambling plastics plant and through the yard where their trucks were parked. He had half expected to find it barricaded, but apparently the rumors that Nick the Croop owned it were true, and it would be protected in other ways, with the trucks used for street fighting, if needed. He threaded his way between two of the trucks.

Then a yell reached his ears, and something swished at him. An egg-sized rock hit the truck behind him and bounced back, just as he spotted a hoodlum drawing back a sling for a second shot.

Gordon was on his knees between heart-beats, darting under one of the trucks. He rolled to his feet, letting out a yell of his own, and plunged forward. His fist hit the thug in the elbow, just as the man's hand reached for his knife. His other hand chopped around, and the edge of his palm connected with the other's nose. Cartilage crunched, and a shrill cry of agony lanced out.

But the hoodlum wasn't alone. Another came out from the rear of one of the trucks. Gordon ducked as a knife sailed for his head; they were stupid enough not to aim for his stomach, at least. He bent down to locate some of the rubble on the ground, cursing his own folly in carrying his knife under his uniform. The easy work on the new beat had given him a false sense of security.

He found a couple of rocks and a bottle and let them fly, then bent for more.

Something landed on his back, and fingernails were gouging into his face, searching for his eyes!

Instinct carried him forward, jerking down sharply and twisting. The figure on his back sailed over his head, to land with a harsh thump on the ground. Brassy yellow hair spilled over Sheila Corey's face, and her breath slammed out of her throat as she hit. But the fall hadn't been enough to do serious damage.

Gordon jumped forward, bringing his foot up in a savage swing, but she'd rolled, and the blow only glanced against her ribs. She jerked her hand down for a knife and came to her knees, her lips drawn back against her teeth. "Get him!" she yelled.

The two thugs had held back, but now they began edging in. Gordon slipped back behind another truck, listening for the sound of their feet. They tried to out-maneuver him, as he had expected. He stepped back to his former spot, catching his breath and digging frantically for his knife. It came out, just as they realized he'd tricked them.

Sheila was still on her knees, fumbling with something, and apparently paying him no attention. But now she jerked to her feet, her hand going back and forward. "Take that—for Hilda!" she shouted.

It was a six-inch section of pipe, with a thin wisp of smoke, and the throw was toward Gordon's feet. The hoodlums yelled and ducked, while Sheila broke into a run away from him. The little home-made bomb land-ed, bounced, and lay still, with its fuse almost burned down.

Gordon's heart froze in his throat, but he was al-ready in action. He spat savagely into his hand, and jumped for the bomb. If the fuse was powder-soaked, he had no chances. He brought his palm down against it, pressing the dampness of the spit onto it, and heard a faint hissing. Then he held his breath, waiting for the explosion.

None came. It had been a crude job, with only a wick for a fuse.

Sheila had stopped at a safe distance and was looking back. Now she grabbed at her helpers, and swung them with her. The three came back, Sheila in the lead with her knife flashing, and the others more cautiously.

Gordon side-stepped her rush, and met the other two head-on, his knife swinging back. His foot hit some of the rubble on the ground at the last second, and he skidded. The leading mobster saw the chance and jumped for him. Gordon bent his head sharply, and dropped, falling onto his shoulders and somersaulting over. He twisted at the last second, jerking his arms down to come up facing the other.

Then a new voice cut into the fracas, and there was the sound of something landing against a skull with a hollow thud. Gordon got his head up just in time to see a man in police uniform kick aside the first hoodlum and lunge for the other. There was a confused flurry, and the second went up into the air and came down in the newcomer's hands, to land with a sickening jar and lie still. Behind, Sheila lay crumpled in a heap, clutching one wrist in the other hand and crying silently.

Gordon came to his feet and started for her. She saw him coming and cast a single glance at the knife that had been knocked from her hands. Then she sprang aside and darted back through the parked trucks, toward the street where she could lose herself in the swarm of Nick's Croopsters. Gordon turned back toward his rescuer.

The iron-gray hair caught his eyes first. Then, as the solidly built figure turned, he grunted. It was Captain Whaler—but now dressed in the uniform of a regular beat cop, without even a corporal's stripes. And the face was filled with the lines of strain that hadn't been there before.

Whaler threw the second gangster up into a truck after the first one and slammed the door shut, locking it with the metal bar which had apparently been his weapon. Then he grinned wryly, and came back toward Gordon.

"You seem to have friends here," he commented. "A good thing I was trying to catch up with you. Just missed you at the precinct house, came after you, and saw you turn in here. Then I heard the rumpus. A good thing for me, too, maybe."

Gordon blinked, accepting the other's hand. "How so? And what happened?" He indicated the bare sleeve.

"One's the result of the other," Whaler told him. "They've got me sewed up, and they're throwing the book at me. The old laws make me a citizen while I wear the uniform—and a citizen can't quit the Force. That puts me out of Earth's jurisdiction. I can't cable for funds, even—and I guess I'm too old to start squeezing money out of citizens who don't have it to hand out. So I can't afford the rooms here. I was coming to ask whether you had room in your diggings for a guest—and I'm hoping now that my part here cinches it."

He had tried to treat it lightly, but Gordon saw the red creeping up into the man's face. "Forget that part," he told Whaler. "There's room enough for two in my place—and I guess Mother Corey won't mind. I'm damned glad you were following me."

"So'm I, Gordon. What'll we do with the prisoners?"

"We couldn't get a Croopster locked up tonight for anything. Let them rot until their friends come along."

He started ahead, leading the way through the remaining trucks and back to the street that led to Mother Corey's. Whaler fell in step with him. The man's voice was dead with fatigue, now that the excitement had worn off. "This is the first time I've had free to look you up," he said. "I've been going out nights to help the citizens organize against the Stonewall gang. But that's over now—they gave me hell for inciting vigilante action, and confined me inside the dome. The way they hate a decent cop here, you'd think honesty was contagious."

"Yeah." Gordon preferred to let it drop. Whaler was being given the business for going too far on the

Stonewall gang, not for refusing to take normal graft. Anyhow, Gordon had never seen any evidence that honesty was catching. He'd been an honest rooky on Earth himself; and the men who'd gotten farthest had been the very ones against whom most of the evidence had turned up when he was ferreting out corruption as a reporter. Honesty was fine—in its place.

They came to the gray three-story building that Mother Corey now owned. Gordon stopped, realizing for the first time that there was no sign of efforts to safeguard it against the coming night and day. The entrance was unprotected by even a sign of a gate. Then his eyes caught the bright chalk marks around it—signs to the gangs to keep hands off. If they were authentic, Mother Corey had pull enough to get every mob in the neighborhood to affix its seal.

As he drew near, though, he found that other steps had been taken. Two men edged across the street from a group watching the beginning excitement. Then, as they identified Gordon, they moved back again. Some of the Mother's old lodgers from the ruin outside the dome were inside now—and obviously posted where it would do the most good.

Corey stuck his head out of the door at the back of the hall as Gordon entered, and started to retire again, until he spotted Whaler. Gordon explained the situation hastily.

"It's your room, cobber," the old man wheezed. He waddled back, to come out with a towel and key, and handed them to Whaler. "Number forty-two."

His heavy hand rested on Gordon's arm, holding the younger man back. Whaler stared at them a second, then took the hint. He gave Gordon a brief, tired smile, and started for the stairs. "Thanks, Gordon. I'm turning in right now."

Mother Corey shook his head, stirring the few hairs on his head and face, and the wrinkles in his doughy skin deepened. "Hasn't changed, that one. Must be thirty years, but I'd know Ira Whaler anywhere. Took me to the spaceport, handed me my yellow ticket, and sent me off for Mars. A nice, clean kid—just like my

72

own boy was. But he wasn't like the rest of the neighborhood. He still called me 'sir,' when my boy was walking across the street so he wouldn't know they were sending me away. Oh, well, that was a long time ago, cobber. A long time."

He rubbed a pasty hand over his chin, shaking his head ponderously, wheezing heavily. Gordon waited, vaguely curious about the reasons behind Corey's being sent off. But on Mars, that was a man's private business. Corey grimaced, and chuckled. "Well, how—?"

Something banged heavily against the entrance seal, and there was the sound of a hot argument, followed by a commotion of some sort. Corey seemed to prick up his ears, and began to waddle rapidly toward the entrance.

But it broke open before he could reach it, the seal snapping back to show a giant of a man outside holding the two guards from across the street, while a scar-faced, dark man shoved through briskly. Corey snapped out a quick word, and the two guards ceased struggling, and started back across the street. The giant pushed in after the smaller thug.

"I'm from the Ajax Householders Protection Group," the dark man announced officially. "We're selling election protection. And, brother, do you need it, if you're counting on those mugs. We're assessing you—"

"Not long on Mars, are you?" Mother Corey asked. The whine was entirely missing from his voice now, though his face seemed as expressionless as ever. "What's your boss Jurgens figure on doing, punk? Taking over *all* the rackets for the whole city?"

The dark face snarled, while the giant moved a step forward. Scarface's fingers twitched nervously toward a knife that rested on his hip. Then he shrugged. "Okay, Fatty. So Jurgens is behind it. So now you know. And I'm doubling your assessment, right now. To you it's—"

A heavy hand fell on the man's shoulder, and Mother Corey leaned forward slightly. Even in Mars' gravity, his bulk made the other buckle at the knees.

73

The hand that had been reaching for the knife yanked the weapon out and brought it up sharply.

Gordon started to step in, then, but there was no time. Mother Corey's free hand came around in an open-palmed slap that lifted the collector up from the floor and sent him reeling back against a wall. The knife fell from the crook's hand, and the dark face turned pale. He seemed to sag down the wall, to end up on the floor, out cold.

The giant opened his mouth and took half a step forward. But the only sound he made was a choking gobble. Mother Corey moved without seeming haste, but before the other could make up his mind. There was a series of motions that seemed to have no pattern. The giant was spun around, somehow; one arm was jerked back behind him, then the other was forced up to it. Mother Corey held the wrists in one hand, put his other under the giant's crotch, and lifted. Carrying the big figure off the floor, the old man moved toward the seal. His foot found the button, snapping the entrance open. He pitched the giant out overhanded, to land squarely on the flat face and skid across the rough surface of the street. Holding the entrance, he reached for the dark man with one hand and tossed him on top of the giant.

"To me, it's nothing," he called out. "Take these two back to young Jurgens, boys, and tell him to keep his punks out of my house."

The entrance snapped shut then, and Corey turned back to Gordon, wiping the wisps of hair from his face. He was still wheezing asthmatically, but there seemed to be no change in the rhythm of his breathing. "As I was going to say, cobber," he said, "we've got a little social game going upstairs—the room with the window. Fine view of the parades. We need a fourth."

Gordon started to protest that he was tired and needed his sleep. Then he shrugged. Corey's house was one of the few that had kept some relation to Earth styles by installing a couple of windows in the second story, and it would give a perfect view of the street. He followed the old man up the stairs.

Two other men were already in the surprisingly well-furnished room, at the folding table set up near the window. Gordon recognized one as Randolph, the publisher of the little opposition paper. The man's pale blondness, weak eyes, and generally rabbity expression totally belied the courage that had permitted him to keep going at his hopeless task of trying to clean up Marsport. The *Crusader* was strictly a one-man weekly, against the strength of Mayor Wayne's *Chronicle,* with its Earth-comics and daily circulation of over a hundred thousand. Wayne apparently let Randolph keep in business to give him a talking point about fair play; but the little paper's history had been filled with trouble—wrecked presses, ruined paper, and everything the crooks whom Randolph had attacked had been able to think of. The man himself walked with a limp from the last working over he had received.

"Hi, Gordon," he said. His thin, high voice was cool and reserved, in keeping with the opinion he had expressed publicly of the police as a body. But he did not protest Corey's selection of a partner. "This is Ed Aimsworth. He's an engineer on our railroad."

Gordon acknowledged the introduction automatically. He'd almost forgotten that Marsport was the center of a thinly populated area stretching for a thousand miles in all directions beyond the city, connected by the winding link of the electric monorail. "So there really is a surrounding countryside," he said.

Aimsworth nodded. He was a big, open-faced man, just turning bald. His handshake was firm and friendly. "There are even cities out there, Gordon. Nothing like Marsport, but that's no loss. That's where the real population of Mars is—decent people, men who are going to turn this into a real planet some day."

"There are plenty like that here, too," Randolph said. "They just don't get a chance to show it. That your door, Mother?"

Mother Corey shook his head sadly and went out and down the stairs, his heavy tread shaking the floor. There was a low mutter of voices from below.

Aimsworth leaned back in his chair and began stuffing a pipe with Marsweed. "You're lucky, Gordon. Why, I dunno. But the Mother seems to have adopted you. And that's good enough for me. Stick with him. He's the best man in this whole stinking city."

Gordon expected the publisher to disagree, but the little man nodded quickly.

"I thought he was supposed to be in the middle of half the crime here, according to the legends," Gordon suggested.

"Nope." Randolph's smile was bitter, but his voice was positive. "That's his cover. He has his own code, and there are worse—as I should know. If there were any justice on this cockeyed planet, he'd be running for mayor instead of Murphy. He'd win, too—no matter what Wayne's organization cooked up."

Gordon filed the idea away for future thought. It didn't fit with what he'd seen—and yet . . .

Mother Corey came back then, making no explanation for the interruption. Randolph picked up the cards. "First ace deals. Damn it, Mother, sit downwind from me, won't you? Or else take a bath."

Mother Corey chuckled and wheezed his way up out of the chair, exchanging places with Gordon. In spite of the perfume, his effluvium was still thick and sour.

"I got a surprise for you, cobber," he said, and there was only amusement in his voice. "I got me fifty gallons of water today, and tomorrow I do just that."

"What about your vow?" Aimsworth asked. "Thought you'd sworn never to clean up until they cleaned up Marsport."

Corey chuckled. "I'll be dead by then, looks like. I'm getting old, boys. So I made up my mind there was going to be one cleanup in Marsport, even if Wayne does win. And stop examining the cards, Bruce. I don't cheat my friends. The readers are put away for old times' sake."

Randolph shrugged and went back to the original subject, as if there'd been no interruption. "Ninety percent of Marsport is decent, particularly outside the dome. They have to be. It takes at least nine honest men to support one crook. They come up here to start

76

over—maybe spent half their life savings to pay for the trip. They hear a man can make fifty credits a day to start in the factories, or strike it rich crop prospecting. What they don't realize is that things cost ten times as much here, too. They plan, maybe on getting rich and going back to Earth . . ."

"Nobody goes back," Mother Corey wheezed. *"I know."* His eyes rested on Gordon.

"A lot don't want to," Aimsworth said. "I never meant to go back. I've got a good job, a farm up north, and a pretty good thing in acting as officer for the farm grange. Another ten years and I'll quit the railroad— maybe sooner. My kids are up on the farm now—grand-kids, that is. They're Martians. Maybe you won't believe me, Gordon, but they can breathe the air here for an hour or so without a helmet."

The others nodded, and Gordon found that a fair number of third-generation people got that way. Their chests were only a trifle larger and their heart-rate only a few beats faster; it was an internal adaptation, like the one that had occurred in test animals reared at a simulated forty-thousand-foot altitude on Earth, before Mars was ever settled.

"I passed out pretty quickly when I—when I lost my helmet once," he protested.

"You expected to," Mother Corey said, raking in the pot. "A man should be able to last a few minutes, if he doesn't panic."

Gordon nodded thoughtfully. It was worth thinking about—it should give a man time enough to fix almost any suit puncture. He had reacted in panic at the idea of breathing Mars air, he realized; maybe he'd be able to take it better next time. "But how do the kids adapt? They're never exposed to it without their suits, are they?"

"Not exactly." Randolph's mouth tightened. "Not by choice. But replacement batteries and those foot gener-ators cost a lot for replacement and repairs. So when things are tough, you turn your aspirator down as low as you can. Gets to be pretty low sometimes. Has to be."

Aimsworth nodded, his face bitter as if remembering too much. Then his face brightened. "Those kids are going to take the planet away from Earth some day. Marsport is strictly artificial. Like the dome, for instance."

"Dome won't last forever," Mother Corey said. "Takes more repairs every year. Whenever we get a decent wind, this fine stuff they call sand here etches it a bit more. One big crack somewhere and it'll go to pieces."

"Maybe it's lasted too long already. It's the cost of the dome that ruined the city. That and the graft of getting it put up." Randolph folded and waited until the hand was finished.

"The dome and the shipping," Aimsworth said. "Marsport is kept going only because it's the only place where Earth will set down her ships. So if we want to trade with Earth, we have to do it here. There's graft in that, too. If Security doesn't do something, time will."

"Security!" Gordon muttered bitterly. Security was good at getting people in trouble, but he had seen no other signs of them.

Randolph frowned over his cards. "Yeah, I know. The governments of Earth set Security up to look pretty, gave them a mixture of powers without any real backing, and have been trying to keep them from working ever since. But somehow, they did clean up Venus. Earth had a dozen nations trying to get that planet, but Security got it. And every crook here is scared to death of the name. How come a muck-raking newspaperman like you never turned up anything on that story, Gordon?"

Gordon shrugged. It was the first reference he'd heard to his background, and he preferred to let it drop. Up here, the usual tradition was that you started life the minute you stepped on Mars. That suited him.

Mother Corey cut in, his voice older and hoarser, and the skin on his jowls was even grayer than usual. "Don't sell them short, cobber. I did—once . . . You forget them, here, after a while. But they're around . . ."

Gordon felt something run down his armpit, and a chill creep up his back. His trick report suddenly floated up in front of his mental eye, along with the way he'd been handled and the deadly sureness of the Security man back on Earth. If they were here—and if they were a geniune power . . .

Out on the street, a sudden whooping began, and he glanced down. The parade was finally outside. The Croopsters were in full swing, already mostly drunk. The main body went down the street, waving fluorescent signs, while side-guards preceded them, armed with axes, knocking aside the flimsier barricades as they went. He watched a group break into a small grocery store to come out with bundles. They dragged out the storekeeper, his wife, and young daughter, and pressed them into the middle of the parade.

"If they're so damned powerful, why don't they stop that?" he asked bitterly.

Randolph grinned at him. "They might do it, Gordon. They just might. It can't go on much longer. But are you sure you want it stopped?"

"All right," Mother Corey said suddenly. "This is a social game cobbers."

Outside, the parade picked up enthusiasm as smaller gangs joined behind the main one. There were a fair number of plain citizens who had been impressed into it, too, judging by the appearance of little frightened groups in the middle of the mobsters.

He couldn't understand why the police hadn't at least been kept on duty, until Honest Izzy came into the room. The little man found a chair and bought chips, silently, shaking his head. He looked tired, as if he'd had a rough time working his way back from the station without being caught in the swarm down there.

"Vacation?" Mother Corey asked.

Izzy nodded. "Trench took forever giving it to us, Mother. But it's the same old deal. All the police gees get tomorrow off. You, too, gov'nor. No cops to influence the vote, that's the word. We even gotta wear civvies when we go out to vote for Wayne. A bloody mess, that's what it is."

Gordon looked down at the rioters, who were now only keeping up a pretense of a parade. It would be worse tomorrow, he supposed. And there would be no cops. The image of the old woman and her husband in the little liquor store where he'd had his first experience came back to him. He wondered how well barricaded they were.

He felt the curious eyes of Mother Corey dancing from him to Izzy and back, and heard the old man's chuckle. "Put a uniform on some men and they begin to believe they're cops, eh, cobber?"

He shoved up from the table abruptly and headed for his room, swearing to himself. Damn it, if the couple couldn't take care of themselves, they had no business in a town like this. If . . .

He kicked open his door and began shucking off his uniform, cursing the lot of them. Randolph and his incessant, hopeless crusading; Mother Corey and his needling; Izzy and his tangled ethics; and even Whaler, sleeping peacefully on the bed, as if he didn't have a thing to worry about.

Damn the whole stupid planet. Somehow, once the elections were over, he'd have to step up his collections. He'd have to get in better with Trench, too. Another three months on Mars and he'd be as crazy as the rest of them.

He lay down on the bed, fuming, and listening to the quiet snoring of Whaler, while the distant sounds of the mob outside came through the walls.

It was just beginning to quiet down a little toward morning when he fell asleep.

VIII

Izzy was up first the next morning, urging them to hurry before things began to hum. From somewhere, he dug up a suit of clothes that Whaler could wear. He found the gun Gordon had confiscated from O'Neill and filled it from a box of ammunition he'd apparently purchased.

"I picked up some special permits," he said. "I knew you had this cannon, gov'nor, and I figured it'd come in handy. Wouldn't be caught dead with one myself. Knives, that's my specialty. Come on, Cap'n, we gotta get out the vote."

Whaler shook his head. "In the first place, I'm not registered," he began.

Izzy grinned. "Every cop's registered in his own precinct. Wayne got the honor system fixed for us. Show your papers and go into any booth in your territory. That's all. And you'd better be seen voting often, too, Cap'n. What's your precinct?"

"Eleventh. But I'm not voting." Whaler brushed Izzy's protest aside. "I'd like to come along with you to observe, but I wouldn't butt into any choice between two such men as Wayne and Murphy."

Downstairs, the rear room was locked, with one of Mother Corey's guards at the door. From inside came the rare sound of water splashing, mixed with a wheezing, off-key caterwauling. Mother Corey was apparently making good on his promise to take a bath. But they had no time to exchange jokes with the man on guard. As they reached the hall, one of Trench's lieutenants came through the entrance, waving his badge at the protesting man outside.

He spotted the three, and jerked his thumb. "Come on, you. We're late. And I ain't staying on the streets when the action gets going."

A small police car was waiting outside, and they headed for it. Gordon looked at the debacle left behind the drunken, looting mob. Most of the barricades were down. Here and there, a few citizens were rushing about trying to restore them, keeping wary eyes on the mobsters who had passed out on the streets. Across the way, a boy of about sixteen sat with his arm around a girl of under nine. She was crying softly, and he was trying to comfort her, his own face pinched white with fear and horror. Trailing down the steps were the garments of a woman, though there was no sign of what had happened to her.

Suddenly a siren blasted out in sharp bursts, and the lieutenant jumped. He leaped into the car. "Come on, you gees. I gotta be back in half an hour."

They piled inside, and the little electric car took off at its top speed. But now the quietness had been broken. There were trucks coming out of the plastics plant, and mobsters were gathering up their drunks, and chasing the citizens back into their houses. Some of them were wearing the forbidden guns, but it wouldn't matter on a day when no police were on duty.

In the Seventh Precinct, the Planters were the biggest gang, and all the others were temporarily enrolled under them. Here, there were fewer signs of trouble. The joints had been better barricaded, and the looting had been kept to a minimum.

The three got off. A scooter pulled up alongside them almost at once, with a gun-carrying mobster riding it. "You mugs get the hell out of—oh, cops! Okay, better pin these on."

He handed out gaudy armbands, and the three fastened them in place. Nearly everyone else already had them showing. The Planters were moving efficiently. They were grouped around the booths, and they had begun to line up their men, putting them in position to begin voting at once.

Then the siren hooted again, a long steady blast. The

bunting in front of the booths was pulled off, and the lines began to move. Izzy led the way to the one at the rich end of their beat, and moved toward the head of the line. "Cops," he said to the six mobsters who surrounded the booth. "We got territory to cover."

A thumb indicated that they could go in. Whaler remained outside, and one of the thugs reached for him. Izzy cut him off. "Just a friend on the way to his own route. Eleventh Precinct."

There were scowls, but they let it go. Then Gordon was in the little booth. It seemed to be in order. There were the books of registration, with a checker for Wayne, one for Murphy, and a third supposedly neutral behind the plank that served as a desk. The Murphy man was protesting.

"He's been dead for ten years. I know him. He's my uncle."

"There's a Mike Thaler registered, and this guy says he's Thaler," the Wayne man said decisively. "He votes."

The Murphy man was starting a protest again when one of the Planters shoved his way inside. He passed his gun to the inspector for the Wayne side, and went out. The Murphy man studied the gun, gulped, and nodded. "He votes. Heh-heh, yes, just a mix-up. He's registered, so he votes."

The next man was one that Gordon recognized from one of the small shops on his beat. The fellow's eyes were desperate, but he was forcing himself to go through with it. "Murtagh," he said, and his voice broke on the second syllable. "Owen Murtagh."

"Murtang. Murtang. No registration!" The Wayne man shrugged. "Next!"

"It's Murtagh. M-U-R-T-A-G-H. Owen Murtagh, of 738 Morrisy . . ."

"Protest!" The Wayne man cut off the frantic wriggling of the Murphy man's finger toward the line in the book. "When a man can't get the name straight the first time, it's pretty damned suspicious."

The supposedly neutral man nodded. "Better check

the name off, unless the real Murtagh shows up. Any objections, Yeoman?"

The Murphy man had no objections—outwardly. He was sweating, and the surprise in his eyes indicated that this was all new to him. He was probably a one-year man, unaware of what he'd been getting into.

Gordon came next, showing his badge. He was passed with a nod, and headed for the little closed-off polling place. But the Wayne man touched his arm and indicated a ballot. There were two piles, and this pile was already filled out for Wayne. "Saves trouble, unless you want to do it yourself," he suggested.

Gordon shrugged, and shoved it into the slot. He went outside and waited for Izzy to follow. It was raw beyond anything he'd expected—but at least it saved any doubt as to how the votes were cast.

The procedure was the same at the next booth they tried, though they found there was more trouble. The Murphy man there was a fool—which meant he was neither green nor agreeable. He protested vigorously, in spite of a suspicious bruise along his temple. Finally, he made some of his protests stick. There was a conference going on among the Planters as they left, and more were arriving. They couldn't get all their votes put through—but they could scare off all opposition voting.

Gordon began to wonder how it could be anything but a clear unanimous vote, at that rate. But Izzy shook his head. "Wayne will win. But not that easy. The sticks don't have strong mobs, and they pile up a heavy Murphy vote. And you'll see things hum soon!"

Gordon had voted three times under the "honor system," before he saw. They were just nearing a polling place when a heavy truck came careening around a corner. Men came piling out of the back before it stopped—men armed with clubs and stones. They were in the middle of the Planters almost at once, striking without any science, but with a surprising ferocity. The line waiting to vote broke up, but the citizens had apparently organized carefully. A good number of the men in the line were with the attackers.

There was the sound of a shot, and a horrified cry. For a second, the citizens broke. Then a wave of fury seemed to wash over them at the needless risk to the safety of all. The horror of rupturing the dome was strongly engrained on every citizen of Marsport. They drew back, and then made a concerted rush. There was a trample of bodies, but no more shots.

In a minute, the citizens' group was inside the voting place, ripping the fixed ballots to shreds, and racing to fill out and drop their own. They were paying no attention to the registration clerks.

A whistle had been shrilling for minutes. Now another group of trucks came onto the scene, and the Planters men began getting out, rapidly. Some of the citizens looked up and yelled, but it was too late. From the approaching cars, pipes projected forward. Streams of liquid jetted out, and there was an agonized cry from the mob that had not yet escaped.

Even where he stood, Gordon could smell the fumes of ammonia. Izzy's face tensed, and he swore. "They're poisoning the air. Inside the dome!"

But the trick worked. In no time, men in crude masks were clearing out the booth, driving the last few struggling citizens away, and getting ready for business as usual. All the registration clerks were missing, but the head Planters man picked out three at random and installed them. Probably all the ballots from that booth would be declared invalid, but they were taking no chances.

Whaler turned on his heel. "I've had enough. I've made up my mind," he said. "The cable offices must be open for the doctored reports on the election to Earth. Where's the nearest?"

Izzy frowned, but supplied the information. Gordon pulled Whaler aside. "Come off the head cop role," he told Whaler. "It won't work. They must have had reports on elections before this. And nothing came of it."

"Damn the trouble. It's never been this raw before. Look at Izzy's face, Gordon. Even he's shocked. Something has to be done about this, before worse happens. I've still got connections back there—"

"Okay," Gordon said bitterly. He had liked Whaler, like a fool. He had begun to respect him. It hurt to see that what he'd considered hard-headedness was just another case of a fool fighting dragons with a paper sword. But he should have expected it. The publisher of the newspaper back on Earth had been carrying on a fight to the bitter end against exploitation of the planets—but when Gordon was picked up by Security for digging up the one thing that could do most for the cause, he'd gone off in a spasm of horror at the idea of Gordon's using top secret stuff.

"Okay, it's your death certificate," he said, and turned back toward Izzy. "Go send your sob stories, Whaler."

They taught a bunch of pretty maxims in school—even slum kids learned that honesty was the best policy, while their honest parents rotted in unheated holes and the racketeers rode around in fancy cars. They made pretty speeches over the radio, and showed pretty stories on television. It got the suckers. It had got him once. He'd refused to take a dive as a boxer, and wound up as a cop. He'd tried to play honest cards and count on his wits, and had almost starved—and he had had to give up because he couldn't pay off the police. He'd tried honesty on his beat back there, and been made a scapegoat for his sergeant. He'd tried to help the suckers in his column, and he was here as a result.

And he still felt himself slipping back. He'd been proud to serve under Whaler, at a cop's salary. Okay, he'd seen enough; all they had to offer a man was things on paper and an appeal to an outside justice that never came. From now on, he'd go back to taking care of number one. Let them depend on their damned rule books. A man's own muscle was all that counted, and he was going to need plenty of muscle.

"Come on, Izzy," he said. "Let's vote!"

Izzy shook his head. "It ain't right, gov'nor."

"Let him do what he damn pleases," Gordon told him.

Izzy's small face puckered up in lines of worry. "No, I don't mean him. I mean this business of using ammonia. I know some of the gees trying to vote. They been paying me off—and that's a retainer, you might say. Now this gang tries to poison them. I'm still running an honest beat, and I bloody well can't vote for that! Uniform or no uniform, I'm walking beat today. And the first gee that gives trouble to the men who pay me gets a knife where he eats. When I get paid for a job, I do the job."

Gordon watched him head down the block, and started after the little man. Then he grimaced.

He went down the row, voting regularly. The Planters had things in order. There were a few skirmishes here and there, and a small mob had obviously been hired to help the citizens in one place, toward the cheaper end of the beat. But the mess had already been cleaned up when he arrived. It was the last place where he expected to do his duty by Wayne's administration, and he waited in line, watching the feet of the thug ahead of him.

Then a voice hit at his ears, and he looked up to see Sheila Corey only two places in front of him. "Mrs. Mary Edelstein," she was saying. The Wayne man nodded, without bothering to check, and there was no protest. She picked up a Wayne ballot, and dropped it in the box.

Then her eyes fell on Gordon, and creased to slits. She hesitated for a second, bit her lips, and finally moved out into the crowd.

He could see no sign of her as he stepped out a minute later, but the back of his neck prickled. Now, in the crowd of her own type, she'd have a chance that she couldn't miss. Even if she'd only rented her services to the Planters, they'd protect her. And one cop, more or less, wouldn't matter.

He started out of the crowd, trying to act normal, but glancing down to make sure his gun was in its proper position. Satisfied, he pivoted suddenly. For a second, he spotted her behind him, before she could slip out of sight.

Then a shout went up, yanking his eyes around with the rest of those standing near. The eyes had centered on the alleys along the street, and men were beginning to run wildly, while others were jerking out their weapons. He saw a gray car, almost big enough to be the mayor's, coming up the street; on its side were painted the colors of the Planters. Now it swerved, while someone hit a siren button.

But it was too late. Trucks shot out of the little alleys, jamming forward through the people. There must have been fifty of them. One hit the big gray car, tossing it aside. It was Trench himself who leaped out, together with the driver. The trucks paid no attention, but bore down on the crowd. From one of them, a machine gun opened fire.

Gordon dropped and began crawling in the only direction that was open, toward the alleys from which the trucks had come. A few others had tried that, but most were darting back as they saw the colors of Murphy's Star Point gang on the trucks.

Other guns began firing, and men were leaping from the trucks and pouring into the mob of Planters, forcing their way toward the booth in the center of the mess.

It was a beautifully timed surprise attack. And it was a well armed one, even though guns were supposed to be so rare here. Gordon stumbled into someone ahead of him, and saw it was Trench. He looked up, and straight into the swinging muzzle of the machine gun that had started the commotion.

Trench was reaching for his revolver, but he was going to be too late. Gordon brought his up the extra half inch, aiming by the feel, and pulled the trigger. The man behind the machine gun dropped, with a sick expression, his fingers clutching at the blood that was beginning to saturate the clothing around his stomach.

Trench had his gun out now, and was firing, after a single surprised glance at Gordon. He waved back toward the crowd.

But Gordon had spotted the open trunk of the gray car, and it offered better safety than the emptying street. He shook his head, and tried to indicate it. Trench jerked his thumb, and leaped to his feet, rushing back. Some kind of a command sounded over the fighting, but Gordon had no time to try to puzzle it out.

He saw another truck go by, and felt a bullet miss him by inches. Then his legs were under him, and he was sliding into the big luggage compartment, where the metal would shield him from most of the danger.

Something soft under his feet threw him down. He felt a body under him, and coldness washed over him before he could get his eyes down. The cold went away, to be replaced by shock.

Between his spread knees lay Whaler, bound and gagged, and with his face a bloody mass of torn and bruised flesh. Only the man's open eyes showed that he was alive.

Gordon reached for the gag, but the other held up his hands and pointed to the gun. It made sense; the gag could wait. The knots were tight, but Gordon managed to get his knife under the rope around Whaler's wrists and slice through it. The older man's hands went out for the gun, and his eyes swung toward the street, while Gordon attacked the rope around his ankles. Then Gordon's eyes swept what he could see from the opened lid of the trunk.

The Star Point men were winning, but it was tough going. They had fought their way almost to the booth, but there a *V* of Planters gang cars had been gotten into position somehow, and gun fire was coming from behind them. As he watched, a huge man reached over one of the cars, picked up a Star Point man, and lifted him behind the barricade.

Whaler's gag had just come out when the Star Point man jumped into view again, waving a rag over his head and yelling. Captain Trench followed him out, and began pointing toward the gray car where Gordon and Whaler were.

"They want me," Whaler gasped thickly. "Get out, Gordon, before they gang up on us!"

It made no sense, yet there was a small nucleus of men from both gangs trying to head toward the car. Gordon jerked his eyes back toward the alley on the

89

other side. It went at an angle and would offer some protection, if they could make it.

He looked back, just as bullets began to land against the metal of the car. Whaler held up one finger and put himself into a position to make a run for it. Then he brought the finger down sharply, and the two men leaped out.

Trench's ex-Marine bellow carried over the fighting. "Get the old man!"

Gordon had no time to look back. He hit the alley in five heart-ripping leaps and was around the bend. Then he swung just as Whaler made it. Bullets spatted against the walls, but at first Gordon thought they had both escaped uninjured. Then he saw the blood pumping under Whaler's right shoulder.

"Keep going!" Whaler ordered.

A fresh cry from the street cut into his order, however. Gordon raised a quick look, and then stepped further out to make sure.

The surprise raid by the Star Pointers hadn't been quite as much of a surprise as they'd expected. Coming down the street, with no regard for men trying to get out from their way, the trucks of the Croopsters were roaring all out, battering aside the few who could not reach safety. There were no machine guns this time, but the straightforward drive of the trucks themselves was danger enough.

They smacked into the tangle of Star Point trucks, and came to a grinding halt, with men piling out ready for battle. Gordon nodded. In a few minutes, Wayne's supporters would have the booth again, and there'd be a long delay before any organized search could be made for the two of them. He looked down at Whaler's shoulder, and calculated as rapidly as his still-scant knowledge of the city permitted.

"Come on," he said finally. "Or should I carry you?"

Whaler shook his head. "I'll walk. Get me to a place where we can talk—and be damned to this. Gordon, I've got to talk—but I don't have to live. I mean that!"

Gordon started off, disregarding the words. A place of safety had to come first. And for whatever reason, sooner or later Trench would be looking for them. It had taken something pretty serious to get the nucleus of Star Pointers working with the Planters. Nobody would trust a strange couple on a day like this—but there was one faint chance, if he was right.

He picked his way down alleys and small streets, with Whaler following. The older man kept trying to stop to speak, but Gordon gave him no chance. He was lucky to be in a poor section, where a few thugs would be enough to control things, and where there was little chance of gang wars to hold him up. Too, the defeated, hopeless condition of the poorer inhabitants of Marsport would make most of the streets deserted at a time like this.

It was further than he thought and he began to suspect he'd missed the way, until he saw the drugstore. Now it all fell into place—the beat he'd first had with Izzy, before he was pulled off it and shipped out to the Nineteenth Precinct.

He ducked down back alleys, until he reached the right section. Then there was no choice; he wouldn't have known the rear entrance if there had been one. He scanned the street and jumped to the door of the little liquor store and began banging on it. There was no answer, though he was sure the old couple lived just over the store. Here there had been no looting, apparently, since the section was too poor to provide a good target.

He began banging again. Finally, a feeble voice sounded from inside. "Who is it?"

"A man in distress!" he yelled back. There was no way to identify himself as the man who had chased off the racketeers and returned their money. He could only hope she would look.

The entrance seal opened briefly. Then it flashed open all the way. Gordon motioned to Whaler, and jumped to help the failing man to the entrance. The old lady looked, then moved quickly to the other side. Whaler was about done in. He leaned on the two of them, panting.

"Ach, God," she breathed. Her hands trembled as

91

she closed the seal. Then she brushed the thin hair off her face, and pointed. He followed her up the stairs, carrying Whaler on his back. She opened a door, passed through a tiny kitchen, and threw open another door to a bedroom.

The old man lay on the bed, and this time there was no question of concussion. A club had bashed in his head, bringing almost instant death. The woman nodded. "Yes. Papa is dead, God forbid it. He *would* try to vote. I told him and told him—and then . . . With my own hands, I carried him here."

Gordon felt sick. He started to turn, but she shook her head quickly. "No. Papa is dead. He needs no beds now, and your friend is suffering. Put him here."

She lifted the frail old body of the man from the bed and lowered him onto the floor with a strength that seemed impossible to her. Then her hands were gentle as she helped lower Whaler where the corpse had been. "I'll get alcohol from below—and bandages and hot water."

Whaler opened his eyes, breathing stertorously. His face was blanched, and his clothes were a mess. But he protested as Gordon tried to strip them. "Let them go, kid. There's no way to save me now. And listen!"

"I'm listening!"

"With your mind, Gordon, not your ears. You've heard a lot about Security. Well, I'm Security. Top level—policy for Mars. We never got a top man here without his being discovered and killed—a leak, somehow. That's why we've had to work under all the cover—and against our own government, as always. Damned nationalism! Nobody knew I was here—men we thought loyal to us are with the grafters. Trench was our man—we sent him here. Thought he was still levelling. Sold us out! We've got junior men—down to your level, clerks, such things. We've got a dozen plans. But we're not ready for an emergency, and it's here—now! Gordon, you're a self-made louse, but you're a man underneath it somewhere. That's why we rate you higher than you think you are. That's why I'm going to trust you—because I have to."

He swallowed, and the thin hand of the woman lifted brandy to his lips. "Papa," she said slowly. "He was a clerk once for Security. But nobody came, nobody called . . ."

She went back to trying to bandage the bleeding bluish hole in his chest. Whaler nodded faintly.

"Probably what happened to a lot—men like Trench, supposed to build an organization, just leaving the loose ends hanging. But—anyhow, they had me trailed since—since they yanked me off the Nineteenth —maybe before. When I headed for the cable office, they picked me up, fast." He groaned, gritted his teeth, and grimaced. Sweat oozed out on his forehead, but his eyes never left Gordon's. "Hell's going to pop. The Government's just waiting to step in and chuck the government here out the window. Earth *wants* to take over."

"It should," Gordon said.

"No! We've studied these things. Mars won't give up—and Earth wants a plum, not responsibility. You'll have civil war and the whole planetary development ruined. Security's the only hope, Gordon—the only chance Mars had, has, or will have! Believe me, I know. Security has to be notified. There's a code message I had ready—a message to a friend—even you can send it; and they'll be watching. I've got the basic plans in the book here—*Aaah!*"

He slumped back. Gordon frowned, then found the book and pulled it out as gently as he could. It was a small black memo book, covered with pages of shorthand. The back was an address book, filled with names—many crossed out, as he could see. A sheet of paper in normal writing fell out.

"The message," Whaler said. His voice was getting thick and faint. He took another swallow of brandy. "Take it. You're head of Security on Mars now. It's all authorized in the plans there. You'll need the brains and knowledge of the others—but they can't act. You can—we know that much about you."

The old woman sighed, and shook her head over the

bandages. She put down the hot water and picked up the bottle of brandy, starting down the stairs.

"Gordon!" Whaler said faintly.

Gordon turned to put his head down. From the stairs, a sudden cry and thump sounded, and something hit the floor. He jumped toward the sound, to find the old lady bending over the inert figure of Sheila Corey.

"I heard someone," the woman said. She stared at the brandy bottle sickly. "God in heavens, look at me. Am I a killer too that I should strike a young and beautiful girl? She comes into my house, and I sneak behind her . . . It is an evil time, young man. Here, you carry her inside. I'll get some twine to tie her up. The idea, spying on you!"

Gordon picked the girl up roughly. This capped it, he thought. There was no way of knowing how much she'd heard, or whether she'd tipped others off to his escape route. He should have guessed she would follow him, even if no one else did. And in the business of getting Whaler inside, they hadn't locked the door seal properly.

She seemed to be still out. He dropped her near the bed and went over to Whaler. The man was dying now.

"So Security expects me to contact the others in the book and organize things?" he asked.

"Yes." Whaler swallowed. His eyes were becoming unfocused, but his mind was still on his duty. "Not a good chance, it seemed—but a chance. So they asked me to decide. I had—time enough—I think. Gordon?"

"What else can I do?" Gordon asked.

It was an evasion, but Whaler apparently accepted it as a promise. The gray-speckled head relaxed and started to roll sideways on the bloody pillow. Then his eyes cleared and he forced himself up, pointing toward the book that was lying where it had been dropped.

"Gordon! Inside—inside . . ."

But it was too late to finish whatever was on his mind. The hand that had touched the book dropped. He slumped back and the blood stopped seeping from around the hole in his chest. Gordon leaned forward, trying to detect a sign of a pulse, but he could find none.

"Dead," he said to the woman as she came up with the twine. "Dead, fighting windmills. And maybe winning. I don't know."

Then he turned toward Sheila.

But in that, he was a split second too late. The girl came up from the floor with a single push of her arm. She pivoted on her heel, hit the door, and her heels were clattering on the stairs. Before Gordon could reach the entrance, she was whipping around into an alley. There, in the confusion of the maze of backstreet Marsport, nobody could catch her.

He watched her go, sick inside, and the last he saw was the hand she held up, waving the little black book at him!

He turned back into the liquor shop, where the woman stood on the stairs watching. She seemed to read his face, and her own expression darkened. "I should have watched her. It is a bad day for me, young man. I failed Papa. I failed the poor man who died—and now I have failed you. It is better . . ."

He caught her as she fell toward him. She relaxed after a second. "Upstairs, please," she whispered. "Beside Papa. There was nothing else. And these Martian poisons—they are so sure, they don't hurt—much. Fifteen minutes more, I think. Stay with me, I'll tell you how Papa and I got married. I want somebody should know how it was with us once, together."

He stayed. Then he picked the two bodies up and moved them from the floor onto the bed where he had first seen the old man. He moved Whaler's body aside, and covered the two gently. Finally, he went down the stairs, carrying Whaler with him. The man's weight was a heavy load, even on Mars, but somehow he couldn't leave it with the old couple to add to the scandal around their death.

He stopped finally, ten blocks of narrow alleys away, and put Whaler down.

Security, if it ever came, would probably blame him for the death of Whaler—with some gentle hints from

Trench. If it didn't come, Trench knew that he had run off with Whaler, and there was already a suspicion in the captain's mind that he was somehow involved with the hated Solar Security. Sheila had the book, for that matter, with his name probably in it. And she'd almost certainly heard Whaler call him the head of Security.

He heard the sound of a mobile amplifier, and strained his ears toward it at last. There was a bustle from above beginning now, as if the tenements around the alley were coming to life, and it took time to focus through to the sound of the speaker. Then he got enough to hear that Wayne had won a thumping victory of better than three to two. Murphy had conceded.

Which meant that Trench was still captain of the Seventh Precinct.

He stared around, realizing it was dark. It must have been dark when he carried Whaler's body out, now that he thought of it; he'd taken no precautions against being seen, at least. How long had he sat after the old lady died, battling with the same problem that was confronting him now?

It didn't matter. He summed it up once again. Head of the hated Security on Mars, with an enemy to testify to it against him, and with no information—that, too, was in enemy hands. A cop who had aided the escape of the one man his captain most wanted to keep. A man who was exiled by Security until his good behavior could win him a pardon, and who was the obvious fall guy for the murder of the head of Security's whole Martian project.

Whaler had been right. He was a man who got things done. Well done, in fact—cooked to a frazzle, with himself as the chief frazzle.

Look out for number one, he told himself grimly!

He dusted himself off, leaving Whaler where he lay, and went looking for a phone booth.

IX

Elections were over, but the few dim lights along the street showed only boarded-up and darkened buildings. There were sounds of stirring, but no one was trusting that the election-day brawls were completely ended yet. It was a nervous, lost sort of unquiet that lay over Marsport, as if the city knew what the next four years under the administration of Mayor Wayne would bring.

Gordon hesitated, then swung glumly toward a corner where he could find a police call-box. He'd have preferred a public phone, where he could get away if the answers sounded wrong. But the automatic signal turned in by the box probably wouldn't matter. If Trench were looking for him, he'd be picked up sooner or later, anyhow.

He heard a cruising patrol car turn the corner and ducked back into another alley to wait for it to go by. But the men inside weren't looking for him. Their spotlight caught a running boy, clutching a few thin copies of the *Crusader* under a scrawny arm.

After the cops had dumped the unconscious kid into the back of the small squad car and gone looking for more game, Gordon went over to look at the tattered scraps left of the opposition paper, with dirt smudged into its still-wet ink.

Randolph wasn't preaching this time, but was content to report the facts he'd seen. There had been at least ninety known killings, outside of gangsters, and an uncounted number not reported. Mobs had fought citizens outside the main market for three solid hours, though that had been done with comparatively little gunfire. And there was a poorly reproduced photo of a group of mobsters lining citizens up under drawn guns for a propaganda movie of Mayor Wayne watching the "orderly" elections!

Yet in spite of all the ballot-stuffing and intimidations, the outlying vote had almost won. Wayne hadn't returned by a landslide; according to Randolph, he'd barely squeaked through by a four-percent majority rather than by what was being claimed. Even some of the mobsters must have sneaked in honest votes against Wayne.

It was obvious that the current administration could never win another election, and that this was their last chance. They'd really have to concentrate all their efforts into the next four years. Marsport wasn't going to be a pleasant place to live.

It also meant that the chances of a cop who might be somehow mixed up with Security would be practically nil. If Sheila Corey turned him in, they wouldn't bother asking whether her story was true or not—they'd get him on the chance it might be.

But as long as he was stuck on Mars, he couldn't do much but play along and hope. He lifted the cradled phone from the box. "Gordon reporting," he announced.

A startled grunt came from the instrument, followed by the clicks of hasty switching. In less than fifteen seconds, Trench's voice barked out of the phone. "Gordon? Where the hell you been?"

"Up an alley between McCutcheon and Miles," Gordon told him. "With a corpse. Whaler's corpse. Better send out the wagon."

Trench hesitated only a fraction of a second. "Okay, I'll be out in ten minutes."

Gordon clumped back to the alley and bent for a final inspection of Whaler's body to make sure nothing would prove the flaws in his weakly built story. Using Trench's flight from the Star Point mob, he could claim he'd thought Whaler had just been rescued from them, which was why he'd freed the man. The time lapse could be taken care of by claiming they'd gotten lost in backstreet Marsport, which was possible enough. But

98

he'd have to go carefully in hinting that Whaler had first tried to get him to send a message to Earth and then had admitted he was a Security agent—letting Trench think he'd been killed by Gordon, without saying so.

It seemed like a pretty thin alibi, now that he thought it over. But it was too late to think up a new one. Trench was better than his word. He swung his gray car up to the alley in seven minutes.

The door slammed behind him, a beam snapped out from his flashlight into the alley, and then he was beside Whaler's body. He threw the light to Gordon and stooped to run expert hands over the corpse and through the pockets.

Finally he stood up, frowning. "He's dead, all right. I don't get it. If you hadn't reported in . . . Gordon, did he try to make you think he was—"

"Security?" Gordon filled in. "Yeah. Claimed he was head of it here, and wanted me to send a message to Earth for him."

Trench nodded, with a touch of relief on his face. "Crazy! Must have been the beating the Star Pointers gave him before my men and I got to him."

Gordon grimaced faintly. Apparently part of his explanation had been obvious enough a distortion that Trench had also chosen it. It was unexpected, but it made things simpler.

"Crazy," Trench repeated. "He must have been to spin that story around men who just might have a few grudges against the whole Security goon squad . . . By the way, thanks for killing that sniper. You're a good shot. I'd be dead if you weren't, I guess."

Gordon made no comment, and Trench worried it around in his mind for a minute more. When he spoke, the edge was gone from his voice, leaving a grim amusement in it. "I could start a nasty investigation, I guess. I'll take care of it. Good thing you got him before he went completely berserk. These guys who crack up after being in authority for years aren't safe loose. Give me a hand, and I'll take care of all this . . . Want me to drop you off?"

They wangled the body into the trunk of the car. Then it was good to relax while Trench drove along the rubble-piled and nearly deserted streets. Gordon heard a sigh from beside him, and realized Trench must have been under tension, too, with Whaler free and trying to call Earth with the news that Isiah Trench had betrayed Security.

But it hadn't hurt the man's thinking, Gordon reflected bitterly. He had Whaler's body—and he'd take care of it, all right; he'd probably have it mummified out in the dry sands, to use as evidence that Gordon had murdered the man—an extra ace in the hole, if necessary.

They didn't speak until Trench stopped in front of Mother Corey's place. Then the captain turned and stuck out his hand. "Congratulations, by the way. I forgot to tell you, but you won the lottery; you're sergeant from now on. Keep your nose clean, and you'll do all right!"

Gordon watched the car disappear down the street. Trench had the body of Whaler. Sheila had the notebook. His nose was already a long ways from clean. One word from her and he'd probably be killed without knowing it; or a change of heart from Trench and he'd be in the gentler hands of Security—and wish he had been killed.

Then he grimaced. He'd forgotten that he *was* Security here, according to what Whaler had delegated to him. The white hope of Mars! He spat on the step and went past the two guards Mother Corey still had posted.

Inside, a thick effluvium hit his nose, and he turned to see Mother Corey's huge bulk waddling down the hall. The old man nodded. "We thought you'd gone on the lam, cobber. But I guess you've cooled. Good, good. As a respectable man now, I couldn't have stashed you from the cops—though I might have been tempted—mighty tempted." His face was melancholy. "Tell me, lad, did they get Whaler?"

Gordon nodded, and the old man sighed. Something suspiciously like a tear glistened in his eyes. He shook his head from side to side, stirring up the odor about him again.

"I thought you were taking a bath," Gordon commented.

The old man chuckled, without changing his expression, though the gray folds of flesh drew back to expose his snaggled teeth. "Fate's against me, cobber. With all the shooting, some punk put a bullet clean through the wall and the plastic of the tub. Fifty gallons of water, all wasted!"

He turned back toward the end of the hall, sighing again, as if he could read the other's hunch that he'd made up the story to cover his loss of nerve. Gordon went up the stairs, noticing that Izzy's door was open. The little man was stretched out on the bunk in his clothes; filthy; one side of his face was swollen to double size.

"Hi, gov'nor," he called out, and his voice was still cheerful. "I had odds you'd beat the ticket, though the Mother and me were worried there for awhile. How'd you grease the fix?"

Gordon sketched it in, without mentioning Security. "What happened to you, Izzy?"

"Price of being honest. I got this, and I lost a couple of knives, you might say. But the gees who paid me protection didn't get hurt, gov'nor. When you get paid for something, you gotta deliver." He winced as he turned his head, then grinned. "So they pay double tomorrow. Honesty pays, gov'nor, if you squeeze it once in a while ... Funny, you making sergeant; I thought two other gees won the lottery."

So the promotion had come from Trench, as he'd suspected. It bothered him. When a turkey sees corn on the menu, it's time to start wondering when Thanksgiving comes.

He shut the door as he came out of Izzy's room and started down the hall. But the sound of heavy breathing near the stairs made him swing back, to see little Randolph literally crawling toward his room.

The pale, rabbity face turned up to meet him, and the watery eyes shook off some of the agony. There was a sneer in them as he worked his crushed lips and forced a hoarse whisper through them. "Congratulations, muck-raker. Your boy's back in the saddle!"

Then he collapsed. But he came to before Gordon could finish trying to patch him up and put him to bed. His lips were stuck now, and he had to point to his clothes. Gordon found a copy of Wayne's official *Chronicle,* with a full page on how Wayne had triumphed over a combination of bribed votes and outlawry among the Star Point and smaller opposition gangs. The paper was an extra, smeared and battered by what Randolph had been through, but still legible. On an inside page, the little man located what he wanted and held it out—a brief paragraph on how Bruce Gordon had been promoted to sergeant for bravery in overcoming a dangerous maniac.

Randolph's lips finally came open. "Get out!" he said flatly.

Gordon got. He found Mother Corey and sent him to look after the publisher, grumbling and fuming that this was a rooming house, not a rest home. Then Gordon slipped through the entrance seal and out onto the street. Some signs of life were appearing again. He located a tricycle cab and gave the address of Fat's Place without thinking about it.

The streets were still in a shambles from the struggles for control of the voting booths, but Fats was open, and nothing seemed to have been harmed. From the way the man greeted him, Gordon suspected Izzy must have had something to do with that.

"Tables are open," Fats suggested. "Grab yourself a stack of chips on the house. Or maybe you'd like an intro to one of the duchesses?"

Gordon started to ask for beer, and then changed his mind. "How's the chance of getting some food, Fats?" He still hadn't eaten.

Fats looked slightly shocked, but he nodded. "Sure. Grab a seat at the bar. Kitchen's closed, but I'll have Mike dig up something. Coming up!"

It was a rough crowd in the place, Gordon saw— mostly men from the gangs getting rid of their spoils, with only a scattering of normal citizens, all either driven by fevered urgency or gloomy resignation. Gordon caught himself looking for Sheila and cursed himself. He'd already stayed too long on this damned planet.

When the steak and fried Marsapples came, he ate half of the meal automatically, but without any real appetite. Damn it, he'd never been a muck-raker. He'd been dirty at times, but as a reporter he'd played for clean stakes. He'd been able to look himself in the mirror when he shaved. But what was the use here? Whaler and his crusading had proved the same thing Randolph was proving with his.

He downed a couple of needled beers and then got up in disgust to head back to his room. He'd make collections tomorrow. And they'd better be good.

They were good, all week, probably as a result of Izzy's actions. Even after he arranged to pay his income tax and turned over his "donation" to the fund, he was well ahead for the first time since he'd landed here. In a couple of months, he could begin to think about hunting up illegal passage back to Earth.

He had become almost superstitious about the way he was always left with no more than a hundred credits in his pockets. This time, he stripped himself to that sum at once, depositing the rest in the First Marsport Bank. Maybe it would break the jinx.

Then collections fell off. The Mayor had wangled a special tax to take care of the election damage, and the cops were being driven hard to collect it. The joints met it with resignation, but the poorer section of his beat was a problem. People had reached the limit. Even Blaine from the Tenth, who had a reputation for being too free with brass knuckles on slow payers, was said to be behind his quota.

In the end, they were forced to tap the joints to make up for the people who couldn't pay. That started the day Gordon collected finally from one small shopkeeper and came back two hours later to find the man hanging by a rope from the ceiling of his store.

"No guts," Izzy commented. "Hell, if you think he

had it tough, gov'nor, you shoulda seen the way my old man went to work the day he died. Starved to death. Fell over dead on the job. You gotta have it under the belt here." But he went along with Gordon's suggestion about tapping the joints.

They were one of the few teams in the Seventh Precinct to make full quota. Trench was lavish in his praise. He was playing more than fair with Gordon now, but there was a basic suspicion in his eyes. He had decided to accept things—but he hadn't been convinced. And he was waiting warily for further developments.

The next day, he drafted them for a trip outside the dome. "It's easy enough, and you'll get plenty of credit in the fund for it. I need two men who can keep their mouths shut."

They idled around the station through the morning. In the late afternoon, they left in a big truck capable of hauling what would have been fifty tons on Earth— about twenty here. Trench drove. Outside the dome, the big machine carried them along at a steady thirty miles an hour, almost silently.

For the first couple of hours, they ran along a track through the sandy waste that was fairly well traveled. Except once, when they swung out to avoid one of the eroded, shallow craters, the track paralleled the monorail railway. They saw a train, pulling about forty small freight cars, but it soon left them behind, running rapidly with a comparatively light load on its way back to the outlands.

This was Gordon's first look at the real Mars. He saw small villages where crop prospectors and hydro farmers lived, with a few small industrial sections scattered over the desert. As they moved out, he saw the slow change from the beaten appearance of the city to something that seemed no worse than would be found among the share-croppers back to Earth. It was obvious that Marsport was the poison center here.

Further out, they began passing farms. Much of the land was still devoted to the tough native plants; apparently the air, richer than was natural to them, had no adverse effect on the things. Mixed with them were plots of ground devoted to those Earth plants that had been successfully adapted to Mars. Cabbages were doing fine in the open, but some other plants still required the big plastic tents that had been the prototype of the dome over Marsport.

Some of the younger children out here were running around and playing normally without helmets, confirming Aimsworth's claim that third-generation Martians somehow learned to adapt to the atmosphere. In them, the sure end of Marsport was being spelled out—but it would take at least another thirty years, and Gordon never expected to see it.

Trench must have noticed his interest. "Show you something, Gordon," he said. "It's only a little out of the way."

He swung the truck off the track onto the desert. The ride was now less smooth, but their speed remained the same. They moved for perhaps fifteen miles through scrub plants. Ahead was something that looked like a cloud near the ground. As they drew nearer, it began to show some huge, solid object behind a screen of dust.

"Air machine," Trench said simply.

Gordon could see it now—a huge affair on gigantic treads that moved forward about a foot a minute, with a giant scoop and conveyor digging into the sand. Behind it lay a swath of grayish-yellow sand and rubble, quite different from the normal desert.

"Sand has a lot of oxides in it," Trench explained. For once, he seemed genuinely pleased and oddly proud. "These things—and there are a lot of them now—break it down, freeing the oxygen and a fair amount of nitrogen from nitrates. Carbonates get converted to coke and oxygen. And the metals that are recovered pay for the whole operation. My grandfather helped develop them."

Then he headed back away to rejoin the track. Darkness fell as they headed out into the dunes. When they stopped, it was beside a small spaceship. Boxes were coming out, and Trench motioned them to help him begin loading. It took about an hour of hard work until they were finished with it. Then Trench went up to one of the men from the ship, handed over an envelope, and came back to start the truck back toward Marsport. As the dunes dwindled behind them, Gordon could see the brief flare of the little rocket taking off.

They drove back through the night as rapidly as the truck could manage. Finally, they rolled into City Hall, down a ramp, and onto an elevator that took them three levels down. Trench climbed out and nodded in satisfaction. "That's it. Take tomorrow off, if you want, and I'll fix credit for you. But just remember you haven't seen anything. You don't know any more than our old friend Whaler!"

He led them to a smaller elevator, and then swung back to the truck.

"Guns," Gordon said slowly. "Guns and contraband ammunition from Earth for the administration. And they must have paid half the graft they've taken for that. It's still considered treason to ship anything bigger than a revolver off Earth. What the hell do they want all that stuff for?"

Izzy jerked a shoulder upward and a twist ran across his pockmarked face. "War, what else? Gov'nor, Earth must be boiling about the election. Maybe Security's getting set to spring. And we're going to be caught in a revolution—right where the big push is gonna hit!"

The idea of Marsport rebelling against Earth seemed ridiculous. Even with guns, they wouldn't have a chance if Earth sent a force of any strength to back Security. But it was the only explanation. Things got better all the time. In such a rebellion, he couldn't join Earth without having Trench spread the word that he'd killed Whaler; and he couldn't risk sticking to Trench and then having Sheila claim he was a spy!

He took the next day off to look for her, but nobody would admit having seen her. He couldn't understand why she hadn't already struck at him. Or had she already gone to Trench, and was Trench just baiting him, fattening him for the kill?

He had seen the crowds beginning to assemble all afternoon, but had paid no attention to them. Now he found the way back to Corey's blocked by a mob, and it finally registered. He studied them for a moment. This was no gang movement; there was too much desperation among them as they milled and fought to move forward.

Then he saw that the object of it all was the First Marsport Bank. It was only toward that building that the shaking fists were raised. Gordon managed to get onto a pile of rubble where he could see over the crowd. The doors of the bank were locked shut, but men were attacking it with an improvised battering ram. As he watched, a pompous little man came to the upper window over the door and began motioning for attention. The crowd quieted almost at once, except for a single yell. "When do we get our money?"

"Please. Please." The voice reached back thinly as the bank president got his silence. "Please. It won't do you any good. Not a bit. We're broke. Not a cent left! And don't go blaming me. *I* didn't start the rush. Your friends did that. They took all the money, and now we're cleaned out. You can't . . ."

A rope rose from the crowd and settled around him. In a second, he was pulled down, and the crowd surged forward. They used only their hands on him—but his shrieks cut off a moment later in a final wild cry.

Gordon dropped from the rubble, staring at the bank. He'd played it safe this time—he'd put his money away, to make sure he'd have it. And now he was back to the old familiar pattern—less than a hundred credits to his name!

A heavy hand fell on his shoulder, and he turned to see Mother Corey there. "That's the way a panic is, cobber," the man said. "There's a run, then everything is ruined. I tried to get you when I first heard the rumor, but you were gone. And when this starts, a man has to get there first." He patted his side, where a bulge showed. "And I just made it, too. Bound to come, but who'd guess it was going to be so soon? Started here and spread. By now there won't be a bank in Marsport that isn't busted."

The mob was beginning to break up now, but it was still in an ugly mood. Gordon stepped into a narrow passageway at the side, and Mother Corey followed. "But what started it?"

"Rumors that Mayor Wayne got a big loan from the bank—and why not, seeing it was his bank! Nobody had to guess that he'd never pay it back, so—" Mother Corey swept his hand toward the crowd. "Ever see a panic, cobber? Well, you will."

"Where's Izzy?" Gordon asked. He was sick at the loss of his money, but somehow the stark tragedy on the faces around made him even sicker. "Never mind, I can guess. See you later."

Somehow, he managed to avoid most of the shouting groups as he headed back for his beat. He found Izzy organizing the bouncers from the joints and some of the citizens into a squad. Every joint was closed down tightly already. Gordon began organizing his own squad.

Izzy slipped over as he began to get them organized. "If we hold past midnight, we'll be set, gov'nor," he said. "They go crazy for a while, and the gangs come out for the pickings, too. But give 'em a few hours, and they stop most of it. A lot of them will probably hit for the food stores or the liquor shops. But a few smart gees are gonna figure the joints have money, and money always talks. I figure you know where all the scratch went?"

"Sure—guns from Earth! The damned fools!"

"Yeah. But not fools. Just bloody well informed, gov'nor. Earth's sending a fleet—got official word of it. No way of telling how big, but it's coming." The little man spat onto the ground, and felt for his knives. Then he grinned crookedly, and headed back to his group.

It gave Gordon something to think about while they patrolled the beat. But he had enough for a time without that. The mobs left the section alone, apparently scared off by the organized group ready and waiting for them. But every street and alley had to be kept under constant surveillance to drive out the angry, desperate men who were trying to get something to hang onto before everything collapsed. He saw stores being broken into beyond his beat, and brawls as one drunken, crazed crowd met another. But he kept to his own territory, knowing that there was nothing he could do beyond it.

By midnight, as Izzy had promised, the people had begun to quiet down, however. The anger and hysteria were giving way to a sullen, beaten hopelessness. Most of them had never had any money to lose; they would suffer in the general depression that must follow, but it was a vague threat still, now that the first shock had worn off.

Honest Izzy finally seemed satisfied to turn things over to the regular night men. Gordon waited around a while longer, but finally headed back to Mother Corey's place. There were still clumps of people about, but their muscles were now slack with defeat instead of taut with fury. He wondered how many would be on the breadlines within a month—and whether there would be any breadlines, with the battle between Earth and Marsport draining the administration's funds.

He met Randolph coming out of the house, and tried to avoid him. But the little man stopped squarely in front of him. The scars were still livid, but he seemed fit enough again.

"Gordon," he said quickly, "I behaved like a louse. I had no business dragging your Earth record into things here. Anyhow, it was a damned swinish thing to make use of your help and then chase you out. I'm apologizing!"

"Forget it," Gordon began. But the publisher had already gone down the steps. Gordon went inside, weary in every bone of his body. "Hi, Mother."

Mother Corey motioned him back and put a cup of steaming coffee into his hands. "You look worse than I do, cobber. Worse than even that granddaughter of mine. She was here looking for you!"

"Sheila?" Gordon jerked the word out.

"Yeah. She left a note for you. I put it up in your room." Mother Corey chuckled. "Why don't you two get married and make your fighting legal?"

109

"Thanks for the coffee," Gordon threw back at him. He was already mounting the stairs.

He tossed his door open and found the letter on his bed. He knew it would be bad news, but he had to find out how bad. He ripped the envelope open.

A single sheet of paper fell out, together with the torn-off front cover of the notebook. He spread the sheet out, and glanced at the writing on it.

"I'd rather go to Wayne," it said. "But I need money. If you want the rest of this, you've got until three tonight to make an offer. If you can find me, maybe I'll listen."

He crushed it savagely and tossed it into the corner. It was a quarter after three already, he was practically broke—and he had no idea where she could be found.

X

Gordon jerked the door open to yell for Izzy while he tucked the notebook cover into his pocket. Then he stopped as something nibbled at his mind. Finally he closed the door silently. Izzy might know the answers, but he regarded it as dishonest to give away valuable information free—that was cutting the rates, and simply not done.

Then the odor Gordon had smelled before registered. He yanked out the cover of the notebook and sniffed. It hadn't been close enough for any length of time to be contaminated by Mother Corey, so the smell could only come from one place. And it was logical enough, when he thought about it.

He checked the batteries on his suit and put it on quickly. There was no point in wearing the helmet inside the dome, but it was better than trying to rent one at the lockers. There was no reason he should conceal going outside, anyhow. He buckled it to a strap. The knife slid into its sheath, and the gun holster snapped onto the suit. As a final thought, he picked up the stout locust stick he'd used under Whaler.

There were no cabs outside tonight, of course. But he hadn't expected to find one. He'd have had to walk from the dome entrance, anyhow. It wouldn't matter. He had to gamble on the fact that Sheila wouldn't actually try to see Wayne or one of his assistants until morning, in spite of the note. As for the other details, he'd take care of them when the need arose.

He struck out at a steady lope. He hadn't been exercising his Earth muscles, but they were still better than those of most of the people here, and the light gravity helped. Exhausted as he had been, he could still put a good six miles behind him every hour.

The streets were almost deserted now, except for some prowler or desperation-driven drug addict. The people who had been hit by the failure had retired at last to lick their wounds in private.

He proceeded cautiously, however, realizing that it would be just like her to lay an ambush for him. He was half hoping she would, since it would save time. But he reached the exit from the dome with no trouble.

"Special pass to leave at this hour," the guard there reminded him. "Of course, if it's urgent, pal . . ."

Gordon was in no mood to try bribes. He let his hand drop to the gun. "Police Sergeant Gordon, on official business," he said curtly. "Get the hell out of my way."

The guard thought it over without taking time to draw a breath and reached for the release. Gordon swung back as he passed through. "And you'd better be ready to open when I come back," he warned the guard.

He was in comparative darkness almost at once, and tonight there was no sign of the lights of patrolling cops. They'd all been pulled back into the dome to keep down trouble there, probably. Nobody cared too much what happened outside. There were only the few phosphor bulbs at the corners. Gordon let his own light remain unlighted, threading his way along. He'd have to depend on the faint markers and on his own memory.

A vague shadow moved out of the darker inkiness around him, and a whining voice came from the other's Marspeaker. "Got a credit, gov'nor? Lost my money in the crash 'n I got three starving kids, 'n—".

The faint tightening of his voice gave him away. Gordon sidestepped, flicking on his helmet light, just as the heavy bludgeon crashed forward in the hand of the man behind him. He stepped in again as the man went off balance, and brought the locust stick down sharply across the back of the helmet.

He swung without waiting to see whether the neck or the helmet had given—the results would be the same out here. The set-up man was just drawing his knife back for a long, awkward overhand throw. Gordon sent the club sailing toward him. The other ducked, pulling his arm down, and Gordon was on him.

Whaler had taught him one more thing that was probably more valuable for survival here than anything else, and that was complete ruthlessness when dealing with such men. It was the man who didn't care how badly he hurt the other who would usually win—and even the supposedly tough customers usually had some squeamishness. He flipped the other over with a single heave and went to work with his recovered club on the small of the back. It wasn't until the screams faded out that he stopped.

He didn't look back as he walked on. The parasites went on killing, robbing and terrorizing in the night out here against thousands of citizens who were honest and just out of luck. Yet a hundred men willing to handle them properly could probably clean up the whole mess—a hundred men and a government that would back them up.

Then three specks of glaring blue light suddenly appeared in the sky, jerking his eyes up. They were dropping rapidly, and the tongues of flame were blazing wider now. Rockets, landing at night. The rocket field

112

in the distance was glaring brightly in the downward wash of fire from them.

Rockets that flamed bright blue . . . the forces from Earth, arriving in military rockets! He wished he knew more of the force each might carry, but that was of only secondary importance. The major thing was that Earth was finally taking a hand! And he was no more ready for it than was the administration of Wayne, if as much so.

He crouched in a hollow that had once been some kind of a basement, out of reach of prowlers, until the ships had landed and cut off their jets. Then he stood up, blinking his eyes until they could again make out the pattern of the dim bulbs. He'd seen enough by the rocket glare to know that he was headed right, at least. Now, more than ever, he had to take care of the immediate situation.

Twice he heard the sounds of someone near, but none came close enough to bother him. And finally the ugly half-cylinder of patched brick and metal that was the old Mother Corey's Chicken Coop showed up against the faint light from the rocket field. It looked even more of a wreck than before, if that were possible.

He moved in cautiously and as silently as he could, wondering if there would be sentries staked outside. Not unless Sheila had expected him, but he couldn't be sure. He finally located the semi-secret entrance to the building without meeting anyone. Once in the tunnel that led to the building, he felt a little safer. He could still stumble on someone, but the element of surprise would be all on his side in that event.

He started to remove his helmet, once he reached the dimness of the old mainfloor hall, but the stench made him change his mind. Then he reconsidered again—without it, he'd seem more like one of whatever inmates there still were. He removed it and strapped it to the back of his suit, out of the way. The old hall was in worse shape than before. For a second, he resented the way the place had gone to pot, before the ridiculousness of the idea hit him.

Yet it wasn't entirely ridiculous. Mother Corey had

run a somewhat orderly place, with constant vigilance; he could never have come into the hallway without being seen in the old days. And there was the feeling of petty criminal evil here now. Before, the "guests" had been mostly those who lived by their wits, just outside the law, rather than muggers and cut-throats.

Then a pounding sound came from the second floor, and Gordon drew back into the denser shadows, staring upward. There were shouts and more bangings, but nothing he could see. A heavy, thick voice picked up the exchange of shouts.

"You, Sheila, you come outa there! You come right out or I'ma gonna blast that there door down with gunpowder. You open up."

Gordon was already moving up the stairs when a second voice reached him, and this one was familiar. "Jurgens don't want you, you outland bat! All he wants is this place—we got use for it. It don't belong to you, anyhow! Come out now, and we'll let you go peaceful. Or stay in there and we'll blast you out—in pieces."

It was the voice of Jurgens' henchman who had called on Mother Corey before elections. The thick voice must belong to the big ape who'd been with him.

"Come on out," the little man cried again. "You don't have a chance. We've already chased all your boarders out!"

Gordon tried to remember which steps had creaked the worst, but he wasn't too worried, if there were only two of them. Then his head projected above the top step, and he hesitated. Only the rat and the ape were standing near a heavy, closed door. But four others were lounging in the background, apparently amused by the trouble their chief was having.

He knew he'd be a fool to go on against that number. He lifted his foot to put it back down to a lower step, just as Sheila's muffled voice shrilled out a fog of profanity. He grinned, and then he saw that he'd lifted his foot to a higher step. All right, then, he decided.

There was a sharp yell from one of the men in the background and a knife sailed for him, but the aim was poor. Gordon's gun came out. Two of the men were dropping before the others could reach for their own weapons, and while the rat-faced man was just turning. The third dropped without firing, and the fourth's shot went wild. Gordon was firing rapidly, but not with such a stupid attempt at speed that he couldn't aim each shot. And at that distance, it was hard to miss.

Rat-face jerked back behind the big hulk of his partner, trying to pull a gun that seemed to be stuck; a scared man's ability to get his gun stuck in a simple holster was always amazing. The big guy made no attempt to reach for a weapon. He simply lunged, with his big hands out.

Gordon sidestepped and caught one of the big arms, swinging the huge body over one hip. It sailed over the broken railing, to land on the floor below and crash through the rotten planking. He heard the man hit the basement, even while he was swinging the club in his hand toward the rat-faced man.

There was a thin, high-pitched scream as a collarbone broke. Rat-face slumped onto the floor, and began to try hitching his way down the steps, holding onto his shattered shoulder with the other hand and whimpering with each movement, his eyes fixed in glazed horror on Gordon's club.

Gordon picked up the gun that had dropped out of the holster as the man fell and put it into his pouch. He considered the two, and decided they would be no menace. The big guy had probably broken his neck, and the smaller one was thinking only of getting away.

"Okay, Sheila," he called out, trying to muffle his voice. "We got them all."

"Pie-Face?" Her voice was doubtful. "Did you decide to come back?"

He considered what a man out here who went under that name might be like, and finally guessed at the proper expression. "Sure, baby. Open up!"

"Wait a minute. I've got this nailed shut." There was the sound of an effort of some kind going on as she talked. "Though I ought to let you stay out there and rot. Damn it, if you'd stuck with me, we could have chased them off in the first place. I told you when I rented rooms to you and your boys that you'd have to give a hand. But no, the first time there's any trouble . . . uh!"

The door heaved open then, and she appeared in it, working herself up into a fine rage. Then she saw him, and her jaw dropped open slackly. *"You!"*

"Me," he agreed. "And lucky for you, Cuddles."

Her hand streaked to a gun in her belt, and she let out a cry to someone behind her. "Kill him!"

This time, he didn't wait to be attacked. He went for the door, knocking her aside with his shoulder. His knee caught the outside of her hip as she spun, and she fell over, the gun spinning out of her hand.

The two men in the room were apparently the same two who had tackled him among Nick the Croop's trucks. They were both holding knives, but in the ridiculous overhand position that seems to be an ingrained stupidity of the human race that will not change until men are taught better. A single flip of his locust club against their wrists accounted for both of the knives. He grabbed them by the hair of their heads, then, and brought the two skulls together savagely. They both continued to breathe, but neither knew about it.

Sheila lay stretched out on the floor where her head had apparently struck against the leg of a bed. Gordon shoved the bodies of the two men aside and looked down at the wreck of a man who lay on the dirty blanket. "Hello, O'Neill," he said. "So they let you out?"

The former leader of the Stonewall gang stared up at the club swinging from Gordon's wrist, and a tongue ran rapidly over dry lips. His voice was almost a whisper. "You ain't gonna beat me this time? I'm a sick man. Sick. Can't hurt nobody. You want some money? I got a few credits. Take it and go away. Don't beat me again."

Gordon's stomach knotted sickly at the product of a thorough lesson in ruthlessness. Doing something under the pressure of necessity or in the heat of a struggle was one thing; but to see the sorry results of it later was another.

"All right," he said. "Just stay there until I get away

from this rat's nest and I won't hit you. I won't even touch you."

He was sure enough that it was no act on O'Neill's part. The man couldn't have acted that well. He'd had the guts ripped out of his soul, and no surgeon would ever be able to put them back. He might have taken worse beatings in and out of combat—but he hadn't been able to take a deliberate, cold-blooded working over on the street where he'd been king.

Gordon wasn't so sure about Sheila. She lay as if stunned, with a slow rising and falling of her chest. But he'd learned to suspect her in all things. He checked the two men on the floor, who were still out cold. Then he stepped through the door carefully, to make sure that the big bruiser hadn't somehow lived and come back.

His ears barely detected the sound she made as she reached for the knife of one of the men. He could follow her movements as she gathered herself together and turned carefully to face him, though he wouldn't have noticed it if he'd been as intent on the stairwell as he seemed.

Then it came—the faintest catch of breath. Gordon threw himself flat to the floor. She let out a scream as he saw her momentum carry her over him. Her heels dug into his ribs, but he'd expected it. Then she was at the edge of the rail, and starting to fall.

He caught her feet in his hands and yanked her back. There was nothing phoney this time as she hit the floor. It was a solid thud that knocked the wind out of her.

"Just a matter of coordination, Cuddles," he told her as she rocked back and forth trying to get her breath back. "Little girls shouldn't play with knives, anyway. They'll grow up to be old maids that way—or worse."

The fury of hell blackened her face, but she still couldn't function. She made a sound that might have been involuntary, or was one she'd heard cats using in the back alleys of Earth, and tried feebly to scratch at his eyes.

He picked her up and tossed her back into the room.

From the broken mattress on the bed, he dug out a coil of wire and bound her hands and feet with it.

"Can't say I think much of your choice of companions these days," he commented, looking toward the bed where O'Neill was cowering. "It looks as if your grandfather picks them better for you."

The funny part was that his own stomach felt as if he'd been bounced on the floor. The prospect of her living with this battered wreck of a man was disgusting to him. It was none of his business, but . . .

She spat out curses at him then, strangling over them. "You filthy-minded hog! D'you think I'd—I'd—I wouldn't eat at the same table with the finest man who ever lived! One room in the place with a decent door, and you can't see why I'd choose that room to keep Jurgens' devils back. You—You—"

He'd been searching the room, but there was no sign of the notebook there. He checked again to see that the wire was tight, and then picked up the two henchmen who were showing some signs of reviving.

"I'll watch them," a voice said from the door. Gordon snapped his head up to see Izzy standing there. He realized he'd been a lot less cautious than he'd thought. It could have been one of her men as easily as the little knifeman. He dropped the two back to the floor.

Izzy grinned at his confusion. "I got enough out of the Mother to case the pitch," he said. "I knew I was right when I spotted the apeman carrying a guy with a bad shoulder away from here. Jurgens' punks, eh?"

"Thanks for coming," Gordon said doubtfully. "But what's it going to cost me?"

"Wouldn't be honest to charge unless you asked me to convoy you, gov'nor. And if you're looking for the vixen's room, it's where you bunked before. I got around after I spotted you here."

Sheila forced herself to a sitting position and spat at Izzy. "Traitor! Scummy half-pint crooked little traitor!"

"Shut up, Sheila," Izzy said. "Your retainer ran out."

Surprisingly, she did shut up. Gordon shook his head and went to the little space where he'd first bunked. He saw that Izzy was right; there were a couple of things there—a nearly-used-up lipstick, a comb, and a cracked mirror. There was also a small cloth bag containing a few scraps of clothes, but he scowled as he pawed through them. He'd learned long ago that a woman without decent underthings will always be more naked than one with no clothes.

He turned the room upside down, but there was no sign of the notebook or papers in it. He hadn't expected to find it here, though. Anything like that would be kept where she could be sure it wasn't found—which meant on her person.

He located her helmet and carried it down with him. "You're going bye-bye, Cuddles," he told her. "I'm going to put this on you and then unfasten your arms and legs. But if you start to so much as wiggle your big toe, you won't sit down for a month. That's a promise."

She pursed her lips hotly, but made no reply. He screwed the helmet on, and unfastened her arms. For a second, she tensed, while he waited, grinning down at her. Then she slumped back and lay quiet as he unfastened her legs.

He tossed her over his shoulder, and started down the rickety stairs. "See the rockets from Earth?" he asked Izzy.

"Yeah. Small ones, though. Can't be more than a hundred men on all three of them."

"Not with blue exhausts," Gordon told him. "With those direct atomic jets, those things are almost all carrying space. They could put a small army in them."

"Oh." Izzy thought it over. "M-Day, eh? Well, I ain't worrying any about it until I learn more, gov'nor."

Gordon wished he could honestly say the same. Those rockets were bothering him plenty. If he could go to them and announce that Whaler had appointed him acting head of Security here . . . But he had no proof, and there might be embarrassing questions about what he'd been doing since his appointment.

There were the beginnings of light in the sky. Five minutes later, it was full daylight, which should have been a signal for the workers to start for their jobs. But today they were drifting out unhappily, as if already sure there would be no jobs by nightfall. For a lot of them, it might be true. Most of the businesses of Mars had been mortgaged, and the bank failure would ruin a lot of them.

A few stared at Gordon and his burden, but most of them didn't even look up. The two men trudged along silently. Sheila had seemed light at first, but her weight was growing with every step. But Gordon was too stubborn to put her down.

"Prisoner," he announced crisply to the guard, but there was no protest this time, and she apparently knew it would be useless to put on a scene. They went through, and he was lucky enough to locate a broken-down tricycle cab.

Mother Corey let them in, without flickering an eyelash as he saw his granddaughter. Gordon dropped her onto her legs. "Behave yourself," he warned her as he took off his helmet, and then unfastened hers.

Mother Corey chuckled. "Very touching, cobber. You have a way with women, it seems. Too bad she had to wear a helmet, or you might have dragged her by her hair. Ah, well, let's not talk about it here. My room is more comfortable—and private."

Inside, she sat woodenly on the little sofa, pretending to see none of them. Mother Corey looked from one to the other, and then back to Gordon. "Well? You must have had some reason for bringing her here, cobber."

"I want her out of my hair, Mother," Gordon tried to explain. It wasn't too clear to himself. "I can lock her up—carrying a gun without a permit is reason enough. But I'd rather you kept her here, if you'll take the responsibility for her. After all, she's your granddaughter."

"So she is. That's why I wash my hands of her. I couldn't control myself at her age, couldn't control my son—bad cess to him, dead though he is—and I don't intend to handle a female of my line. You might get Izzy to watch her, except that he's got a job. It looks as if you'll have to arrest her." The gray flesh shook on his face, and his few hairs bobbed about as he shrugged ponderously. But the little eyes in their heavy lids were amused.

"Okay. Suppose I rent a room and put a good lock on it. You've got the one that connects with mine vacant."

"I run a respectable house now, Gordon," Mother Corey stated flatly. "What you do outside my place is your own business. But no women, except married ones. Can't trust 'em."

Gordon stared at the old man, but he apparently meant just what he said. "All right, Mother," he said finally. "How in hell do I marry her without any rigamarole? I understand you've got some system here."

Izzy's face seemed to drop toward the floor, and Sheila let out a gasp. She came up off the couch with a choking cry and leaped for the door. But Mother Corey's immense arm moved out casually, sweeping her back onto the couch.

"Very convenient," the old man said. "The two of you simply fill out a form—I've got a few left from the last time—and get Izzy and me to witness it. Drop it in the mail, and you are married. Of course, it isn't legal on any other planet, but I don't suppose you'll mind that too much, cobber!"

"If you think I'd marry you, you filthy—" Sheila began.

Mother Corey listened attentively. "Rich, but not very imaginative," he said thoughtfully. "But she'll learn. Izzy, I have a feeling we should let them settle their differences."

As the door shut behind them, Gordon yanked Sheila back to the couch. "Shut up!" he told her. "This isn't a game this time. Hell's popping here—you know that better than most people. And I'm up to my neck in it. I should have killed you. But I'm still squeamish, I guess. If I've got to marry you to keep you out of my hair, I will."

Her face was paste white, but she put her hands together on her lap demurely, bent her head, and fluttered her eyelashes up at him. "So romantic," she sighed. "You sweep me off my feet. You—Why, you—"

"Me or Trench! Take your choice. I can take you to him and tell him you're mixed up in Security, and that you either have papers on you or out at the Chicken Coop to prove it. He'd probably believe you if you got to him first. But not if I take you in. You figure out what will happen. Well?"

She looked at him a long time in silence, and there was surprise in her eyes. "You'd do it! You really would . . . All right. I'll sign your damned papers!"

Ten minutes later, he stood in what was now a connecting double room, watching Mother Corey nail up the hall door to the room that was to be hers. There were no windows here, and his own room had an excellent lock on it already—one he'd put on himself. Izzy came back as Mother Corey finished the door and began knocking a small panel out of the connecting door. The old man was surprisingly adept with his hands as he fitted hinges and a catch to the panel and reinstalled it so that she could swing it open. He had considered Gordon crazy for requesting it, but he was doing a good job.

"They're married," Izzy said. "It's in the mail to the register, along with the twenty credits. Gov'nor, we're about due to report in."

Gordon nodded. "Be with you in a minute," he said as he paid Mother for the materials and work. He jerked his head, and the two men went out, leaving him alone with Sheila.

"I'll bring you some food tonight. And you may not have a private bath, but it beats the Chicken Coop. Here." He handed her the key to the connecting door. "Keep your damned virtue. It's the only key there is."

She stared at it in amazement, and back to him. "I'm going to kill you someday," she told him in a matter-of-fact tone.

"You're going to try," he corrected her.

She nodded dumbly, and he went out, locking his door carefully behind him.

XI

All that day, the three rocket ships sat out on the field. Nobody went up to them, and nobody came from them; surprisingly, Wayne had found the courage to ignore them. But rumors were circulating wildly. If they were putting on a test of nerves, they were winning. Gordon felt his nerves creeping out of his skin and beginning to stand on end to test each breeze for danger.

Izzy seemed to have made up his mind about something, but he wasn't telling anyone. He went about the serious job of patrolling the beat and making his collections as quietly as ever.

And collections were good, in spite of the strains of the bank failure, now spreading like wildfire into all businesses. "Good business to be honest about your job," Izzy pointed out. "They take a look at what happened on other beats, and they figure they're getting something for their money, so they don't mind paying. It always paid me to stay honest, gov'nor."

With the credit they'd accumulated in the fund, nearly all their collection was theirs. Gordon went out to do some shopping. He stopped when his money was down to a hundred credits, hardly realizing what he was doing. When he went out, the street was going crazy.

Izzy had been waiting, and filled him in. At exactly sundown, the rocket ships had thrown down ramps, and a stream of jeeps had ridden down them and toward the south entrance to the dome. They had presented some sort of paper, and forced the guard to let them through. There were about two hundred men, some of them armed. They had driven straight to the

123

huge, barnlike Employment Bureau, had chased out the few people remaining there, and had simply taken over. Now there was a sign in front which simply said MARS-PORT LEGAL POLICE FORCE HEADQUARTERS. Then the jeeps had driven back to the rockets, gone on board, and the ships had taken off, as if their job had been finished in setting up the new Force.

Gordon glanced at his watch, finding it hard to believe it could have been done so quickly. But time had gone by faster than he'd expected. It was two hours after sundown. Apparently the move had been timed to correspond with the change in shift on the police force.

Now a surge in the crowd on the street indicated something, and a car with a loudspeaker on top rolled into view—a completely armored car. It stopped, and the speaker clacked once, and began operating.

"Citizens of Marsport! In order to protect your interests from the proven rapacity and illegality of the administration which has recently gained control again here, Earth has revoked the independent charter of Marsport for due cause. The past elections are hereby declared null and void. In their place, your home world has appointed Marcus Gannett as mayor, with Philip Crane as chief of police. Other members of the council will be by appointment during the interim period until legal elections can be held safely. The Municipal Police Force is disbanded, and the Legal Police Force is now being organized around the nucleus of men who have been established in the building where the mockery of justice known as employment relief has been held previously.

"All police and officers who remain loyal to their legal government, as admitted under Earth charter, will be accepted at their present grade or higher. To those who now leave the illegal Municipal Force and accept their duty with the Legal Force, there will be no question of past conduct or loyalty. Nor will they suffer financially from the change!

"Banks will be reopened as rapidly as the Legal Government can extend its control, and all deposits previously made will be honored in full."

That brought a cheer from the crowd, as the sound truck moved on. Gordon saw two of the police officers nearby fingering their badges thoughtfully.

Then another truck rolled into view, and the Mayor's canned voice came over it, panting as if he'd had to rush to make the recording. He began directly:

"Martians! Earth has declared war on us. She has denied us our right to rule ourselves—a right guaranteed in our charter. We admit there have been abuses; all young civilizations make mistakes. But we've developed and grown.

"This is an old pattern, fellow Martians! England tried it on her colonies four hundred years ago. And the people rose up and demanded their right to rule themselves. They had troubles with their governments, too—and they had panics. But they won their freedom, and it made them great—so great that now that *one* nation—not all Earth, but that single nation!—is trying to do to us what she wouldn't permit to herself.

"Well, we don't have an army. But neither do they. They know the people of this world wouldn't stand for the landing of foreign—that's right, *foreign*—troops. So they're trying to steal our police force from us and use it for their war.

"Fellow Martians, they aren't going to bribe us into that! Mars has had enough. I declare us to be in a state of revolution. And since they have chosen the weapons, I declare our loyal and functioning Municipal Police Force to be *our* army. Any man who deserts will be considered a traitor. But any man who sticks will be rewarded more than he ever expected. We're going to protect our freedom.

"Let them open their banks—our banks—again. And when they have established your accounts, go in and collect the money! If they give it to you, Mars is that much richer. If they don't, you'll know they're lying.

"Let them bribe us if they like. We're going to win this war."

Gordon felt the crowd's reaction twist again, and he had to admit that Wayne had played his cards well.

But it didn't make the question of where he belonged

or what he should do any easier. He waited until the crowd had thinned out a little and began heading toward Corey's, with Izzy moving along silently beside him, carrying half the packages.

In any normal revolution, there should have been good chances for a man to get whatever he wanted. But this was more like a game in which the police would be the pieces.

He remembered the promise of forgiveness for all sins on joining the new Legal Force, but he'd read enough history to know that it was fine—as long as the struggle continued. Afterward, promises grew dim, while the old crimes and faults rose up to plague a man more strongly than ever.

He had no use for the present administration. And yet, there was something to be said for its side. Certainly Earth had no right to take over without a formal examination, investigation, and a chance for the people to state their choice. If Security operated that way, it was blinder than he had thought.

Then he grimaced at himself. He was in no position to move according to right and wrong. The only question that counted was how he had the best chance to ride out the storm, and to get back to Earth and a normal life. Fellow Martians! He'd almost swallowed it, too!

He was still in a brown study as he took the bundles from Izzy and dropped them on his bed. Izzy went out and he stood staring at the wall. Trench? The man might be a dangerous enemy, and he could sweeten the graft for Gordon; the collections were coming in well. Another two months and he might be able to go back— if any ships were operating. Or the new Commissioner Crane? If Earth should win—and they had most of the power, after all—and he fought against Security, the mines of Mercury were waiting for him! It was the old puzzle, going around and around, and getting nowhere. Only now it had to get somewhere.

He picked up the stuff from his bed and started to sweep it aside before he lay down. Then he remembered at last. He knocked on the panel. For a second, he thought she had somehow escaped. Then there was a sound. He rattled the panel again, until it finally opened a crack.

"Here," he told her. "Food, and some other stuff. There are some refuse bags there, too. Yell when you want me to take them out."

She took the bundles woodenly until she came to a plastic can. Then she gasped. "Water! Two gallons!"

"There are heat tablets there, and a skin tub." The salesgirl had explained how one gallon was enough in the plastic bag that served as a tub; he had his doubts. "Detergent. The whole works."

She hauled the stuff in and started to close the panel. Then she hesitated. "I suppose I should thank you, but ... But I don't like to be told I stink so much you can't stand me in the next room!"

"Hell, I've gotten so I can stand your grandfather," he answered. "It wasn't that."

The panel slammed shut. For some reason, she was cursing to herself. But he heard the gurgle of water after a while—at eight credits a bottle, and then for reprocessed stuff instead of redistilled. It was a fine time to take on more responsibility.

But his body was dead from the lack of sleep the night before. He stretched out without taking off his clothes to worry about things, and then stopped worrying. He'd just reached the blissful stage of knowing he was almost asleep when he heard the key turn in the lock, and snapped up.

"Did you eat?" she asked. He nodded, rubbing his eyes. She was framed in the doorway, in a robe of some plastic fabric that was sold in the bargain basements on Earth, but came in only the one department store here. She hesitated, cleared her throat, and took a step into his room, to jump back as he sat up. "I—how does it look?"

"Looks fine," he told her. They were new clothes, clean, and they'd last a long time with reasonable care. He hadn't even considered getting her the fancy stuff the women he'd known wanted, after one look at the price tags. But something about her attitude convinced him more was expected. "You're a knockout," he added.

She turned the edge of the robe over to feel the softness of the garments underneath. "If I only had someone to show it all to . . ."

He felt a pulse in his throat, but he tried to keep his tone brusque. "Go ahead. After all, we're married!"

She came a step closer. "Maybe . . . if I didn't feel like an animal in a cage . . . If I had a key of my own, like other women . . ."

It was too obvious. He caught her arm, and saw her face whiten. The robe fell half open, and she caught it together again with a movement of desperation. Gordon laughed suddenly, and spun her around away from him. "Go back to your safety, Cuddles. All I want from you is that notebook. When you tell me how to get it, you can go anywhere you want."

She jerked out of his grasp and leaped to the door. Her face was a mask of flaming eyes and teeth exposed beneath taut lips. "Then I'll die here. Because you'll never get it. Never!" She slammed and locked the door, and he heard her break into almost hysterical sobs. He stood there irresolute, and then headed toward the bed.

The panel flopped open suddenly, and she stuck a tearstained face against it. "And I was going to give you your d-damned b-book, too!" Then the panel went up again, to come down a second later as she began stuffing boxes and clothes back through it; it shut again, at last, with a note of finality.

Gordon studied the heap of packages, noticing that she hadn't shoved through the nicer things. But he couldn't get any amusement out of it. He couldn't figure out why, but he somehow felt like a pig.

He still hadn't solved his problem in the morning, and he was too logey from the long sleep to think about it. Out of habit, he put on his uniform and went across to Izzy's room. But Izzy was already gone. It was still early. Probably the boy had gone down for early coffee.

Gordon fished into the pocket of his uniform for paper and a pencil to leave a note in case Izzy came back. His fingers found the half notebook cover instead. He drew it out, scowling at it, and started to crumple it. Then he stopped, staring at the piece of imitation leather and paper that wouldn't bend.

His fingers were still stiff as he began tearing off the thin covering with his knife, and he pricked himself; he swore absently, and pried the last scraps of leatheroid off. The paper backing pealed away easily.

Under it lay a thin metal plate that glowed faintly, even in the dim light of Izzy's room! Gordon nearly dropped it. He'd seen such an identification plate once before, in the hands of the head of Solar Security back on Earth. There was no mistaking the flash of colors now. He turned it over, and the second shock hit him.

The printing on it leaped at him: "This will identify the bearer, BRUCE IRVING GORDON, as a PRIME agent of the Office of Solar Security, empowered to make and execute any and all directives under the powers of this office." The printing in capitals was obviously done by hand, but with the same catalytic "ink" as the rest of the badge. Whaler must have prepared it and hidden it in the notebook, ready to use—and then died before the secret could be revealed.

A knock sounded from across the hall. Gordon thrust the damning badge as deep into his pouch as he could cram it and looked out. It was Mother Corey, his old face more like putty than ever.

"You've got a visitor—outside," he announced. "Trench. And I don't like the stench of that kind of cop in my place. Get him away, cobber, get him away!"

Gordon found Trench pacing up and down in front of the house, scowling up at it. But the ex-marine snapped around as the seal opened, and then smiled as he saw Gorden in uniform. "Good. At least some men are loyal. Had breakfast, Gordon?"

Gordon shook his head, and realized suddenly that the decision seemed to have been taken out of his hands. They crossed the street and went down half a block to the hole in the wall that was supposed to be a restaurant. "All right," he said, when the first cup of coffee began waking him, "What's the angle?"

Trench dropped the eyes that had been boring into him. "I'll have to trust you, Gordon. I've never been sure. But either you're loyal now or I can't depend on anyone being loyal. Do you know the situation? No, you wouldn't. Well, things are rough—in fact, hell is popping!"

During the night, it seemed, the Legal Force had been recruiting. Wayne, Arliss, and the rest of the administration had counted on self-interest holding most of the cops loyal to them. They'd been wrong. A few agitators had worked them over, and nearly half of the force had gone over to the Legal side. The administration had also counted on the gangs, but some of them had switched—and all were apparently willing to play both ends against the middle. Legal forces already controlled some of the precincts—and about half of the city. So far, there had been no actual engagements, but that was working itself up.

"So?" Gordon asked. He could have told Trench that the fund was good enough reason for most police deserting, and that only a fool ever counted on gang support. But what was the use?

Trench put his coffee down and yelled for more. It was obvious he'd spent the night without sleep. "So we're going to need men with guts. We need a floating mop-up squad. I finally got Arliss and Wayne to see that, at least. Gordon, you had training under Whaler—who knew his business, damn him. And you aren't a coward, as most of these fat fools are. I've got a proposition, straight from Wayne."

"I'm listening."

"Here." Trench threw across a platinum badge. "Take that—captain at large—and conscript any of the Municipal Force you want, up to a hundred. Pick out any place you want, train them to handle those damned Legals the way Whaler handled the Stonewall boys. And then scour the city until no Legal dares to crawl out of the cellar! In return, the sky's the limit. Name your own salary, once you've done the job. And no kick-backs, either!"

Gordon picked up the badge slowly and buckled it

on, while a grim, satisfied smile spread over Trench's features. The problem seemed to have been solved. Look out for number one, Gordon had told himself; and he couldn't do better. He should have been satisfied. But he felt like Judas picking up the thirty pieces of silver. The picture of the man who'd hung himself after paying his protection got all mixed up with the words of Whaler and the vision of the old woman who had forgotten her own tragedy to help him. He tried to swallow them with the dregs of his coffee, and they stuck in his throat.

Comes the revolution and we'll all eat strawberries and scream!

A hubbub sounded outside, and Trench grimaced as a police whistle sounded, and a Municipal cop ran by. "We're in enemy territory," he said. "The Legals got this precinct last night. Captain Hendrix and some of his men wanted to come back with full battle equipment and chase them out. I had a hell of a time getting them to take it easy. If we can stall for a week until you can get rolling, and avoid any gunplay that might get Earth completely worked up, we'll win this. I suppose that was some damned fool who tried to go back to his beat."

"Then you'd better look again," Gordon told him. He'd gone to the door and was looking out. Up the narrow little street was rolling a group of about seventy Municipal police and half a dozen small trucks. The men were wearing guns. And up the street a man in bright green uniform was pounding his fist up and down in emphasis as he called in over the precinct box.

"The idiot!" Trench grabbed Gordon and spun out, running toward the advancing men. "We've got to stop this. Get my car—up the street—call Arliss on the phone—under the dash. Or Wayne. I'll bring Hendrix."

Trench's system made some sense, and this business of marching as to war made none at all. Gordon grabbed the phone from under the dash. A sleepy voice answered to say that Commissioner Arliss and Mayor Wayne were sleeping. They'd had a hard night, and . . .

"Damn it, there's a rebellion going on!" Gordon told

the man. Rebellion, rebellion! He'd meant to say revolution, but . . .

Trench was arguing frantically with the pompous figure of Captain Hendrix. From the other end of the street a group of small cars appeared and men began piling out, all dressed in shiny green.

"Who's this?" the phone asked. When Gordon identified himself, there was a snort of disgust. "Yes, yes, congratulations, Trench was quite right, you're fully authorized. Did you call me out of bed just to check on that, young man?"

"No, I—" Then he hung up. Hendrix had dropped to his knees and fired, before Trench could knock the gun from his hands. There was nothing Wayne could do about it now!

There was no answering fire. The Legals simply came boiling down the street, equipped with long pikes with lead-weighted ends. And Hendrix came charging up, with his men straggling behind him. Gordon was squarely in the middle. He considered staying in Trench's car and letting the fight roll past him. But he'd taken the damned badge.

"Hell," he said in disgust. He climbed out, just as the two groups met. It all had a curious feeling of unreality, as if none of it mattered. Emotionally, it wasn't his fight.

Then a man jumped for him, swinging a pike, and the feeling was suddenly gone. His hand snapped down sharply for a rock on the street. The pike whistled over his head, barely missing, and he was up, squashing the big stone into the face of the other. He jerked the pike away, kicked the man in the neck as he fell, and unsheathed his knife with the other hand.

Trench was a few feet away. The man might be a louse, but he was also a fighting machine of first order, still. He'd already captured one of the pikes. Now he grinned tightly at Gordon and began moving toward him. Gordon nodded—in a brawl such as this, two working together had a distinct advantage. He shortened his grip and brought the pike head up from underneath against a chin that suddenly rained teeth and blood. The

132

first rush had brought the men too close together for good fighting, and they were only beginning to spread out.

Then a yell sounded as more Legals poured down the street. One of them was obviously Izzy, wearing the same green as the others!

Gordon felt something hit his back, and instinctively fell, soaking up the blow. It sent hot hell lancing up his nerves, but he managed to bend his neck and roll, coming to his feet. His knife slashed upward, and the Legal fell—almost on top of the Security badge that had dropped from Gordon's pouch.

He jerked himself down and scooped it up, his eyes darting for Trench. He stuffed it back, ducking a blow. Then his eyes fell on the entrance to Mother Corey's house—with Sheila Corey coming out of the seal!

Gordon threw himself back, trying to get out of the fight and get to her. He stepped on a face, and stumbled. The battle was moving down the street, though, and it looked as if he might make it. He had to get to her before . . .

He hadn't been watching as closely as he should. He saw the pike coming down and tried to duck. It hit him on the shoulder, driving him to his knees. Pain seemed to weld him to the street, but he fought up through it somehow. The pike went up again, and he forced his hand back with the knife and began the labored effort of the throw.

The knife beat the pike, but only by a microsecond. It went home into the Legal's throat, but the pike came down, carried by momentum. Gordon tried to duck, and almost made it. It was only a glancing blow when it hit, but the side of his head rang with agony, and blackness spread from it.

He fought against unconsciousness, even while he felt himself falling. There was no sensation as he hit the street. He lay there, while consciousness came and went in sick waves. But somehow, he got his hands under him and forced himself to his knees. Inch by aching inch, he struggled to his feet, forcing the blackness away. He stood there, reeling, with a red haze over everything.

Through it, he painfully focussed his eyes and began turning his head. Trench was running toward him, looking like someone in a magenta, slow-motion movie. Back further, Sheila Corey had stooped to recover a fallen pike and now was headed for him. Then Trench stopped as two of the Legal force closed in on him.

Another wave of the blackness rolled over him, but he fought it off and refocused his eyes. Sheila was almost up to him now, with the pike raised for the final stroke. He staggered to meet her, but his feet refused to coordinate. He twisted himself around, to stare at the gleaming point of a knife in the hands of the Legal who had come up behind him.

Then something crashed against his shoulder, and there was the beginning of a scream, followed by a spattering crunch. Something fell on him, driving the breath from his lungs. The knife dropped in front of him and he reached for it. He saw his fingers touch and contract—and then the blackness finally won!

He was vaguely conscious later of looking up to see Sheila dragging him into some entrance, while Trench ran toward them. Sheila and Trench together—and the Security badge was still in his pouch!

XII

Something cold and damp against his forehead brought Gordon part way out of his unconsciousness finally. There was the softness of a bed under him and the bitter aftertaste of Migrainol on his tongue. He tried to move, but nothing happened. The drug killed pain, but only at the expense of a temporary paralysis of all voluntary motion.

There was a sudden withdrawal of the cooling touch on his forehead, and then hasty steps that went away from him, and the sound of a door closing. He fought against the paralysis and managed to open one eye. He was in his own bed, obviously partly undressed, since his uniform lay on the chair beside him. The pouch was on top and half open, but he couldn't see whether the Security badge was still safe.

Steps sounded from outside, and his eyes suddenly shut again. The drug was wearing off, but he had no real control, and couldn't reopen them. The steps reached the door; it opened, and there was the sound of two men crossing the room, one with the heavy shuffle of Mother Corey. But it was the voice of Honest Izzy he heard first.

"No wonder the boys couldn't find where you'd stashed him, Mother. Must be a bloody big false section you've got in that trick matteress of yours!"

"Big enough for him and for Trench, Izzy," Mother Corey's wheezing voice agreed. "Had to be big to fit me. Of course, I'm respectable now—but a poor old man never knows . . ."

"You mean you hid Trench out, too?" Izzy asked. "I thought you had that gee pegged as a dome hole?"

There was a thick chuckle and the sound of hands being rubbed together. "A respectable landlord has to protect himself, Izzy. For hiding and a convoy back, our Captain Trench gave me a paper with immunity from the Municipal forces. I used that with a bit of my old reputation to get your Mayor Gannett to give me the same from the Legals. He didn't want Mother Corey to think the Municipals were kinder than the Legals, and maybe joining forces. So you're in the only neutral territory in Marsport. Not that you deserve it."

"Lay off, Mother," Izzy said sharply. "I told you I had to do it. I didn't owe the Municipals anything. Who paid me? The gees on my beat did—and the administration got a cut on my collection. I take care of the side that pays my cut, and the bloody administration pulled the plug on my beat twice. So I hadda switch sides and hope maybe Gannett's crowd was some better. Only honest thing to do was to join the Legals."

"And get your rating up to a lieutenant," Mother Corey observed. "Without telling cobber Gordon!"

"Like I say, honesty pays, Mother—when you know how to collect. Hell, I figured Bruce would do the same. He's a right gee."

Mother Corey seemed to hesitate. Then he chuckled without humor. "Yeah, quite a man. When he forgets he's a machine. How about a game of shanks?"

The steps moved away, and the door closed again. Gordon mentally spat out the Mother's last words. This time he got both eyes open and managed to sit up. The effects of the drug were almost gone, but it took a straining of every nerve to force his body forward enough to reach his uniform pouch. His fingers were clumsy and uncertain as he fumbled inside, groping back and forth for a badge that wasn't there!

A cold shock ran up his spine as he dropped back wearily. Trench had apparently been hidden with him in a false section of Mother Corey's bed, and the captain hadn't missed the chance. It made everything complete. Sheila was free to spill what she knew on him, he was practically helpless here, and the Municipals were probably ready to shoot him on sight as a Security man. Trench had probably slipped word to the Legals that he'd killed Earth's Captain Whaler, just to make it complete!

He heard the door open softly, but made no attempt to look up. The reaction from his effort had drained him, and the sound probably only meant that Izzy had come back to tuck him in for the night.

Fingers touched his head carefully, brushing the hair back delicately from the side of his skull. Then there was the biting sting of antiseptic, sharp enough to bring a groan from his lips. He forced his eyes open, to see Sheila bending over him, her hair over her face as she bent to replace the bandages on his wound. Her being back made no sense, but he accepted it suddenly with a queer lift of spirits and an almost instant disgust at his own reaction.

Her eyes wandered toward his, and the scissors and bandages on her lap hit the floor as she jumped to her feet. She turned toward her room, then hesitated as he grinned crookedly at her. "Hi, Cuddles," he said flatly.

She bit her lips and turned back, while a slow flush ran over her face. Her voice was uncertain. "Hello, Bruce. You okay?"

The normality of the words jarred him, but he let it go. "How long have I been like this?"

"Fifteen hours, I guess. It's almost midnight." She bent over to pick up the bandages and to finish with his head. Her fingers were clever at it—more so than his own as he explored the swelling there. "Are you hungry? There's some canned soup—I took the money from your pocket. Or coffee . . ."

"Coffee," he said. He forced himself up again, noticing that most of the drug's effects were already gone. Sheila propped the flimsy pillow behind him, then went into her room to come back with a plastic cup filled with brown liquid that passed for coffee here. It was loaded with caffeine, at least, and brought new life to his body.

He sat on the narrow two-by-six bunk, studying her. The years of Mars' half-life still showed. But in a decent dress and with better cosmetics, most of the cheapness was gone. He knew that the voluptuous curves covered muscles capable of killing a man, and that the prettiness of her face hid a mind completely unpredictable. But with the badge gone, and probably all Mars against him, he had to find some way of using any help he could get.

Maybe he should have spent more time on Earth learning about women, he thought, and then grimaced. There had been women enough, of a sort—but something in him had scared off the ones that might have offered any chance for normal relationships. It wasn't experience he lacked, but something inside himself.

"Why'd you come back?" he asked suddenly. "You were anxious enough to pick the lock and get out."

She brought her eyes up slowly, her face whitening faintly. "I didn't pick it—you forgot to lock it."

He couldn't remember what he'd done after he found the badge, but it was possible. He nodded doubtfully. "Okay, my mistake. But why the change of heart?"

"Because I needed a meal ticket!" she said harshly. Her hands lay on her lap, clenched tightly. "What else could I do after what you've done to me? Do you think *decent* people would have anything to do with me? Or that my own kind would, after they heard I'd married the iron cop who beats up hoods for breakfast and makes Izzy and the Mother go straight? You've got a reputation, and it's washed off on me. Big joke! I always knew I'd have to kill you for the rotten devil you are inside. Then, when I see that Legal cop ready to take you, I have to go running out to save you! Because I don't have the iron guts to starve like a Martian!"

It rocked him back on his mental heels. He'd been thinking that she had been attacking him on the street; but it made more sense this way, at that. So he owed her his life, the fact that he was here instead of out on the street with his throat cut open and his ribs caved in. And now she was set to collect his gratitude!

"You're a fool!" he told her bitterly. "You bought a punched meal ticket. You never had enough sense to come in out of the wet! Right now I probably have six death warrants out and about as much chance of making a living as . . ."

"I'll stick to my chances. I don't have any others now." She grimaced. "You get things done. Now that you've got a wife to support, you'll support her. Just remember, it was your idea."

He'd had a lot of ideas, it seemed. "I've got a wife who's holding onto a notebook that belongs to me, then. Where is it?"

She shook her head. "It's safe, where nobody will find it. I'll cook for you, I'll help you whenever I can. I'll swallow your insults. But in case that isn't enough, I'm keeping the notebook for insurance. Blackmail,

Bruce. You should understand that! And you won't find it, so don't bother looking."

His mind twisted over the facts he knew on her, looking for an angle to force her hand. The badge was gone; the notebook might be useless now. But he couldn't overlook any bets. Suddenly he reached out to catch her wrist. "It might be fun looking," he told her. Then, because the attempted amusement didn't quite cover a thickness in his throat, he jerked her forward. "Come here."

"You filthy pig!" She avoided his lips, and her hand darted to the place where a knife should be. Her eyes blazed from the whiteness of her face. The hooked fingers of her other hand came up to claw his head, touched the bandage, and dropped. The straining tenseness went out of her as quickly as it had come. "All right. I—I swore I'd kill any man who touched me, but I guess I asked for this. Okay, I'm your wife. Bruce, all *right*. Only give me a minute first."

Surprised, he released her. Now she stumbled across the room toward her own. But the door didn't slam behind her. Instead, there was the rustle of clothes. A minute later, Sheila came back, forcing herself a step at a time. The dress was gone now, replaced by the negligée, and her hair had been brushed back hastily. It showed beads of sweat glistening on her forehead.

"My first—husband ... he ... I *had* to kill him," she said hoarsely. The effort of speech left her throat muscles tense under the beating arteries. Her eyes were still dark with fear, but now there was an odd pleading in them. "Bruce, don't remind me of *him!* Pretend—pretend this is a real marriage, that you like me—that you think I'm ... pretty in the trousseau you bought me. And I'll tell you what I wanted to say when you first gave it all to me ..."

She swung about, awkwardly at first, and then quickly to display the clothes. The negligée swirled out, revealing smooth limbs and bits of lace and silky fabric.

Gordon stood up and moved toward her without conscious volition: "You're beautiful, Cuddles," he said

139

hoarsely, and this time he meant it. She met his eyes and moved hesitantly into his arms, while her mouth opened slightly and tilted to meet his. Her arms tightened.

But it was only a pretense. Her body was unresisting, but like a dead thing, and her lips were motionless, while her eyes remained open and glazed. She began to tremble in slow shudders. He tightened his arms slowly, trying to awaken some response in her. His arms moved to draw her closer, and then were alive and demanding on her back.

And suddenly she jerked and her mouth opened in a thin, agonized scream!

It hit him like an ice bath, and he stepped back, dropping to his bed while she sank limply into the chair. His hands found a cigarette, and he burned his lungs on a long, aching drag of smoke. Finally he grimaced and shrugged. "All right, Cuddles," he said. "Forget it!"

"Bruce . . ."

"Forget it. Go to bed. I'm not interested in the phony act of a frigid woman!"

She stood up, with her face a death mask and her hands making motions like those of an Aztec priest tearing the heart from a living victim. Her colorless lips parted to show clenched teeth as she tried to speak. "You damned ghoul! You mechanical monster!"

Words boiled up in him as she swung toward her room. He opened his mouth . . .

And the words vanished under the shock of the red stain he saw spreading down the back of the negligée.

He caught her before she reached the door and swung her around, ripping the garment back from her shoulder. There was a rough bandage there, but blood was seeping from beneath it. He lifted it, to stare at an ugly six-inch gash that ran down her back where his hands had been.

She shook free of his grasp and pulled the clothes back quickly. "Yes," she said, in a low, tired voice. "That's why I screamed. The Legal wasn't quite dead when I pulled you out from under. And I don't welch on my bargains—ever! Can I go, now?"

"After I bandage that." He turned back to where the bandages lay and began fumbling for them. But her voice cut off his motions, and he swung to face her.

"Bruce!" She was through the door, holding onto it, and now she caught his glance with hers and held it. "Bruce, forget the cut. There are other things . . ."

"It might get infected."

She sighed, and her lips tightened. "Oh, go to hell!" she said, and shut the door. There was the sound of the lock being worked, and then silence.

He stared at the door foolishly, swearing at all women and at the whole stinking planet. Then he grimaced. Until he was on a better planet, he'd have to face his problems here—and there were plenty of them to face, without Sheila. He started for the door, grunted in self-disgust, and turned back to the chair where his uniform still lay. He could stay here fighting with her, or he could face his troubles on the outside, and maybe bull through somehow. The whole thing hinged on what Trench did with the badge and about him. And unless Trench had shown it to others, his problem boiled down to a single man.

Gordon found a couple of tablets of normal aspirin in a bottle and swallowed them with the dregs of the coffee. He still felt lousy, but events never waited on a man's feelings. He'd already been here too long. Anyhow, it wasn't the first time he'd been knocked out and had to come up fighting on the count of nine.

He made sure his knife was in its sheath and that the gun at his side was loaded. He found his police club, checked the loop at its end, and slipped it onto his wrist.

At the door to the hall, he hesitated, staring at Sheila's room. Wife or prisoner? He turned it over in his mind, knowing that her words couldn't change the facts. But in the end, he dropped the key and half his money beside her door, along with a spare knife and one of his guns. If he came back, he'd have to worry about it then; and if he shouldn't make it, at least she'd have a fighting chance.

He went by Izzy's room without stopping, uncertain of his status now. Technically, the boy was an enemy to all Municipals. This might be neutral territory, but there was no use pressing it. Gordon went down the stairs and out through the seal onto the street entrance, still in the shadows.

His eyes covered the street in two quick scans. Far up, a Legal cop was passing beyond the range of the single dim light. At the other end, a pair of figures skulked along, trying the door of each house they passed. With the cops busy fighting each other, this was better pickings than outside the dome.

Gordon let his eyes turn toward the dimly lighted plastic sheet of the dome above, that kept the full citizens safe as the rabble outside could never be. How much longer, he wondered, with guns being used regularly inside? It was a fragile thing, even though erecting it had wrecked the city economy and led to the graft that now ruled. There was always some danger of it cracking, so that houses were still air-tight and regular drills were held for the emergency. Maybe they'd need that experience.

He saw the Legal cop move out of sight and stepped onto the street, trying to look like another petty crook on the prowl. He headed for the nearest alley, which led through the truckyard of Nick the Croop. There was some danger of an ambush there, but small chance of being picked up by the guarding Legals.

The entrance was in nearly complete darkness. Gordon loosened his knife and tightened his grip on the locust stick. He swung into the alley, moving rapidly and trying to force his eyes to adjust. Once he was past the first few steps, his chances picked up. He felt his scalp tense, but nothing happened, and he moved along more cautiously, skirting garbage and stumbling over a body that had been half stripped.

Suddenly a whisper of sound caught his ears. He stopped, not too quickly, and listened, but everything was still. It *might* have been something falling. But what light there was came from behind him, and he couldn't make out more than the dark walls ahead.

A hundred feet further on, and within twenty yards of the trucks, a swishing rustle reached his ears and light slashed hotly into his eyes. Hands grabbed at his arms, and a club swung down toward his knife. But the warning had been enough. Gordon's arms jerked upward to avoid the reaching hands. His boot lifted, and the flashlight spun aside, broken and dark. With a continuous motion, he switched the knife to his left hand in a thumb-up position and brought it back. There was a grunt of pain, though it obviously hadn't found a vital area. But it gave him the split second he needed. He stepped backward and twisted. His hands caught the man behind, lifted across a hip, and heaved, just before the front man reached him.

The two ambushers were down in a tangled mess. There was just enough light to make out faint outlines, and Gordon brought his locust club down twice, with the hollow thud of wood on skulls. He groped around behind him until luck guided his hand to the fallen knife. Then he straightened.

His head was swimming in a hot maelstrom of pain, but it was quieting as his breathing returned to normal. And with it was an odd satisfaction at the realization of how far he'd come in this sort of business since his arrival. He'd reached the fine peak where instinct seemed to guide his actions, without the need for thought. As long as his opponents were slower or less ruthless, he could take care of himself.

The trouble, though, was that Trench was neither slow nor squeamish.

Gordon gathered the two hoodlums under his arms and dragged them with him. He came out in the truckyard and began searching. But Nick the Croop had ridden his reputation long enough to be careless, and the third truck had its key still in the lock. He threw the two into the back and struck a cautious light.

One of them was Jurgens' apelike follower, his stupid face relaxed and vacant. The other was probably also one of Jurgens' growing mob of protection racketeers—

the ones who could milk out money from the small shopkeepers when even the police couldn't touch them. He was dressed like it, at least. Gordon yanked out his wallet, but there was no identification; it held only a small sheaf of bills.

For a second, Gordon started to put it back. Then he cursed his own habits. On Mars, the spoils belonged to the victors. And with Sheila draining his income, he could use it. He stripped out the money—and finally put half of it back into the wallet and dropped it beside the hoodlum. Even in jail, a man had to have smokes.

He stuck to the alleys, not using the headlights, after he had locked the two in and started the electric motor. Once he reached the main streets, there would be some all-night traffic, but he didn't want to attract attention out this far. He finally passed an entrance to one of the alleys which showed Legals building some kind of a barricade across the street beyond, and guessed that he was now in Municipal territory. He had no clear idea of how the battles were going, but it looked as if the Seventh Precinct was still in Municipal hands.

Finally, he swung onto a main street and cut on his lights, cruising along at the same speed as the few others trucks. Two Municipal cops were arguing beside a call box, but they paid as little attention to him as they did to the sounds of a group looting a store two blocks down. Gordon grumbled, wondering if they really thought they were soldiers now, instead of cops. Once they let the crooks get out of control . . .

There was no one at the side entrance to Seventh Precinct headquarters and only two corporals on duty inside; the rest were probably out fighting the Legals, or worrying about it. One of the corporals started to stand up and halt him, but wavered at the sight of the captain's star that was still pinned to his uniform.

"Special prisoners," Gordon told him sharply. "I've got to get information to Trench—and in private!"

The corporal stuttered. Gordon knocked him out of the way with his elbow, reached for the door to Trench's private office, and yanked it open. He stepped through, drawing it shut behind him, while his eyes checked the position of his gun at his hip. Then he looked up.

There was no sign of Trench. In his place, and in the uniform of a Municipal captain, sat the heavy figure of Jurgens, the man who had been working busily to take over all the illegal rackets on an efficient basis—and a man who already had Gordon marked down in his book. "Outside!" he snapped. Then his eyes narrowed, and a stiff smile came onto his lips as he laid the pen down. "Oh, it's you, Gordon."

"Where's Captain Trench?"

The heavy features didn't change as Jurgens chuckled. "Commissioner Trench, Gordon. It seems Arliss decided to get rid of Mayor Wayne, but didn't count on Wayne's spies being better than his. So Trench got promoted—and I got his job for loyal service in helping the force recruit. My boys always wanted to be cops, you know."

Gordon tried to grin in return as he moved closer, slipping the heavy locust club off his wrist. It was like the damned fools to get mixed up in a would-be palace revolution in the middle of their trouble with the Earth-controlled Legals. It was easy enough to fit Jurgens into the pattern, too. But how had Trench managed to swing the promotion over the other captains—unless he'd offered evidence that he might know how to locate the head of the dreaded Solar Security on Mars? . . .

"I sent Ape and Mullins out to get in touch with you," Jurgens said. "But I guess they didn't reach you before you left."

Gordon shook his head slightly, while the nerves bunched and tingled in his neck. "They hadn't arrived when I left the house," he said truthfully enough. There was no point in mentioning that the two out in the truck must be the men who had been sent to him, in a slight mix-up of identities all around. Or had they been unaware of who he was?

Jurgens reached out for tobacco and filled a pipe. He fumbled in his pockets, as if looking for a light. "Too bad. I knew you weren't in top shape, so I figured a convoy might be handy. Well, no matter. Trench left some instructions about you, and—"

His voice was perfectly normal, but Gordon saw the hand move suddenly toward the drawer that was half-open. And the cigarette lighter was attached to the other side of the desk.

The locust stick left Gordon's hand with a snap. It cut through the air a scant eight feet, jerked to a stop against Jurgens' forehead, and clattered onto the top of the desk, while Jurgens folded over, his mouth still open, his hand slumping out of the drawer. The man's chin scraped along the top of the desk, reached the edge, and let his nose and forehead bump faintly before he collapsed completely under the desk. The club rolled toward Gordon, who caught it before it could reach the floor.

But Jurgens was only momentarily out. As Gordon slipped the loop over his wrist again, one of the new captain's hands groped upward, seeking a button on the edge of the desk.

The two corporals were at the door when Gordon threw it open, but they drew back at the sight of his drawn gun. Feet were pounding below as he found the entrance that led to the truck. He hit the seat and rammed down the throttle with his foot before he could get his hands on the wheel.

It was a full minute before sirens sounded behind him, and Nick the Croop had fast trucks. He spotted the squad car far behind, ducked through a maze of alleys, and lost it for another few precious minutes. Then the barricade lay ahead.

The truck faltered as it hit the nearly finished obstacle, and Gordon felt his stomach squashing down onto the wheel. He kept his foot to the floor, strewing bits of the barricade behind him, until he was beyond the range of the Legal guns that were firing suddenly. Then he stopped and got out carefully, with his hands up.

"Captain Bruce Gordon, with two prisoners—bodyguards of Captain Jurgens," he reported to the three men in bright new Legal uniforms who were approaching warily. "How do I sign up with you?"

XIII

The Legal forces were short-handed and eager for recruits. They had struck quickly according to plans made by experts on Earth, and now controlled about half of Marsport. But it was a sprawling crescent around the central section, harder to handle than the Municipal territory. Gordon was sworn in at once.

Then he cooled his heels while the florid, paunchy ex-politician Commissioner Crane worried about his rating and repeated how corrupt Mars was and how the collection system was over—absolutely over. In the end, Gordon was given a captain's pay and the rank of sergeant. As a favor, he was allowed to share a beat with Honest Izzy under Captain Hendrix, who had simply switched sides after losing the morning's battle.

Gordon's credits were changed to Legal script, and he was issued a trim-fitting green uniform. Then a surprisingly competent doctor examined his wound, rebandaged it, and sent him home for the day. The change was finished—and he felt like a grown man playing with dolls.

He walked back, watching the dull-looking people closing off their homes, as they had done at elections. Here and there houses had been broken into during the night. An old man sat in a wrecked doorway, holding an obviously dead girl child in his arms. His eyes followed Gordon without expression. There were occasional buzzes of angry conversation that cut off as he approached.

Marsport had learned to hate all cops, and a change of uniform hadn't altered that; instead, the people seemed to resent the loss of the familiar symbol of hatred.

He came up to a fat, blowsy woman who was firmly planted in his path. "You're a cop!" she accused him. "Okay, cop, you get them thieves outta my place!"

"See your own beat cop," he suggested.

"Says he's busy with some war or other. Can't be bothered!"

Gordon shrugged and followed her to the doorway of a small beer-hall. Inside, the place was a mess, and two ragged men sat at a table drinking while a sodden wreck that might have been a woman once was sprawled on the floor in drunken stupor. There was a filthy revolver on the table.

"Beat it, copper," the older man said sullenly, and his hand slid for the gun. "The dame usta be my wife, so the joint's half mine. Gotta have some place to stay with you coppers stirring up hell outside, ain't I?"

He watched Gordon advance steadily toward him and licked his lips, fear growing in his eyes. But it was the younger man who grabbed the gun suddenly. Gordon's club swung in a short arc, and the gun clattered to the floor, while the man's scream mixed with the sound of bones breaking in his wrist. He started for the door, and the woman grabbed him and heaved him into the street.

The older man had a knife out, finally. Gordon knocked it aside with his hand and brought his open palm up against the man's face, rocking him sideways. Then the left palm contacted, tossing him over to meet the right again. Gordon counted calmly, focusing his thoughts on the even count. He stopped at twenty, staring at the slow tears oozing from the bruised face, and swung back to the woman.

The raw animal delight in her eyes was sickening. "Don't lock him up," she half-whispered. "Twenty years, and now I find he's yellow. Leave him here, copper!"

Gordon shrugged. It was probably funny, he thought as he shoved through the small crowd outside. But it wouldn't be funny if every two-bit punk in Marsport figured the police war meant he was free to do what he wanted—or if all the cops were too busy to bother.

He found Izzy and Randolph at the restaurant across from Mother Corey's. Izzy grinned suddenly at the sight of the uniform. "I knew it, gov'nor—knew it the minute I heard Jurgens was a cop. Did you make 'em give you my beat?"

He seemed genuinely pleased as Gordon nodded, and then dropped it, to point to Randolph. "Guess what, gov'nor. The Legals bought Randy's *Crusader*. Traded him an old job press and a bag of scratch for his reputation."

"You'll be late, Izzy," Randolph said quietly. Gordon suddenly realized that Randolph, like everyone else, seemed to be Izzy's friend. He watched the little man leave, and reached out for the menu. Randolph picked it out of his hand. "You've got a wife home, muck-raker. You don't have to eat this filth."

Gordon got up, grimacing at the obvious dismissal. But the publisher motioned him back again.

"Yeah, the Legals want the *Crusader* for their propaganda," he said wearily. "New slogans and new uniforms, and none of them mean anything. Umm. Look, I've been trying to tell you I'm grateful for what you did, sorry I blew my stack—and glad you and the girl are making out. Here!" He drew a small golden band from his little finger. "My mother's wedding ring. Give it to her—and if you tell her it came from me, I'll rip out your guts!"

He got up suddenly and hobbled out, his pinched face working. Gordon turned the ring over, puzzled. Finally he got up and headed for his room, a little surprised to find the door unlocked. Sheila opened her eyes at his uniform, but made no comment. "Food ready in ten minutes," she told him.

She'd already been shopping, and had installed the tiny cooking equipment used in half of Marsport. There was also a small iron lying beside a pile of his laundered clothes. He dropped onto the bed wearily, then jerked upright as she came over to remove his boots. But there was no mockery on her face—and oddly, it felt good to him. Maybe her idea of married life was different from his.

She was sanding the dishes and putting them away when he finally remembered the ring. He studied it again, then got up and dropped it beside her. He was surprised as she fumbled it on to see that it fitted—and more surprised at the sudden realization that she was entitled to it, and that this wasn't just a game they were using against each other.

She studied it under the glare of the single bulb, and then turned to her room. She was back a few seconds later with a small purse. "I got a duplicate key. Yours is in there," she said thickly. "And—something else. I guess I was going to give it to you anyway. I was afraid someone else might find it—"

He cut her off brusquely, his eyes riveted on the Security badge he'd been sure Trench had taken. "Yeah, I know. Your meal-ticket was in danger. Okay, you've done your nightly duty. Now get the hell out of my room, will you?"

He didn't watch her leave, but he heard the door close several minutes later. With a snort of disgust, he bent down to his bag, located the bottle of cheap whiskey there, and tilted it to his lips. It was time he got drunk—stinko enough to wash out the shock of the badge in her purse, and the stupidity he'd made of his whole damned life on Mars.

Play it smart, be ruthless, look out for number one! The original kukla, only with less free-will than a ventriloquist's dummy. The man who could almost save himself from a danger that didn't exist. If he'd stayed put, Jurgen's punks would have convoyed him back to a set-up where Trench was Commissioner and Gordon might have been his right-hand man, as Jurgens had probably been trying to tell him. And when the silly war was over, he'd have had the money to stow away back to Earth, hire the best plastic surgeon, and set himself up on easy street.

Instead he'd gone over to the other side without any choice in the matter. He'd thrown a seven with his own evens dice! Trench was probably busy right now, planning when the exact worst time would be to tip the Earth forces off to his phoney evidence that Gordon had killed the Solar Security aee Whaler! It might take a week or two, just to give him time to squirm. And even without that, the graft was gone, taking with it his last chance to go back to Earth. Sure, he'd joined the Earth forces—but so had a lot of others, and it wouldn't make them revoke his yellow ticket!

Security was probably sour on him, anyway, or they'd have gotten in touch with him. They were through with him, and he'd either go to Mercury, or wind up forty years from now out there in the slums, scavenging. He tilted the bottle up, downing the rest as fast as his throat would handle it. It had finally begun to hit him, and he debated throwing Sheila out. There was something wrong with that idea. Then it occurred to him that when he had to hide out beyond the dome, he'd just put her to work, make her his mealticket. Big joke! Have to hang onto her. Be nice to Cuddles . . .

He staggered across the room, but it was too far, and the bare floor looked too soft. He had a single final thought, though, before he passed out. While he lasted, he'd be the best damned cop this planet of his ever saw!

Somehow he was in bed and it was morning again when Sheila woke him. He'd slept past his hangover, and he ate the breakfast she had ready, split the money he had with her, and went out to join Izzy.

The week went on mechanically, while he gradually adjusted to the new angles of being a Legal. The banks were open, and deposits honored, as promised. But it was in the printing press scrip of Legal currency, useful only through Mayor Gannett's trick exchanges. All orders had to be placed and paid for at the nearest exchange if the total came to more than five credits, and the exchange then purchased and had them delivered. Water went up from fourteen credits to eighty credits for a gallon of pure distilled. Other things were worse. Resentment flared up, but the script was the only money available, and as long as it had any value it still bound the people to the new regime.

Supplies were scarce, salt and sugar almost unavailable. Earth had cut off all shipping until the affair was settled, and nobody in the outlands would deal in scrip.

He came home the third evening to find that Sheila had managed to find space for her bunk in his room, cut off by a heavy screen, and had closed the other room to save the rent. It led to some relaxation between them, and they began talking impersonally.

Gordon watched for a sign that Trench had passed his evidence of the murder of Whaler to the Earth forces, but there was no sign. Most of the time, the pressure of the beat took his mind from it. Looting had stepped up, and between trying to keep order and the constant series of minor fracases with Municipal men at the borders, he began to acquire a shield of fatigue that nothing could cut.

Izzy had cooperated reluctantly at first, until Gordon was able to convince him that in the long run it was the people who paid his salary. Then he nodded. "It's a helluva roundabout way of doing things, gov'nor, but if the gees pay for protection any bloody way, then they're gonna get it!"

They got it. Hoodlums began moving elsewhere toward easier pickings. The shops now opened promptly as Gordon and Izzy came on duty, and they could time the end of their beat by the sudden emptying of the streets. People spoke to them now; and once, when a small gang decided to wipe out the nuisance of the two cops, men from the surrounding houses came pouring out to join in and turn it into a decisive victory.

Hendrix took time out for a pompous lecture on loyalty to the government first, but couldn't find any proof that they had weakened the Legal position, and finally disregarded it, except to warn them that the limited jail facilities had to be reserved for captured Municipals who wouldn't switch sides. The two henchmen of Jurgens had already been released.

Gordon turned his entire pay over to Sheila; at current prices, it would barely keep them in food for a week. He could get lunch and cigarettes along his beat from people eager to offer them. But if inflation kept on, his salary would mean nothing. "I told you I was a punched meal ticket," he said bitterly.

"We'll live," she answered him. "I got a job today—bar-maid, on your beat, where being your wife helps."

He could think of nothing to say to that, but after supper he went to Izzy's room to arrange for a raid on Municipal territory. Such small raids were nominally on the excuse of extending the boundaries, but actually matters of out-and-out looting. It was tough on the people near the border, but no worse than the constantly increasing gang fights.

The people endured it, somehow. On Mars, they couldn't simply pack and move on; the planet gave them life, but only of a marginal sort. And they had been conditioned to a hopeless acceptance of corruption and abuse that no Earth citizen could ever understand.

He came back from Izzy's room to find her cleaning up, and shoved her away. "Go to bed. You look beat. I'll sand these."

She started to protest, then let him take over. It occurred to him that there was no need for her to stay, now. But their life was getting to be a habit, with even the bitterness a bond between them. And with conditions as they were, there was more financial safety in pooling their incomes.

Maybe some day, with the Earth forces probably winning, things would be better. Marsport was the only place on the planet under Earth charter, but as the funnel for all trade it was valuable enough to justify rebuilding into what it could have been.

They never made the looting raid. The next morning, they arrived at the Ninth Precinct headquarters to find men milling around the bulletin board, buzzing over an announcement there. Apparently, Chief Justice Arnold had broken with the Wayne administration; and the mimeographed form was a legal ruling that Wayne was no longer Mayor, since the charter had been voided. He was charged with inciting a riot, and a warrant had been issued for his arrest.

Hendrix appeared finally. "All right, men," he shouted. "You all see it. We're going to arrest Wayne. By jingo, they can't say we ain't legal now! Every odd-numbered shield goes from every precinct. Gordon, Isaacs—you two been talking big about law and order. Here's the warrant. You two take it and arrest Wayne! And by jimminy, shoot if you gotta! It's all legal now."

It took nearly an hour of pep talks and working themselves up to get the plans settled, and the men weren't too happy then. There was no profit to such a raid, and it had been entirely too warlike a feeling. But finally they headed for the trucks that had been arriving. Most of them belonged to Nick the Croop, who had apparently decided the Legals would win.

Gordon and Izzy found the lead truck and led the way. The little man was busy testing his knives as they rolled. "Honest Izzy, that's me. Give me a job and I do it. Only remind me to see a crazy-doctor, gov'nor."

They neared the bar where Sheila was working, and Gordon swore. She was running toward the center of the street, frantically trying to flag him down, and he barely managed to swerve around her. "Damned fool!" he muttered.

Izzy's pock-marked face soured for a second as he stared at Gordon. "The princess? She sure is," he said flatly.

The crew at the barricade had been alerted, and now began clearing it aside hastily, while others kept up a covering fire against the few Municipals. The trucks wheeled through, and Gordon dropped back to let scout trucks go ahead and pick off any Municipals rash enough to head for the call boxes. They couldn't prevent advance warning, but they could delay and minimize it. Hendrix or Crane had done a good job of organizing.

They were near the big Municipal Building when they came to the first real opposition, and it was obviously hastily assembled. The scouts took care of most of the trouble, though a few shots pinged against the truck Gordon was driving.

154

"Rifles!" Izzy commented in disgust. "They'll ruin the dome yet. Why can't they stick to knives?"

He was studying a map of the big building, picking their best entrance. Ahead, trucks formed a sort of *V* formation as they reached the grounds around it and began bulling their way through the groups that were trying to organize a defense. Gordon found his way cleared and shot through, emerging behind the defense and driving at full speed toward the entrance Izzy pointed out.

"Cut speed! Left sharp!" Izzy shouted. "Now, in there!"

They sliced into a small tunnel, scraping their sides where it was barely big enough for the truck. Then they reached a dead end, with just room for them to squeeze through the door of the truck and into an entrance marked with a big notice of privacy.

There was a guard beside an elevator, but Izzy's knife took care of him. They ducked around the elevator, unsure of whether it could be remotely controlled, and up a narrow flight of stairs, down a hallway, and up another flight! A Municipal corporal at the top grabbed for a warning whistle, but Gordon clipped him with a hasty rabbit-punch and shoved him down the stairs. Then they were in front of an ornate door, with their weapons ready.

Izzy yanked the door open and dropped flat behind it. Bullets from a submachine gun clipped out, peppering the entrance and the door, ricocheting down the hall. The yammering stopped, finally, and Izzy stuck his head and one arm out with a snap of his knife. Gordon leaped in, to see a Municipal dropping the machine gun and strangling around the knife in his throat.

There were about thirty cops inside, gathered around the Mayor, with Trench standing at one side. Izzy's arm was flicking steadily, unloading his knives, and Gordon was busy picking off the men in the order in which they tried to draw their guns. The fools had obviously expected the machine gun to do all the work.

Izzy leaped for the machine gun and yanked it from the dead hands, while the cops slowly began raising their arms. Wayne sat petrified, staring unbelievingly, and Gordon drew out the warrant. "Wayne, you're under arrest!"

Trench moved forward, his hands in the air, but with no mark of surprise or fear on his face. "So the bad pennies turn up. You damned fools, you should have stuck. I had big plans for you, Gordon. I've still got them, if you don't insist . . ." His hands whipped down savagely toward his hips and came up sharply! Gordon spun, and the gun leaped in his hands, while the submachine gun jerked forward and clicked on an empty chamber. Trench was tumbling forward to avoid the shot, but he twitched as a bullet creased his shoulder. Then he was upright, waving empty hands at them, with the thin smile on his face deepening. He'd had no guns—it had been a pure bluff, and it had worked.

Gordon jerked around, but Wayne was already disappearing through a heavy door. And the cops were reaching for their guns again. Gordon estimated the chances of escape instantly, and then leaped forward into their group, with Izzy at his side, seeking close quarters where guns wouldn't work.

Gun butts, elbows, fists and clubs were pounding at him, while his own club lashed out savagely. In ten seconds, things began to haze over, but his arms went on mechanically, seeking the most damage they could work. It almost seemed that they could win through to the shelter of the door beyond.

Then a heavy bellow sounded, and a seeming mountain of flesh thundered across the huge room. There was no shuffle to Mother Corey now. The huge legs pumped steadily, and the great arms were reaching out to knock aside clubs and knives. Men began spewing out of the brawl like straw from a thresher as the old man grabbed arms, legs or whatever was handy. He had one cop in his left arm, using him as a flail against the others, and seemed to be completely unaware of danger to himself.

The Municipals broke. And at the first sign, Mother Corey leaped forward, dropping his flail and gathering

Izzy and Gordon under his arms. He hit the heavy door with his shoulder and crashed through without breaking stride. Stairs lay there, and he took them three at a time.

He dropped them finally as they came to a side entrance. There was a sporadic firing going on there, and a knot of Municipals were clustered around a few Legals, busy with knives and clubs. Corey broke into a run again, driving straight into them and through, with Gordon and Izzy on his heels. The surprise element was enough to give them a few seconds, before hasty, ill-aimed bullets snapped after them.

Then they were around a small side-building, out of danger. Sheila was holding the door of a large three-wheeler open, and yelling for them to hurry. They ducked into it, while she grabbed the wheel.

They edged forward until they could make out the shape of the fight going on. The Legals had never quite reached the front of the building, obviously, and were now cut into sections. Corey tapped her shoulder, pointing out the route, and she gunned the car.

They were through too fast to draw fire from the busy groups of battle-crazed men, accelerating across the square and into the first side street they could find. Then she slowed, and headed for the main street back to Legal territory.

"Lucky we found a good car to steal," Mother Corey wheezed. He was puffing now, mopping rivulets of perspiration from his face. "I'm getting old, cobbers. Once I broke every strongman record on Earth—still stand, too—before it went to my head. But not now. Senile!"

"You didn't have to come," Izzy said, but there was a grin on his battered face.

"When my own granddaughter comes crying for help? When she finally breaks down and admits she needs her old grandfather?"

Gordon was staring back at the straggling of trucks he could see beginning to break away. The raid was over, and the Legals had lost. Trench had tricked him, and life under Hendrix was going to be rough from now on.

Izzy grunted suddenly. "Gov'nor, if you're right and the plain gees pay my salary, who's paying me to start fighting other cops? Or is it maybe that somebody isn't being exactly honest with the scratch they lift from the gees?"

"We still have to eat," Gordon said bitterly. "And to eat, we'll go on doing what we're told."

It was all life meant now—a bare existence. And in his case, even that was uncertain.

XIV

Hendrix had been wounded lightly, and was out of his office when Gordon and Izzy reported. But the next day, they were switched to a new beat where the trouble had been thickest and given twelve-hour duty—without special overtime.

Izzy considered it slowly and shook his head. "That does it, gov'nor. It ain't honest, treating us this way. It just proves what I've been thinking. If the crackle comes from the people and these gees give everybody a dome cracking, then they're crooks. And who's letting 'em get away with it? We are, gov'nor. But not me; it ain't honest, and I'm too sick to work. And if that bloody doctor won't agree . . ."

He turned toward the dispensary. Gordon hesitated, and then swung off woodenly to take up his new beat. At least, it still made living possible; and perhaps, if he did his best, when it was all over Security would let him stay here. Returning to Earth seemed impossible now, but he might duck the threatened mines of Mercury.

He plunged into the work on his new beat, trying to numb himself by exhaustion. Apparently, his reputation had gone ahead of him, since most of the hoodlums had decided pickings would be easier on some beat where the cops had their own secret rackets to attend to, instead of head busting. They probably expected Izzy to show up later. Once they learned he was alone . . .

But the second day, two of the citizens fell into step behind him almost at once, armed with heavy clubs. Periodically during the shift, replacements took their place, making sure that he was never by himself. It surprised him even more when he saw that a couple of the men had come over from his old beat. Something began to burn inside him, but he held himself in, confining his talk to vague comments on the rumors going around.

There were enough of them, mostly based on truth. The Croopsters were busy with a three-day gang war with the Planters, and the cops on both sides were doing nothing about it, though seventy bystanders had been killed. Part of Jurgens' old crowd had broken away from him and had established a corner on most of the available drugs; they had secretly traded a supply to Wayne, who had become an addict, for a stock of weapons.

Gordon remembered the contraband shipment of guns, and compared it to the increase he'd noticed in weapons, and to the impossible prices the pushers were demanding. It made sense.

All kind of supplies were low, and the outlands beyond Marsport had cut off all shipments. Scrip was useless to them, and the Legals were raiding all cargoes destined for Wayne's section. And the Municipals had imposed new taxes again.

Gordon bolstered himself with the thought that it couldn't go on forever, and that the Legals seemed to be winning slowly. Once the war was over and the charter officially turned over to Security, it would have to act. Things were at their worst now, and later . . .

He came back from what should have been his day off to find Izzy in uniform, waiting grimly. Behind the screen, there was a rustling of clothes, and a dress came sailing from behind it. While he stared, Sheila came out, finishing the zipping of her airsuit. She moved to a small bag and began drawing out the gun she had used and a knife. He caught her shoulders and shoved her back, pulling the weapons from her.

"Get out of my way, you damned Legal machine!" she spat at him. "Do you think I never knew where you got the ring? Do you think I can go on forever with no feelings at all? All right, I've been your obedient servant—and no thanks from you! Now you can take it and stuff it . . ."

"Easy, princess," Izzy said. "He hasn't seen it yet, I guess. Here, gov'nor!"

He picked up a copy of Randolph's new little *Truth* and pointed to the headline. Gordon read it, and blinked. It glared up at him in forty-eight point ultrabold:

SECURITY DENOUNCES
RAPE OF MARSPORT!

The story was somewhat cooler than that, but not much. Randolph simply quoted what was supposed to be an official cable from Security on Earth, denouncing both governments, and demanding that both immediately surrender. It listed the crimes of Wayne and his gang and then tore into the Legals as a bunch of dupes, sent by North America to foment trouble while they looted the city, and to give the Earth government an excuse for seizing military control of Marsport officially. Citizens were instructed not to cooperate, and all members of either government were indicted for high treason to Security!

He crushed the paper slowly, tearing it to bits with his clenched hands, and seeing in each bit a yellow ticket to Mercury. He'd swallowed the implication that the Legals were Security, or from it. He'd been suckered in . . .

Then it hit him slowly, and he looked up. "Where's Randolph?"

"At his plant. At least he left for it, according to Sheila."

Gordon picked up Sheila's gun and buckled it on beside his own. She grabbed at it, but he shoved her back again. "You're staying here, Cuddles." He grimaced as she spat at him, and a touch of the almost forgotten amusement twisted his lips. "You're supposed to be a woman now, remember!"

She was swearing hotly as they left, but she made no attempt to follow. Gordon broke into a slow trot behind Izzy, until they could spot one of the remaining cabs. He stopped it with his whistle, and dumped the passenger out unceremoniously, while Izzy gave the address. There was a stream of protest from the driver, but it cut off at the sudden appearance of the knife in Izzy's hand.

"That damned fool Randolph opened up on the border—figured he'd circulate to both sections," Izzy said. "We'd better get out a block up and walk. And I hope we ain't *too* bloody late!"

The building was a wreck, outside; inside it was worse. Gordon ripped open the door to the sound of metal crashing. Men in the Municipal uniform were working over the small job press and dumping the hand-set type from the boxes. On the floor, a Legal cop lay under the wreckage, apparently having gotten there first and been taken care of by the later Municipals. Randolph had been sitting in a chair between two of the cops, but now he leaped up with a cry at the new interruption and tried to flee through the back door.

Izzy started forward, but Gordon pulled him back, as the cops reached for weapons. There was no use brawling here when the others had been caught flat-footed. The gun in his hand picked them out at quarters too close for a miss, starting with the cop who had jumped to catch Randolph. Izzy had ducked around the side, and now came back, leading the little man.

Randolph paid no attention to the dead men, nor to the bruises on his own body. He moved forward to the press, staring at it, and there were tears in his eyes as

161

he ran his hands over the broken metal. Then he looked up at them. "Arrest or rescue?" he asked.

"Arrest!" a voice from the door said harshly, and Gordon swung to see six Legals filing in, headed by Hendrix himself. The captain nodded at Gordon. "Good work, Sergeant. By jinx, when I heard the Municipals were coming, I got scared they'd get him for sure. Crane wants to watch this guy shot in person! Come on, you damned little traitor!"

He grabbed Randolph by the arm, twisting it sadistically and grinning at the scream the torture produced.

"You're overlooking something, Hendrix," Gordon cut in. He had moved back toward the wall, to face the group. "If you ever look at my record, you'll find I'm an ex-newspaperman myself. This is a rescue. Tie them up, Izzy."

Hendrix was faster than Gordon thought possible. He had his gun almost up before Gordon could fire. A bluish hole appeared on the man's forehead, and one thick hand reached for it, while surprise ran briefly over the features. He dropped slowly, the back of his head a gory mess. Randolph bent over, throwing up over the broken metal on the floor, and the other Legals looked almost as sick. But they made no trouble Izzy bound them with baling wire.

"And I hope nobody finds them," he commented. "All right, Randy, I guess we're a bunch of refugees heading for the outside, and bloody lucky at that. Proves a man shouldn't have friends."

Randolph's face was still greenish white, but he straightened and managed a feeble smile. "Not to me, Izzy. Right now I can appreciate friends. But you two better get going. I've got some unfinished business to tend to." He moved to one corner and began dragging out an old double-cylinder mimeograph. "Either of you know where I can buy stencils and ink and find some kind of a truck to haul this paper along?"

Izzy stopped and stared at the rabbity, pale little man. Then he let out a sudden yelp of laughter. "Okay, Randy, we'll find them. Gov'nor, you'd better tell the

Mother I'll be using the old sheets. Go on. You've got the princess to worry about. We will be along later."

He grabbed Randolph's hand and ducked out the back before Gordon could protest. Gordon hesitated, and then moved toward the front exit. There would be little chance of catching another cab, but that didn't much matter now. He found a small car finally, kicked the glass out, and shorted the switch hastily.

Izzy could only have meant that they were going to hole up in Mother Corey's old Chicken Coop. So Gordon had managed to make a full circle, back to the beginnings on Mars. But then he'd been only a yellow-ticket firster. Now he was branded as a traitor by Security, a deserter and would-be assassin by the Municipals, and a criminal on too many counts to list by the Legals. And even in the outlands he had a reputation —the iron cop, without a heart. He'd started with a deck of cards, and now he was going back with a single club. He wondered if one would be better than the other.

He had counted on at least some regret from Mother Corey, however. But the old man only nodded after hearing that Randolph was safe. "Fanatics, crusaders and damned fools!" he said. He shook his head sadly and went shuffling back to his room, where two of his part-time henchmen were waiting.

Sheila had been sitting on the bunk, still in her air-suit. Now she jerked upright, and then sank back with a slow flush. Her hands were trembling as she reached out for a cup of coffee and handed it to him, listening to his quick report of Randolph's safety and the fact that he was going back outside the dome.

"I'm all packed," she said. "And I packed your things, too."

He shot his eyes around the room, realizing that it was practically bare except for a few of her dresses. She followed his gaze, and shook her head. "I won't need them out there," she said. Her voice caught on that, but she covered quickly. "They'll be safe here."

"So will you, now that you've made up with the Mother," he told her. "Your meal-ticket's ruined, Cuddles. And you made it clear a little while ago just where you stand. Remind me to tell you sometime how much fun it's been. Makes me think marriage is a good idea. I'll have to try it sometime."

She bit her lips and struggled with herself. Then she grinned with her lips, bitterly. Her voice was low and almost expressionless. "Your mother was good with a soldering iron, wasn't she? You even look human." She bent to pick up a shoulder pack and a bag, and her face was normal when she stood up again. "You might guess that the cops would be happy to get ahold of your wife now, though. Come on, it's a long walk."

He hesitated for a moment, and then picked up the rest of the luggage, surprised at how much they had managed to accumulate, light though it was. Corey could have protected her, he thought; but he let it go, and moved out of the room quietly. Somehow, it hurt to leave, though he couldn't figure why—nor why something in his head insisted he had expected it to hurt more.

Mother Corey wasn't around, and that did hurt. He shrugged it off and led Sheila to the car he had stolen. Without a pass, he couldn't take it through the locks, but it would be useful until then. Without thinking, he swung through his beat. His lights picked out a small group of teen-age punks working on the window of a small shop, and his hand groped automatically for his gun. Then he sighed and drove on. It wasn't his job now, and he couldn't risk trouble.

He left the car beyond the gate, and they pushed through the locker room toward the smaller exit, stopping to fasten down their helmets. The guard halted them, but without any suspicion.

"Going hunting for those damned kids, eh?" he said. He stared at Sheila, deliberately smacking his lips. "Lucky devil! All I got for a guide was an old bum. Okay, have fun!"

It made no sense to Gordon, but he wasn't going to argue over it. They went through and out into the waste and slums beyond the domes, heading out until there were only the few phosphor bulbs to guide their way. It was as if they were in a separate world, where squalor was a meaningless term. Even in the darkness, there was a feeling that came across to them.

Gordon was moving cautiously, using his helmet light only occasionally, with his gun ready in his hand. But it was Sheila who caught the faint sound. He heard her cry out and turned to see her crash into the stomach of a man with a half-raised stick. He went down with almost no resistance. Sheila shot the beam of her light on the thin, drawn face. "Rusty!"

"Hi, Princess." He got up slowly, trying to grin. "Didn't know who it was. Sorry. Ever get that louse you were out for?"

She nodded. "Yeah, I got him. That's him—my husband! What's wrong with you, Rusty? You've lost fifty pounds, and . . ."

"Things are a mite tough out here, Princess. No deliveries. Closed my bar, been living sort of hand to mouth, but not much mouth." His eyes bulged greedily as she dug into a bag and began to drag out the sandwiches she must have packed for the trip. But he shook his head. "I ain't so bad off. I ate something yesterday. But if you can spare something for the kid—Hey, kid!"

A thin boy of about sixteen crept out of the corner of some rubble, staring uncertainly. Then at the sight of the food, he made a lunge, grabbed it, and hardly waited to get it through the slits of his suit before gulping it down. Rusty sat down, his lined old face breaking into a faint grin. He hesitated, but finally took some of the food.

"Shouldn't oughta. You'll need it. Umm." He swallowed slowly, as if tasting the food all the way down. "Kid can't talk. Cop caught him peddling one of Randolph's pamphlets, cut out part of his tongue. But he's all right now. Come on, kid, hurry it up. We gotta convoy these people."

They went on finally, with Gordon turning it over in his head. He hadn't completely believed the stories he had heard about life out here; unconsciously, he'd figured it in terms of previous experience. But with the bank failure, most of the workers had been fired. And the war inside the dome must have cut people off completely.

They were following a kind of road when headlights bore down on them. Gordon's hand was on his gun as they leaped for shelter, but there was no hostile move from the big truck. He studied it, trying to decide what a truck would be doing here. Then a Marspeaker-amplified voice shouted from it. "Any muckrakers there?"

"One," Gordon shouted back, and ran toward the truck, motioning the others to follow. He'd always objected to the nickname, but it made a good code. Randolph's frail hand came down to help them up, but a bigger paw did the actual lifting.

"Why didn't you two wait?" Mother Corey asked, his voice booming out of his Marspeaker. "I figured Izzy'd stop by first. Here, sit over there. Not much room, with my stuff and Randolph's, but it beats walking."

"What in hell brings you back?" Gordon asked.

The huge man shrugged ponderously. "A man gets tired of being respectable, cobber. And I'm getting old and sentimental about the Chicken Coop." He chuckled, rubbing his hands together. "But not so old I can't handle a couple of guards that are stubborn about trucks, eh, Izzy?"

"Messy, but nice," Izzy agreed from the pile above them. "Tell those trained apes of yours to cut the lights, will you, Mother? Somebody must be using the Coop."

They stopped the truck before reaching the old wreck. In the few dim lights, the old building still gave off an air of mold and decay. Gordon had a sudden picture of an ancient, evil old crone chuckling over her past, with a few coarse gray hairs sticking out from under a henna-red wig. But the Chicken Coop had memories no single crone could have contained within her mind. He shuddered faintly, then followed Izzy and the Mother into the semi-secret entrance.

Izzy went ahead, almost silent, with a thin strand of wire between his hands, his elbows weaving back and forth slowly to guide him. He was apparently as familiar with the garrotte as the knife, and this would be faster. But they found no guard. Izzy pressed the seal release and slid in cautiously, while the others followed.

There were no guards, but in the beam of Gordon's torch, a single figure lay sprawled out on the floor half-way to the rickety stairs of the main house. Mother Corey grunted, and moved quickly to the coughing, battered old air machine. His fingers closed a valve equipped with a combination lock, and he shook his head heavily.

"They're all dead, cobbers," he wheezed. "Dead because a crook had to try his hand on a lock. Years ago I had a flask of poison gas attached, in case a gang should ever squeeze me out. A handy thing to have."

In the filthy rooms above, Gordon found the corpses—about fifteen of them, and some obviously former members of the Jurgens organization. They had been dead for long enough to have grown cold, at least, apparently dying without ever realizing they were in danger. He found the apelike bodyguard stretched out on a bunk, still staring at a book of low-grade pornography, a vacant smile on his face.

A yell from the basement called him back down to where Izzy was busily going through piles of crates and boxes stacked along one wall. He was pointing to a plastic-covered box. "Dope! And all that other stuff's ammunition! You know what, gov'nor? All that scuttlebutt about the gang cornering the dope supply and dealing with Wayne must've been on the level! And now we got it!"

He shivered, staring at the fortune in his hands. Then he grimaced and shoved the open can into its case. He threw it back and began stacking ammunition cases in front of the dope. Gordon went out to get the others to start moving in the supplies and transferring the corpses to the truck for disposal. Randolph scurried off to start setting up his makeshift plant in the basement.

Mother Corey was staring about the filthy, decrepit interior when they returned. His puttylike skin was creased into wrinkles of horrified disgust, and his wheezing voice was almost sobbing. "Filthy," he wailed. "A pig-pen. They've ruined the Coop, cobber. Smell that air—even I can smell it!" He sniffed dolefully. It was pretty bad, Gordon had to agree. Nothing would ever remove the rank, sour staleness. But it looked a good deal better to his eyes than it had been before the gang took it over.

Mother Corey sighed again. "Well, it'll give the boys something to do," he decided. "When a man gets old, he likes a little comfort, cobber. Nice things around him . . ."

Gordon found what had been his old room and dumped his few things into it. Sheila watched him uncertainly, and then took possession of the next room. She came back a few minutes later, staring at the ages-old filth. "I'll be cleaning for a week," she said. "What are you going to do now, Bruce?"

He shook his head, and started back down the stairs. It was an unanswerable question. Originally, he'd intended to set up the Coop and run it as Mother Corey had done; but now the Mother would be attending to that. And it hadn't been too good an idea, anyhow. He ran over his occupations bitterly in his mind. Gambler, fighter, cop—he'd tried in one way or another everything except reporting, and failed at each.

For a second, he hesitated. Then he hurried, past the first landing, and down into the basement where Randolph was arranging his mimeograph.

The printer listened to only the first sentence, and shook his head impatiently. "I was afraid you'd think of that, Gordon. Look, I'm grateful for what you've done—but not that grateful. You never were a reporter—you ran a column. You slanted, sensationalized, shouted, and hunted publicity for yourself. You killed and maimed with words. You're good at fighting, killing and maiming—and at finding good excuses for it, maybe. You can write up what every man here feels, and make him nod his head and swear you're dead right. But you never dug up news that would help people, and they need a lot of help and inspiration now. I can't use you!"

"Thanks!" Gordon said curtly. "Too bad Security didn't think I was as lousy a reporter as you do."

Randolph shrugged. He dropped to the chair, pulled the battered portable to him, and became extremely busy writing about a quick brown fox that jumped over the lazy dog. Then he let his hands fall and swung back. "Okay, you were good at what you did. I read some of your stuff. You were a first-class muckraker; you had all the virtues of a cop turned crusading reporter. Oh, don't scowl at me! I've done a lot of muckraking myself. But what's going on here doesn't need exposing now—it exposes itself. You're a good cop, Gordon—as others have said, you get things done. But you're no source of inspiration. So why not stick to what you know?"

"Because I can't support a wife without a job," Gordon told him bitterly.

Randolph sighed. "Yeah. I'm glad you feel that way. Maybe you're human, after all. But we're in the same boat. I can't support myself now. I'm flat busted, Gordon. I wouldn't even have supplies for my worn mimeo machine without the Mother's help. If you want charity, go see Mother Corey! You can't find it here."

Gordon felt his arm jerk back, and the knotted fist started up at the pinched, nervous little face in front of him. But at the last second, he killed the punch, feeling his muscles wrench from the effort. Finger by finger, he unclenched his hand and dropped it to his side, while the anger dulled and became only a bruise on his soul. "Okay. Maybe I deserved that," he said finally.

But Randolph was jumping the quick brown fox over the lazy dog again.

Rusty and one of Mother Corey's men were on guard, and the others had turned in. Gordon went up the stairs, breathing the rancid, musty odor and watching the rotten boards below him. As a kid in the slums, it had been the smell of cabbage and soaking diapers, and he had watched rats fighting over garbage, while men made pious speeches of horror over the tenements, as they had done for five hundred years.

He threw himself onto his bed in disgust. He'd

fought his way out of those slums. He'd fought the petty crooks, the cops who lived on them, and the whole blasted set-up that made such misery possible. He'd fought his way to a filthy bed in a hovel where no rat could live, already asking for charity on the long way to the ultimate bottom, without a genuine friend to his name. Sure, he was good at fighting!

"Bruce!" Sheila stood outlined in the doorway against the dim glow of a phosphor bulb. Her robe was partly open, and an animal hunger in him burned along his arms and tautened the muscles of his abdomen. Then, before he could lift himself, she bent over and began unfastening his boots. "You all right, Bruce? I heard you tossing around."

"I'm fine," he told her mechanically. "Just making plans for tomorrow."

He watched her turn back slowly, then lay quietly, trying not to disturb her again. Tomorrow, he thought. Tomorrow he'd find some kind of an answer; and it wouldn't be anyone's charity.

XV

There were three men, each with a white circle painted on chest and left arm, talking to Mother Corey when Gordon came down the rickety steps. He stopped for a second, but saw no sign of trouble. Then the words of the thin man below reached him.

"We had a vote right after we found the stiffs you cleaned out from here; figured it had to mean you were back at the Coop, Mother. Damn good thing we were right, and I don't mean just the ammunition, though we can sure use that. A lot of people are going to feel better now. And if this Gordon guy you mentioned is any good, maybe that'll help. Where is he, anyhow?"

"Here!" Gordon broke into the group. He'd recognized the little man finally as Schulberg, one of the grocers from his old Nineteenth Precinct.

The man swung suspiciously to face him, then grinned suddenly. There was hunger and strain on his face, but an odd authority and pride were there too. "I'll be doggoned! You! Why didn't you tell us he was the one with Whaler, Mother? Sure, he'll do just fine!"

"They want someone to help them get organized out here, cobber," Mother Corey told him. "All the cops got pulled back from outside the dome, so they're trying to build up some kind of volunteer organization. But they need someone with more experience. I told them you were just the man."

"What's in it?" Gordon asked, but he was already reaching for his helmet. Almost anything would be better than begging for charity.

There was a surprised exchange of glances from the others, but Mother Corey chuckled. "Heart like a steel trap, cobbers," he said, almost approvingly. "Well, you'll be earning your bare keep here in the Coop— yours and that granddaughter's, too. I got that all fixed up with these men. As long as any food lasts, you'll eat. They sort of want you to come along with them, get the feel of things out here. After that, you'll maybe know better what needs doing."

Outside, a battered little truck was waiting. Rusty and two of Corey's henchmen were busy loading it with ammunition from the pile they had found in the cellar.

Schulberg motioned him into the cab of the truck, and the other two citizens climbed into the closed rear section. "All right," Gordon asked, "what goes on?"

The little man shrugged and began explaining between jolts as he picked a way through the ruin and rubble. Before Whaler was killed, he had done all he could at nights in helping his old precinct. He'd laid out a program for a citizen's vigilante committee to police their own area and had drilled them as best he could in the ruthless use of clubs and what weapons they could find to keep the gangs down.

Once the police were all pulled back inside the dome, busy with their private war, the committee had been the only means of keeping order in the district. And little by little, it had extended its control, until now about half the areas beyond the dome were being patrolled by voluntary police. For a time, the leanness of pickings out here had made the job easier by driving most of the gangs into coalition with the others inside the dome. But now . . .

Schulberg pointed outside. They were now on the outskirts of the Nineteenth Precinct, in somewhat familiar territory. It had changed, Gordon saw. There were fewer people outside. And where belligerence and sullen hate had been the keynotes along with hopelessness before, now there was the desperation that marked those who had finally given up completely. The few kids on the filthy streets simply sat staring with hungry eyes, while their parents moved about sluggishly without any apparent destination. Gordon had never seen group starvation before, but the ultimate ugliness of it in the gaunt faces and bloated stomachs was unmistakable.

They passed a crowd around a crude gallows, and Schulberg stopped. A man was already dead and dangling. But the fire of mob savagery was cooled to a dull hatred in the eyes watching him. "Should turn 'em over to us cops," Schulberg said. "What's he hung for?"

"Hoarding," a voice answered, and other supplied the few details. The dead man had been caught with a half bag of flour and part of a case of beans. Schulberg nodded slowly, staring at the corpse with contempt. He found a scrap of something and penciled the cime on it, together with a circle signature, and pinned it to the dangling body.

"All food should be turned in," he explained to Gordon as they climbed back into the truck. "We figure community kitchens can stretch things a bit more. And we give a half extra ration to the guys who can find anything useful to do."

The bank failure had apparently thrown nearly everyone here out of jobs, since there had been no appreciable capital left to meet payrolls. And the police war had ended work at the few places that had been open, since it was unsafe to leave the dome in the view of most plant managers and technicians, and workers from outside were barred from any jobs inside. Now the only ones permitted to leave or enter were the police and the occasional trains from the outlands.

They passed another hanging corpse with a sign that proclaimed him to be a ghoul. Schulberg shrugged. "Sure, we get cannibalism sometimes. What can you expect? Turned up a woman yesterday. Husband missing, kids looking a little better fed than they should be. But she proved her old man killed himself for the kids. He left her a note. And she hadn't touched him herself. So we hadda let her go. Sometimes, when I see my own kids . . ."

"Forget it," Gordon told him. He should have been sickened, but too much experience with this miserable little world had blunted his feelings. "It's bad business, the way things are, even forgetting the taboos. Sure, cannibalism may work sometimes, but only when the victim has been reasonably well fed and has a normal amount of fat in his tissues. If you try to use someone who's been suffering from starvation until his tissues are depleted, you wind up getting protein poisoning—and you die faster than you would from simple starvation."

"Yeah. I've heard that. But maybe they'd feel a little better while they were dying. Oh, hell—we got enough so most people won't quite starve for a while, I guess. Everybody we can reach is on rations—with extra for the ones that do the work that needs doing. And we've been dickering with the outland farmers, too. Nothing so far, but maybe we can get a little food in. We'd better. Well, here we are."

He had pulled up to the old building that Whaler had used as a precinct house. Now it bore a crude sign proclaiming it to be the volunteer police and government center. Inside, a group of worried, haggard men were going clumsily through a course on the use of crude weapons, while others were holding some kind of a discussion—mutual sharing of problems, from the few words Gordon heard.

Schulberg moved toward the center and yelled for their attention. "Okay," he announced when things were quiet. "I got a report. We were right. The Mother's back, and with us all the way. He found a bunch of ammo, and he's turning that over to us, too." He waited for the faint cheers to subside. "And he's sent Bruce Gordon out here to help us. He worked under Whaler, so some of you know him."

There were ugly looks from some men at sight of his police airsuit, but a few nodded; they looked vaguely familiar to him. Word was passed from them, and someone motioned for him to join their discussion.

So he was back in police work again, serving with the third force in about as many weeks. Maybe he should have been pleased to find a place where he was welcome. But there was no future for him that he could see. While the trouble lasted, he'd be entitled to the little that the others received. After that—if there ever was an after—well, he'd have to face it when it came.

There was speculation rife in the little volunteer force that Security was going to save them. It seemed to give them some needed hope. But if it were true, then it probably meant no release except the hell-world of Mercury for him. Look out for number one, he'd told himself. Too bad he hadn't been able to do it.

He spent the afternoon leading and training a patrol on work that was desperately needed and yet somehow futile. It was late when he returned to the Chicken Coop, and he turned toward the stairs that led to his room. All he wanted was to lie down and feel sorry for himself—if there was any pity left over in him, after what he'd seen during the day!

Mother Cory hailed him. "Hi, cobber. We're back this way."

The old man shuffled ahead, leading toward what had been his quarters in the old days. There was a big table set up there now, with Randolph and a couple of others sitting around it. The place had been cleaned up more than he expected, and there must have been new plants installed in the basement, since the air was somewhat fresher, in spite of the sounds from above that indicated most of the rooms were filled.

The others had obviously finished eating, but Mother Corey came wheezing back from a smaller room that must serve as a kitchen, carrying a plate. "Sheila left this for you. She's our cook now, but I sent her upstairs a while ago. Better eat."

Gordon's stomach told him that he was hungry, but the sight of the food was curiously unwelcome. There wasn't much, but it was still twice what could be expected by most of the people out here. He shoved the plate back in sudden disgust. "Where did all this come from?"

"I sort of stocked up before I left the dome," Mother Corey said. He chuckled, running his hands over his paunch. "And I always had a cellar nobody knew about, with a lot of things that wouldn't spoil. I've seen a mite of trouble before."

"Any idea what they do to hoarders here?" Gordon asked grimly. "I should arrest you right now. And if Schulberg . . ."

Randolph cut him off impatiently. "Don't be a fool, Gordon. Schulberg and the Mother split things up this morning. Nobody's hoarding anything. Most of us get standard rations. But the men who need their strength and alertness get more. That's the way it has to be. Eat your dinner. This is no time to waste food."

It made sense, Gordon realized. Probably the idea of all sharing equally sounded noble, but it wouldn't work. Somebody had to be operating at full efficiency, if there were ever to be any solution to this mess. But the food still seemed to stick in his craw as he forced it down. He finished as quickly as he could and left without another word.

He found his own room and turned in automatically, his head thick and his emotions churning under a confusing blanket of disgust. He needed sleep. After that, maybe he could think.

"Bruce?" A dim light snapped on, and he stared down at Sheila. Then he blinked. His bunk had been changed for a wider one, and she lay under the thin covering on one side where the bed was pressed up against the wall to fit into the room. Down the center of the cover, crude stitches of heavy cord showed where she had sewed the blanket to the mattress to divide it into two sections. And in one corner of the room, a torn sheet formed an inadequate screen for dressing.

She caught his stare and reddened slowly, drawing the cover up over her more tightly. Her voice was scared and apologetic. "I had to, Bruce. The Coop is full, and they need every room ... and I couldn't tell them that—that ..."

"Forget it," he told her. Her face looked as tired as he felt, and he wondered vaguely what sort of ration she drew—standard single, probably. He dropped to his own side of the bed, trying to consider that, and began dragging off his boots and uniform. She started up to help him, then jerked back and turned her head away.

He grimaced in minor wonder at her strange mixture of codes and ideas. "Forget all you're thinking, Cuddles. I'm still not bothering unwilling women—even if I had enough energy left to think about it. I'll even close my eyes when you dress, if that'll make you feel better."

She sighed and relaxed.

There was a faint touch of humor in her voice. "They called it bundling once, I think. I ... Bruce, I know you don't like me, so I guess it isn't too hard for you. But—sometimes ... Oh, damn it! Sometimes I think you're—nice!"

"Nice people don't get to Mars. They stay on Earth, being careful not to find out what it's like up here," he told her bitterly. For a second, he hesitated; then he began telling her about the things he had seen during the day. There'd been the young girl with the dead baby; they hadn't been able to prove it, but her neighbors were sure the baby had died because the mother was eating her child's meager food allowance. And the boy who'd be maimed for life because a Legal cop had found him too near the dome.

Sheila dropped a hand onto his, nodding. "I know. The Kid—Rusty's friend—wrote down what they did to him."

Gordon grunted. He'd almost forgotten the matter of the tongueless kid. Hell, if he had any sense, he would forget everything. But he couldn't. His thoughts went churning on, until fatigue overcame him.

Fatigue, as he found during the next few days, was almost a blessing, since it served as some anodyne for the ache of living. Some of Izzy's philosophy seemed to have rubbed off on him. He was being paid better than most others in the only way that counted out here—the food that was waiting him each night at the Coop. And a twist of his mind forced him to work longer and harder to give value for value.

His small squad was getting good at their job, too. They handled the poor, starving fool who went berserk at an assembly almost as well as professionals from Earth could have done. Under normal circumstances, he could have enjoyed knowing them. But there was no time for that. A gang of desperate citizens from a territory outside the organized sections made a raid, and it took the volunteers most of a day to track them down and recover what was left. And then there was the mad old woman in the basement . . .

Randolph located Gordon early in the evening, just as he was finishing the sign for the woman's body. "Schulberg told me where to find you, Gordon. I'm supposed to bring you back to Mother Corey. He's expecting Aimsworth some time tonight, and he wants you to tell him how things really are out here."

Gordon nodded and climbed wearily into the little three-wheeled scooter the man was driving. One of the windows had been broken, but it was crudely repaired and the compressor was whining busily behind him. He took his helmet off in relief.

"Yeah. He told me this morning." It should have been good news, maybe. Aimsworth was apparently the shipping agent for the farm grange in addition to his other positions.

Randolph took a careful look at him, reached inside his jacket, and handed over a small bottle of what passed for whiskey. Gordon took a long pull at it. The raw stuff seemed to help a little. "How come you're chauffeuring?"

"Why not? The single sheet of mimeo news I put out doesn't take up my full time. Anyhow, everyone else at the Coop is busy."

"Doing what?" Gordon asked. There was always a bustle of coming and going there when he left in the morning, but he had no idea of what it was about.

Randolph grinned crookedly. "Running outer Marsport. Don't keep selling the Mother short, Gordon. He's the only man everyone knows and trusts—his word has never been broken that anyone can remember. So he's acting as mayor generally out here. Heard about Mayor Wayne, incidentally?"

Gordon shook his head, not caring, but the man went on. "He must have had his supply of drugs looted somehow. He holed up a day or so, until it really hit him that he couldn't get any more and the jerks were about due. Then he went gunning for Trench with some idea that Trench had swiped his stuff. Trench had to shoot him, so Trench is now running the Municipal bunch. And I hear the gangs are just about in control of both sections lately."

It seemed like another world already, a fantasy world where Wayne's idea of shooting Trench was no worse than others. Wayne had been mad or a fool. On Mars, where weapons had been supposedly taboo, almost nobody knew how to use them accurately; otherwise, Gordon would have been killed in any of a dozen confrontations. But Trench was a skilled marksman.

Randolph took the long way back to Corey's to avoid the more dangerous sections. They passed near the dome, close to one of the smaller entrances. Gordon stared at it, noticing that fewer lights were burning than before, except in one place, where a group of men seemed to be working.

"Inspection and repair," Randolph said in answer to his vague question. "It's the only job where the Legals and Municipals cry truce and let the workers alone. The inspection gang has to go around it every three months, patching anything that looks dangerously weak where it's attached to the base. There's another gang that services the quick-release mechanism—though I don't suppose anyone will ever use that. Still, the switches are there, and they have to be serviced."

Damn the dome, Gordon thought. Out in the frontiers where the farms lay was one Mars. Here, in the section beyond the dome, was another. And inside was still a third. There was no similarity, except for the common misery of the last two. A world, an isolated city—and beyond, the sweepings of that city! No wonder hell had popped.

Then he jerked upright as a searchlight lashed out from inside the dome. In it was caught the figure of a boy of perhaps ten, running wildly, with a small bundle of papers under his arm. From the side of the entrance, a man in Legal uniform broke into a run after him, with a ragged bum behind him. Guns were erupting from the holsters of the two men, and the helmetless boy began screaming as the bullets whined by.

Gordon shoved Randolph's helmet over his head, clapped his own down, and was out of the scooter at a jump. His gun bucked in his hand as he hit the ground. The Legal dropped. The second shot caught the bum in the helmet, cracking it. The man staggered on a few steps, gasping, and then fell, to die slowly from lack of adequate oxygen.

The boy vanished into a pile of rubble and was gone. The searchlight swung to cover Gordon and the scooter, and there was the thin crack of a rifle. He ducked back inside, while Randolph hit the throttle and the machine lurched away. "That kid—he wasn't wearing a helmet!"

"Third generation, doesn't need one. A lot of kids here can get along on Mars air. You think that adaptation only happens out on the farms?" The publisher sighed heavily as they passed beyond range of the bullets. "One of my delivery boys. Probably trying to slip up to the dome and paste one of my sheets to it. They count coup on such tricks. I've tried to stop it, but they won't listen. And the Legals have put a bonus on the kids. For once, Gordon, I was glad to see men killed. Funny, I never thought I would be."

There were a lot of unthinkable things these days—and violent death was the least of them. But Gordon let it pass.

Aimsworth was already sitting at the table with Mother Corey when they arrived. There was a bottle of the brandy made in the outlands between them. He nodded to them and waited while Sheila brought out Gordon's rations from the kitchen, staring in disgust at the plate. Then he shrugged and turned back to Corey.

"We're not taking credits of any kind, Mother. Credits are all worthless scrap now. And your junk wouldn't buy much." He pointed to a collection of cheap jewelry and baubles that had been collected. "Wayne's group—what used to be Wayne's group—and the Legals have oil and chemicals we need. What have you got to barter?"

"That doesn't sound like the Ed Aimsworth I know," Mother Corey said sadly. He sighed heavily, his jowls shaking pendulously with the weight of all his disillusion with the man.

"It's not, damn you!" Aimsworth answered. He caught himself and grimaced. "Cut it out, Mother. I'm only shipping agent for the grange in my quadrant of the outlands. I tried to get you a shipment when I got your note—but they vetoed it, and we act as a group. All that stuff I brought you out in the truck came from my own stocks, and I had to sneak that through. Most of the members are pretty bitter about you people. One of our trains was looted last week here in outer Marsport. If your people won't let us trade for what we need, why should we feed them?"

"Ever see real starvation?" Gordon asked, wishing the story could be told by someone else who could do it justice. He told about the man who'd committed suicide for his kids, not stopping as Aimsworth's face sickened slowly. "Hell, who wouldn't loot your trains when their kids are dying? Besides, it wasn't our group; I've talked with the men enough to know that."

"Maybe so—but you can't expect us to keep up with which group is which here." Aimsworth reached for his glass and downed the contents as if he needed it. "Look, I'd like to do business with you. We've got stuff about to rot in the tanks, and most of us have kids of our own. But I donno . . ."

"The volunteer police here are shaping up. Suppose they agreed to give your trains an armed escort through the dome?" Gordon suggested.

Aimsworth considered that slowly, then shrugged. "It might help. Yes, that's a talking point, if the Mother will back up the agreement. We could let you have a few cars of the stuff that won't keep in the next shipment, maybe—and a car or two from each following shipment. I think I could talk the men in my quadrant over to that."

"Give us the stuff that's already spoiling to fill up the train," Corey said. "We can use it—it's better than some of the food we have now."

Aimsworth shook his head. "Half a train, maybe. We've got to send some stuff through to the dome."

Gordon sat back weakly and reached for a glass of the brandy, surprised at the relief that washed over him at even this small victory. The food shipment wouldn't be enough—not even a fraction of what they needed. But it would bring some hope to those who were dying without it. And it might make the difference between death and a kind of survival.

Aimsworth seemed equally relieved to have this distasteful business settled. He began stuffing his pipe with Marsweed. "Be a good thing when we can go back to dealing in honest credits. It's a relief to know Security's sending a ship. Currency won't be worth carrying until they can get this mess straightened out."

"You're sure they're coming?" Randolph asked.

Aimsworth nodded. "They're on the way. We picked up the news of that a week ago on the equatorial dish.

They must have heard it inside the dome, too—though I suppose they wouldn't let word of it get out."

Gordon felt the hair at the back of his neck tingle, remembering that the kindest reports Security would get of his actions would be enough to send an angel to hell. He grinned bitterly, then shrugged it off. "What makes you think Security can do anything? They haven't shown a hand yet."

"They will," Aimsworth said, and there was conviction in his voice. "You guys in Marsport under your own charter fed yourselves so many lies you began to believe in them. But Security took Venus—and I'm not worried here, in the long run. Don't ask me how. All I know is that Security gets results." His voice was a mixture of bitterness and an odd certainty. "They set Security up as a nice little debating society, Gordon, to make it easy for North America to grab the planets by doing it through that agency. Only they got better men on it than they wanted. So far, Security has played one nation against another enough to keep any from daring to swipe power on the planets. And this latest trick went sour, too. North America figured on Marsport folding up once they got a police war started with a bunch of chiseling profiteers as their front; they expected the citizens to yell uncle all the way back to Earth. But out here, nobody thinks of Earth as a place to yell to for help, so they missed. And now Security's got Pan-Asia and United Africa balanced against North America, so the swipe won't work. We got dope in full from our equatorial receiver. North America's called it all a mistaken emergency measure and turned it back to Security."

"Along with how many war rockets?" Gordon asked.

"None. They never gave Security any real power, never will. The only strength Security's ever had comes from the fact that it always wins, somehow. It's developed a reputation. No, there's just one ship coming, with a group of authorized agents." He studied Gordon, then grunted. "Forget the crooks and the crooked cops, man! Ask the people who've been getting kicked around on the planets about Security. You'll find that

182

even most of them here in outer Marsport—yes, and under the dome—are for it. It's the only hope we've got of not having all the planets turned into colonial Empire possessions."

Even Mother Corey nodded at that. "The only hope. There was a time when I might not have said it, but . . . Well, I just wish they get here soon enough."

"All right," Gordon said. "Suppose Security were here right now, and suppose they were sitting here with us. Aimsworth, would their guarantee buy us the food we need? Can Security do that for us? Because right now, nothing else matters."

Aimsworth frowned. "Until they could establish hard credit . . ." he began. Then he shook his head slowly. "No, you're right. Security can't perform miracles overnight, if that's what you're getting at. But I'll tell you this—if Security ordered it, some of us would feel a lot freer about sending you food. You wouldn't get what you need, maybe, but you'd probably get double what I can offer now."

And that tore it! Gordon grunted, and there was a sickness in his stomach as he stood up and began fumbling in his uniform pouch. Sheila had come to the door and was shaking her head violently at him, as if she could read his mind. But he found what he wanted, and began dragging it from the pouch.

He slapped the little badge onto the table before them. "Then I'm declaring Security in!" he told them coldly. "You know enough about Security badges at top level to know they can't be forged. This one has my name on it, and rating as a Prime—which makes me top Security man on this damned stinking planet and gives me complete authority to act for the agency. All right, Aimsworth, I've called your bluff. What are you going to do about it?"

Schulberg came in then and had to be briefed quickly, while Aimsworth turned the badge over and over in his hands, scowling in concentration.

Mother Corey chortled gleefully at the expressions on the men's faces. "Imagine the brother of Lanny

Gordon being Security Prime! Sheila, aren't you impressed with your husband?"

"She knew about it," Gordon told him curtly. "Well, Aimsworth?"

The outlander nodded reluctantly. "I guess I'm going back and start spreading the word. And maybe when I tell them about this, you'll get enough. Maybe. Mother, have an escort for me at the Third Station Friday noon."

He left, shaking his head, and Randolph picked up the badge; he fumbled at an inside pocket, drawing out a tattered bit of another badge and comparing them. His eyes were shocked. "I lost connection years ago. But I guess this makes you my boss."

"Then get busy cranking out the news. Write about the ship coming and everything else you heard from Aimsworth. And say I'm an advance agent, that I've just declared war on the whole damned dome section, and that I'm recruiting every man with a badge. Mother, is there any way we can get men into the dome with the news?"

Mother Corey nodded, his puttylike face creased in a frown. He picked up the badge, shuddered, and then grinned slowly. "There are ways, cobber. We've still got the dope we found. For that, there are places where we can get men in and out without trouble."

Schulberg dropped onto a chair, sighing. "If your deal with Aimsworth works out, there's plenty here who'd follow you anyhow. But with a Security ship coming and this authority—well, I've never cottoned to Security, Gordon, but those devils in there have been killing our kids! So I guess maybe it's time outer Marsport turned itself in to Security."

Mother Corey heaved his bulk up slowly, wheezing, and indicated his chair at the head of the table. But Gordon shook his head. He'd made his decision. He'd named himself Security, and now he had to play the part as best he could guess a real Security man would decide. But now his mind was emptied, and he wanted nothing more than a chance to hit the bed and forget the whole business until morning.

Sheila followed him up and stared at him in some brown study as he shucked off his outer clothes mechanically and crawled under the blanket. She let the robe fall to the floor and slid into her side of the bed without taking her eyes off him. "Do you think it's true about Security sending a ship?" she asked at last. He nodded, and her breath caught. "What happens when they arrive and find out everything about us, Bruce?"

She was shivering. He rolled over and patted her shoulder. "Who knows? Who cares? Stop worrying about it. I'll see that they don't blame you for things, somehow."

She threw herself sideways, as far from him as she could get. Her voice was thick, but muffled in the blanket. "Damn you, Bruce Gordon. I should have let you die that first time!"

Gordon turned back to his own side, letting the sting of her words disappear into the chasing circle of his thoughts. He was a fool for even trying to understand her. He'd always been a fool, it seemed. He'd started fighting for himself back on Earth and somehow wound up trying to fight for all the others like himself against the forces of corruption. It had gotten him a yellow ticket to Mars and had led him into this mess. Here, he'd started in grim determination to fight for number one, and the same old drive had caught up with him again. Tough, realistic—sure, until he always wound up being as much of a stupid do-gooder as Randolph.

Now he'd jockeyed himself into having to play at being Security, without the least idea of how a trained Security man would operate. And he was planning to take a bunch of other desperate fools into a war that no sane man could hope to win.

Slowly, aided by fatigue, he began forcing his mind to blank out the unwelcome thoughts. Vaguely, he was aware of Sheila's hand on his shoulder. Then sleep finally erased his conscious worries.

XVI

His head was clearer in the morning, and he lay for a few minutes trying to straighten out his ideas. Then he dressed quickly and hastened down the creaking stairs, still pondering.

Mother Corey was waiting for him. "Relax, cobber. You're through patrolling. Izzy's taken over with Schulberg now, so you've got time for breakfast. Then we've got a war to plan—unless you've cooled down?"

Gordon shook his head. He'd cooled down from the bravado of his previous words, but the job still had to be done. With a week left before Security arrived, the forces in the dome would be able to prepare for them. And without weapons from Earth, the thin forces of Security wouldn't have a chance. He'd taken on the position of Security Prime; now he had to prepare the way for the real agents who might offer some hope to this benighted planet. At least others seemed to think so, and nothing could be worse than it was.

He explained his ideas to Mother Corey as he ate what passed for breakfast, realizing from his own words how desperately poor his chances were. Most of his scheme depended on the fact that the people in the Ninth Precinct, the last precinct he had patrolled inside the dome, had come to his aid. They should be even more willing now, ready to seize even the hope he could offer. And with some cooperation from them, he could set up a base from which to spread outward, striking against the slightly more hated Legal forces first, until he could control enough territory to let Security set up and begin taking over. First, of course, he would have to break through the nearest entrance.

"So you need a small army," Corey said. "And a place to train and quarter them. I figured on something like that, so Rusty and a couple others are taking over the old plastics factory and cleaning the squatters out. How about using some of the junkies? We've got dope enough to offer for any that can steal out of the dome and join up."

Gordon nodded. Some of them would be useless, of course. But he'd seen men who would cheerfully fight a wildcat barehanded for a fix.

"And food." The old man sighed more heavily, then shrugged. "Well, I guess we'll have to shorten our reserve and count on what Aimsworth is supposed to send."

Somewhat to Gordon's surprise, the name of Security really did have some value here on Mars. A few volunteers reported to him, and some were gaunt, desperate men from the other quadrants. And three men from the Municipal police arrived, with two of them showing worn low-ranking Security cards. They would be useful, and it was heartening to know that there were still some men willing to strike back finally at the corruption they had endured. They brought reports of utter chaos in large areas of the dome, including the precinct where Gordon hoped to build his base. That might help.

And there was somewhat better news from Schulberg and Izzy than he had let himself expect that evening. Apparently Randolph's little sheet reached widely throughout outer Marsport, and some of his publicity worked. There was less trouble in the other quadrants now, and tentative suggestions of cooperation from a few of the leaders there.

The food from Aimsworth's group came in, and it was as much as he had promised. For a brief time, men smiled as they saw it, before they realized how pitifully little it actually was when divided among all those who needed it desperately. Still, the food lifted some of the immediate pressure of starvation, though Gordon's own stomach told him that the slight increase in rations was

187

not enough—and he was getting more than most of the wretches around him.

Besides, most of the food was the easily produced Mars native type, and that lacked some of the vitamins the human system needed. Those vitamins should have been supplied from Earth, but were now apparently sitting up on Deimos, where the freighters had been rerouted under the ban on shipping to Mars. Signs of scurvy were common, and pellagra was becoming evident.

Gordon whipped himself into forgetting some of that. His tiny army was growing. Or rather, his mob. There was no sense in trying to get more than the vaguest organization, or in trying to teach them to use weapons more sophisticated than clubs and knives, even if he had been blessed with an adequate supply of arms.

There was a fair sprinkling of addicts. They had begun coming out at the first word of the free drugs their systems demanded. But there were fewer than he had expected. Over a half of the junkies had died during the turmoil and deprivation within the dome, and many of the others were in pitiful condition. Then, after the first ones slipped out, the gate guards were given orders to shoot anyone leaving, and most of those remaining died in trying to make it. In the long run, the death of the poor wretches was probably for the good of Mars, Gordon thought—but now it played further hell with his plans.

He grimaced bitterly as he realized that probably Rusty's friend, the Kid, was far more of a man than ninety percent of the others.

Then the recruits stopped coming. Security might be popular as a vague hope, but its practical appeal was limited—though he had seen several other long-hidden badges among the men who did volunteer. Gordon shrugged to himself, facing the fact that his mob was as ready as it could ever be and issued orders that they would leave early the next morning.

He issued extra dope for those who wanted it and managed to get a slight increase in their rations, so they made brave enough a showing as they moved out in the early dawn. He led them through back streets, winding his way under all the cover he could find, until they finally came out near the entrance to the dome.

Then he had a clear view through the dome, and his failure to conceal his plans was immediately obvious.

There were no men standing outside the gate with rifles pointed at his force. But the warning had obviously been given, and the two forces of Legal and Municipal police were mustered inside the gate, waiting for him. For this occasion, obviously, a truce on their war had been arranged.

Stretching north from the gate were the Municipals with members of some of the gangs; the other gangmen were with the Legals to the south. And there were men standing within a few feet of the thin dome, holding axes and long knives at the ready.

A big Marspeaker ran out from the gate. It blatted a sour whistle to catch attention, and then the voice of Gannett came over it. "Go back! Go back to your stinking dens, you cannibals! If just one of you gets within fifty feet of the entrance or any part of the dome, we're going to rip the dome away! We'll destroy Marsport before we'll give in to a doped-up mob of riff-raff. You've got five minutes to get out of sight, before we come out with guns and knock you off. Now beat it!"

Gordon got out of the car the Kid was driving and started toward the entrance, just as the moaning wail of the group behind him built up. He took another step, and some of the axes inside were raised. Then hands were clawing at him, dragging him back.

"You fools!" he yelled. "They're bluffing. They wouldn't dare destroy the dome. Come on!"

But already his men were darting back into the rubble of the streets behind. He stared at the rout and suddenly stopped fighting the hands holding him. Beside him, the Kid was crying, making horrible sounds of it.

Gordon turned slowly back to the car, and felt it get under way. His final sight was that of the Legals and Municipals wildly scrambling for cover from each other while one of the gangs began breaking into the gate locker rooms.

Mother Corey met him, dragging him back to the dining room, where he dug up the last precious bottle of brandy. "Drink it, cobber. Drink it all."

"You know about it?"

The old head nodded sadly. "I know. So one of those Security badges had the wrong man attached to it, and word was sent back. Or somebody else squealed. Probably somebody with a badge, though. Bound to be some with low badges who went all the way wrong or who didn't own the names on them. But you'd probably have been as bad off, no matter what volunteers you used. Don't blame yourself. You just ran into the sacred law of Marsport—the one they teach their kids. Be bad and the dome will collapse. The dome made Marsport, and it's taboo!"

Gordon nodded, tilting the bottle back. The liquor jolted into his too-empty stomach, but he hardly noticed it. The old man was probably right. He'd been forced to use the near dozen men who claimed Security badges as his nucleus of leadership, and one might have been the traitor. "So why encourage me, Mother? If the dome is sacred and gives them a perfect defense, why let me make a fool of myself?"

Corey sank into an opposite chair, setting the heavy folds of flesh to bouncing. "Because it might have worked. And because it gave people here something to live for, cobber. And when you get over this, you're gonna announce you've discovered the traitor and make new plans to try again. Yes, you are! It gives people something to rally around, and maybe inside the dome they'll be so busy worrying about you that they won't have time to prepare against Security before that gets here. But right now, you get yourself drunk!"

He left Gordon and the bottle. After a while, the bottle was empty. Things seemed more blurred but no better by the time Izzy came in.

"Trench is outside in a heavily armored car, Bruce," Izzy announced. "Says he has to see you. Something to discuss—a proposition. Shall I have the boys let him in?"

Sure, Gordon thought—a proposition for outer Marsport to surrender, or maybe for him to use his drug-controlled addicts against the Legals. From all accounts, Trench wasn't in a good position since one of the gangs had switched sides. Gordon stood up, wobbling a little, trying to think. Then he swore and headed for his room. "Tell him to go to hell!"

He saw Izzy leave, with Sheila moving out behind him. He wondered vaguely where she had been since he got back. Through the opening in the seal, he spotted the two moving toward the big car outside. Then he shrugged dully. He finally made the stairs and reached his bed before he passed out.

Sheila was standing over him when he finally awoke. She dumped a headache powder into her palm and held it out, handing him a small glass of water. He swallowed the fast-acting drug and sat up, trying to remember. Then he wished he couldn't.

"What did Trench want?" he asked thickly.

"He wanted to talk to you. Something about knowing what you were and helping you out after Whaler died. And he had a badge." She frowned uncertainly. "He only gave me a quick look, but it seemed to be real, and his name was on it. He wouldn't talk to me much. But maybe you'd better see him if he comes back, as he said he would. I think I remember his name in the book . . ."

Too many details, Gordon thought. And he was still partly drunk. He shook his head to clear it, and then grunted at the pain. He sat up, noticing absently that someone had removed his clothes. The book, he thought, the book Whaler had given him with all the names . . .

"All right, Cuddles," he said finally. "You got your meal-ticket, and you've outgrown it in this mess. Maybe you're a better man than I am, now. But I want that damned book! I've been operating in the dark too long, and it's time I found out how to get in touch with the right people here. Where's the book?"

She shook her head. "It isn't. Bruce, I don't have it. That time I sent you the note about it ... you didn't come when I said, and I thought you wouldn't. Then Jurgens' men broke in, and I thought they'd get it when they reached me, so—so I burned it. I lied to you about using it to make you keep me."

"You burned it?" He turned it over, staring at her, suddenly re-remembering all that had happened before his marriage to her. The time seemed eons away. "Okay, Cuddles, you burned it. You were trying to kill me then, so of course you would burn it to protect me from having Jurgens get it and putting the finger on me! Where is it, Sheila? On you?"

She backed away, biting her lips. "No, Bruce. I burned it. I don't know why. I just did. No!"

She turned from him toward the door as he pushed up from the bed. But his arm caught her wrist, dragging her back. She whimpered once, then shrieked faintly as his hand caught the buttons on the dress, dragging them off. Then suddenly she was a writhing, biting, scratching fury, her clawed fingers striking for his eyes, her teeth reaching for his neck.

He tightened his grip and lifted her to the bed, dropping a knee onto her throat and beginning to squeeze, while he jerked the dress and thin slip off.

She sat up as he released his knee, her hoarse voice squeezed from between her whitened lips. "Are you satisfied now, you mechanical beast? Do you still think I have the book on me?"

He grinned, twisting the corners of his mouth. "You don't. That I can see, Cuddles. But you're being a bad wife still. Don't you know a wife shouldn't keep secrets from her husband? A husband who's getting more warm-blooded and affectionate every minute." He bent down, knocking aside her flailing arms, and pulled her closer to him. "Better tell your husband where the book is, Cuddles."

She cursed and he drew her closer. His breath caught in his throat as his hands slid over her skin. She was fighting against him, perspiring with the effort, and the scent of her hair and her faintly feminine ordor

192

burned its way into his lungs. He bent down, forcing her back and setting his lips on hers.

Then he lifted his head to look into her eyes and managed a final sound of mockery. "To hell with the book, Cuddles," he said. But there was no mockery inside him—only a hunger that had been held back too long, and a rising clamor of excitement that throbbed through his body. He no longer knew whether she was fighting him or clinging to him. He only knew that she was gathered to him, and that yesterday and tomorrow had no reality.

From somewhere, wetness touched his cheek, and it had no business in this world of over-taut emotions. But the wetness was still there. He tried to shake it off, but the cool wetness interfered with his twisted concentration. Finally, he lifted his head and looked down. The wetness came from tears that spilled out of her eyes and ran off onto the mattress. She was making no sound, and there was no resistance, but the tears ran out, one drop seeming to trip over another.

He heaved himself away, and there was a sickness and hollowness through every cell of his body. He caught his aching breath and sat up, to reach for his clothes.

"All right, Sheila," he said. His voice sounded cracked in his ears. "Another week of being a failure on this planet of failures, and I might. Go ahead and tell me I'm the same as your first husband. But tell it to me fast, because I'm through bothering you. If I can't even keep my word to you, I can at least get out and stay out." He shook his head, waiting for her denunciation, but she lay there silently. And suddenly there was another bitterness on top of all the ones that had gone before. He laughed roughly at himself. "For your amusement, I'm going to miss having you around!"

He stood up, lifting his leg to the uniform opening. Something touched his hand, and he looked down to see her fingers. His eyes swung slowly, studying her arm, her shoulder, and finally her face, filled with a strange surprise.

"Bruce," she said faintly. "You meant it! You don't

hate me any more." She rubbed her wrist across her eyes, and the ghost of a smile touched her lips. "I don't think you're a failure. And maybe—maybe I'm not. Maybe I don't have to be a failure as a woman—a wife, Bruce. I don't want you to go!"

He dropped the uniform slowly and bent toward her, until his arm slid beneath her neck and her lips gradually came up to meet his. There was no savage lurch of animal fire this time, but a slow flood of warmth. She caught her breath and tensed, and his hands were gentle as he released her slowly. Then she sighed faintly, and pulled him back, while the warmth seemed to spread from him to her, until it was a shared and precious thing, and they were one in it.

He stared down at her later. She lay sleeping, with the faint smile still tucked in the corner of her mouth. Vaguely, he could understand why she might have burned the book as she claimed. They had been like two worlds, as separate as were inner and outer Marsport, held apart by a dome that neither dared to break. But under it all, they had been the same, and the drive toward completion had always operated before one could harm the other.

He sighed, wishing the two Marsports could have the same protection against mutual ruin. Two worlds. One huddled under its dome, forever afraid of losing the protection and having to face the life the other led; and yet driven to work together or to perish together. The sacred dome!

And suddenly he was sitting up, shaking her. "The dome! It has to be the answer. Sheila, you broke the chain enough for me to think again. We've been blind—the whole damned planet has been blind."

She blinked and then frowned. "Bruce—"

"I'm all right! I'm just half sane instead of all insane for a change." He got up, pacing the floor as he talked and as the truth of his idea began to drive itself home.

"Look, most of the people on this planet are Martians. They've left Earth behind, and they're meeting this world on its own terms. And they're adapting. Third-generation children—not all, but a lot of them—

are breathing the atmosphere we'd die in, and they're doing fine at it. Probably second-generation ones can keep going after we'd pass out. It's just as true out here beyond the dome as it is on the frontier. But inner Marsport has that sacred dome over it. It's still trying to be Earth. And it can't do it. It sits huddled in terror, ripe for the plucking of anyone who will keep the dome going. It has never had a chance to adjust here, and it's afraid to try."

"Maybe," she agreed doubtfully. "But what about this part of Marsport? Why are things such a mess here? Why have they always been so bad?"

"Obvious. Here, they grow up under the shadow of the dome. They live in a half world. There, inside the dome save by the mace of God, live they. There, with luck, they'll move some day. They worship the thing, because it's a symbol they might barely have a chance to live a sheltered life again. They've been infected. And they have to live on the crumbs the dome tosses to them. What we need is to break through, and there's only one way to do it! Fix it so they're all on the same level, so they can live together like people again, not like slave and master—and so they'll have to face the world they're living on. Sheila, if something happened to that dome . . ."

"We'd be killed," she said. "How do we do it?"

They spent the rest of the night discussing it. Sometime during the discussion, they moved downstairs so she could make what passed for coffee. Their need of it was greater than their regret at exceeding their normal allotment. Randolph and the Kid found them there and had to be briefed. Randolph was a willing convert, and the Kid had been alternately worshipping Gordon and Sheila since he'd first been sure they were fighting against the men who'd robbed him of his right to speak. In the end, as the night spread into day, there were more people than they felt were safe and less than they needed. Rusty and Izzy argued hotly against the situation until finally convinced, and then settled down to conviction in the rightness of it that was greater even than Gordon's.

He could feel something boiling inside him that he hadn't felt since the day back on Earth when he'd discovered that the head of one of the most vicious rackets was a leading Congressman and had written his column on it—the one that got him the only prize he'd ever valued.

But later, as some of them stood in partial concealment beyond the dome when night had fallen again, he wasn't so sure. It was huge. The fabric of it was thin, and even the webbing straps that gave it strength were frail things. But it was strong enough to hold back the pressure of ten pounds per square inch, and the webbing was anchored in a metal sleeve that went too high for cutting. They could rip it with a sharp implement, but that might not do more than let out a hiss of air. The job had to be done so that no repair could ever be made. Once gone, the expense of putting up another would be too great for the fraying economy of the city.

Under it, and anchoring it, was a concrete wall all around Marsport.

Behind them lay the wild lands of outer Marsport, with ugly hulks and wrecks of buildings showing faintly in the weak light. Inside, the city was mostly silent, except for the patrolling cops and a few gangsters who moved about boldly, unmindful of the cops.

"You mentioned some kind of release once, Randolph," Gordon suggested.

The publisher nodded. "Yes. The designers were afraid that a rip might spread until the entire dome was ruined. So they put in emergency releases, every fifty yards, with the bottom cable anchored to them. If any part fails, all the trips are supposed to be electrically released together. Cheaper to let the whole dome go, then reinstall it, than to buy a new one. A few years ago, Mayor Wayne had a master control installed in city hall—as a threat against rebellion, I guess. But I don't think he'd have dared use it."

"Suppose someone tossed a bomb against one of the trips," Gordon suggested. "What would happen?"

Randolph shrugged. "Who know? In theory, all would release at once. But they've been there a long time, and the men who maintain them are political appointees. It's a sinecure job. If some released and others stuck, the dome would go all to pieces."

"They've got a release in each gate," Izzy said. "Safest place. But you can spot the next one down there. See how the webbing is thicker?"

The Kid made a gobbling sound and darted off toward the spot Izzy had indicated. He was half-way there when an alarm sounded and lights came on. Some sort of alarm system had been installed outside the dome!

The two nearest guards were snapping down their helmets and rushing through the gate. They began firing at once, but their marksmanship was as bad as usual. The Kid was running all out, away from Gordon's hiding place. He reached a ruin and ducked into it.

"Time to go, gov'nor," Izzy said. "Nothing we can do to help him."

It was sound advice, and Gordon turned reluctantly. The guards had seen only the figure of a youngster and were probably figuring that it was another of Randolph's boys making a crazy attempt at a coup. With any luck, they wouldn't pursue the Kid.

They reached the battered truck and waited there. A few minutes later, the Kid came panting up. There was blood on the back of one hand, but it was from a scratch he'd taken in dashing through the ruins. Gordon started to bawl him out, then shrugged and gave up. He had been a fool himself at that age—and maybe he still was. They piled into the truck and headed back toward the Coop.

"Anybody know how to make a bomb?" he asked.

Randolph and Izzy both snorted, but it was the publisher who answered. "You're new here, Gordon, or you would know more about the Mother. Bombs were his speciality—that's what got him up here a long time ago. With the explosives we've still got at the Coop, he could make you a hundred."

"Yeah," Izzy agreed. "Only who throws it? No matter how you lay a cover, gov'nor, somebody's going to put the finger on you for sure. Guards see a man running toward the dome, they snap down their helmets, so some of them live through the dome rupture. And afterward, some of them are going to remember and spread the word. So everybody makes mincemeat of the man who threw the bomb. Fine mincemeat!"

Gordon shrugged. It couldn't be helped. Anyhow, it didn't matter so much now. With the real Security on the way, his time was being counted in the present tense only. Mincemeat was probably better than Mercury. The important thing was to get the dome down, so he had blanketed his mind to everything else.

"We'll take all our men with us," he said. "Make a second attack, and in the confusion, anything can happen."

Izzy shook his head. "I don't like it, gov'nor. I don't like it at all."

"Nevertheless, get the men ready for an early attack," Gordon ordered. Izzy grumbled, but he nodded.

There was a fair group of men in the Coop, and suspicious looks were directed by a few of them. But Mother Corey waddled over to greet them. "Did you find the stuff, cobber?" he asked quickly, and one of his eyelids flickered.

Izzy answered before Gordon could rise to it. "Not yet, Mother. I think you got a bum steer."

There was a little further discussion of the mythical supplies they were supposed to have searched for, and then the men began leaving, with Izzy heading out to the factory that served as a barracks to pass on word of the coming attack. Eventually, Gordon was alone with Mother Corey and could ask about the possibility of building some kind of small bomb.

The old man stared at him, then grinned slightly. "Don't have to build anything," he said. "Come along." He led the way down to the cellar, where he wheezed his way along one wall until he found a loose section that came away easily. His hand went inside, fumbled, and came out.

"An old man has to have a bit of protection, cobber.

When he gets old and feeble, he has to get himself a little extra security. He . . . hold it!"

There were steps behind them but it was only the Kid. Corey stared at him, then shrugged and passed the object over to Gordon.

It was obviously a professionally made grenade, beautiful in its own ugly way, and no bigger than a fist. Gordon hefted it and shook his head. "I need more than this, Mother."

"Don't be a fool! I know what you need." A swollen hand caressed the object gently. "I put a sort of special explosive in that one—you just pull out this pin when you're ready, hold this lever down, and throw it. It blows in seven seconds. Only don't get too close—that little thing will surprise you, cobber. Who's going to use it?"

Gordon stared at the thing, then stuck it carefully in his pocket. He didn't answer.

"Yeah," Mother Corey said finally. He turned toward the stairs. "You better get some sleep. And tell my granddaughter she married an idiot. Kid, you come with me."

Sheila was undressing when he entered the room, but he only nodded and headed for the bed, not botherng to strip off more than his uniform. She stood at the foot of the bed, staring at him for a moment and fingering the stitches that still ran down the blanket to divide it. Then she grimaced faintly and dropped down beside him on top of the blanket. Her head hit his arm, and she seemed to be asleep almost at once.

He lay there, twisting things about in his mind. The lift of the previous night was gone now, and there were only doubts left.

The people inside the dome had been drilled to seek cover at once, but that was only from a rent in the fabric that would produce a fairly gradual leak. This would be a wild rush of air that would strip the inside of the city down to Mars-normal in bare seconds. He had no idea of the amount of wind there would be, nor whether there would be time for men to snap down helmets or seek cover. The houses had been built to take it, but human bodies were a lot less tough.

Twice he turned over to wake Sheila and tell her it was all off. But he couldn't cancel the only hope he could see. If the idea worked, it would be worth a little death. There shouldn't be much, since alarms would probably be set off when his group approached the dome. Randolph had told him he was good only for murder and killing. Maybe it was true. But if he had to spend his life in fighting, he might as well make it pay off.

Rule books, he thought! Whaler and his willingness to die for what he believed. The old man and his wife who had run the liquor store, and who had never had a chance on this stupid world. He wondered vaguely whether their bodies had ever been found, and whether they had had a decent burial.

Then he looked down at Sheila's face. Some day she'd have children. Probably not his children. He thought of that, and it hurt a little. Sure, maybe it was just his slum background where men had always pauperized themselves to have fine strong sons to support them in their age. In spite of social insurance, the old ideas still stuck in such places. And the sons neglected their parents in trying to have sons for their future! Or maybe it was just a drive that was built into all men. He'd always felt a touch of jealousy when he saw other men with kids.

But it didn't matter. She'd be having children here on this planet, and they had a right to better things than she had found for herself. Her grandchildren would be Martians, able to meet the world on its own terms and to breathe the atmosphere unaided.

What he was doing had to be right.

The same thought was still in his mind when he awoke to find Izzy shaking his shoulder. He looked down for Sheila, but she was gone. Izzy followed his eyes and shook his head.

"The princess took off," he said. "I got back a while ago and found she left in a car with Trench!"

"Trench!"

"Yeah, Trench. But don't get me wrong. I'm not thinking . . ."

"You'd better tell me all about it," Gordon suggested grimly, reaching for his uniform.

The little man nodded. Apparently there wasn't too much to tell. Randolph had seen her when he came downstairs during the night to get hot water for some medicine he took. She had been talking with one of the men from the barracks, one of those with a low-ranking Security badge. Then the guard outside the Coop had seen Trench drive up in the early morning. Sheila had gone out to see him, talked for a couple of minutes, and climbed into the car. They had taken off for the dome.

"She'd never betray us, gov'nor," Izzy said. "Not the princess. I figure maybe she had some idea of helping . . ."

Gordon found himself staring at the leg still only half in the uniform. "Yeah," he agreed. "Trying to save my neck."

"That's it," Izzy agreed. "But what do we do now?"

There wasn't much they could do but stick to plans, Gordon thought, cursing himself for being fooled into believing she had fallen asleep. He pulled up his uniform slowly. She'd probably be as safe with Trench as anywhere; the man had never been a woman chaser. And if the dome was alerted, maybe something could be made of the confusion.

"We go ahead, Izzy. What else? Get the men started while we scout ahead."

There was no sign of alarm inside the dome when Gordon, Izzy and the Kid reached their scouting position. There seemed to be more guards, but hardly enough to stand off a vigorous attack.

"It looks all right," Gordon decided. "We'll get the men to move up and spread out as close as they can be hidden. Then in an hour, we pull a raid. You lead, and make a lot of fuss. Then begin withdrawing. When they see you retreating, they should relax enough for a man to run from that second ruin until he's close enough to toss the grenade."

"That smells!" Izzy told him. "Who elected you to be chief martyr around here? You'll be blown up, gov'nor—and if you ain't, they'll rip you to ribbons for knocking off the dome. And your own men will join in—"

He stopped suddenly, staring. Gordon leaned forward, shoving Izzy out of his way. Then he also saw it.

Standing near the gate was Trench, talking to a Municipal guard. And beside him stood Sheila, with one hand resting on his elbow. Then, as Gordon stared, she looked up and suddenly pointed straight toward him!

He forced back all the nasty thoughts in his mind and turned to face Izzy, aware that the other had also seen.

He could feel the misery between them, but he pushed that aside with his thoughts. "Let's get back, Izzy," he said, and his voice was so level that it sounded like a machine talking.

"You're going through with it, still?"

"In one hour. And you might pass the word along that we're doing it to save the dome. Tell the men we just found out that Trench is losing to the Legals, and that he intends to blow up the dome rather than to let them win."

Rumor would travel fast, he hoped. And the results might give him a few extra seconds before his forces cracked.

The hour passed in a fog. He knew he was issuing orders, posting the men, acting the cold figure of command in person. He had a blurred memory of spreading the story about Trench's plans for the dome, and later of hearing it come back to him curiously twisted.

It wasn't until he stood ready to give the final signal that he snapped into focus again. There was no sign of Sheila this time, or of Trench; and he didn't look for them. His whole mind was concentrated down to a single point. Get the dome, get the dome, get the dome . . .

This time there was no orderly separation of Municipals and Legals. The Municipal forces were rushing about as Legals were arriving in trucks and beginning to pour out. It looked like the beginning of a pitched battle right at the spot where Gordon needed his own cover.

It made no sense to him. If they wanted to fight inside the dome at this spot, it was all to the good. Then a thin wailing began, carried weakly across the distance from inside.

"Dome warning!" Izzy shouted. "Hear that siren, gov'nor? And our men haven't showed yet. That should make them believe what we've been telling them about Trench."

"Then get back and start our men moving!" Gordon ordered. "Kid, go back with Izzy."

The Kid shook his head, beginning to make gobbling noises. Gordon shrugged and let him stay. Inside the dome, a heavy truck carrying Municipal colors began moving up, carrying a big Marspeaker on its roof. There were sounds coming from it, and the voice seemed to be that of Trench. But the words were being muffled by the distance through the thin air out here. Now Izzy was just moving out toward the gate with Gordon's men behind him. They seemed to be yelling, from the few faces he could see through their helmets. By now they were convinced of the planted rumor.

But nobody paid attention inside the dome. The Municipals were drawing back toward the truck, which began backing up. The Legals seemed uncertain, then began to move closer to the dome, making threatening signs. And a sudden sharp whistle from the big Marspeaker cut the air. Abruptly, some of the Municipal forces lifted guns and began firing at the Legals.

Now, Gordon decided. He reached into his pocket for the grenade, turning it so the little lever would fit firmly in his hand. He could pull the pin with his teeth as he ran.

Then he turned his head to order the Kid back, just in time to see the other move. One thin hand snapped down against Gordon's wrist and the other jerked forward to catch the grenade as it fell. The Kid's legs doubled, and he was running frantically forward.

Inside the dome, everything was a mêlée, with both

forces firingly crazily. Bullets were hitting the dome and driving through, but they seemed to be causing no serious damage to the fabric. Gordon stole a quick glance at his men, to see them running madly forward, shaking their fists and weapons. Then he turned back to stare toward the running Kid.

The Kid was close enough to the dome, and so far no one seemed to have noticed him. A shot hit the ground in front of his feet, but it was not intended for him. Still he ran on.

"Throw it," Gordon whispered. Then he began screaming uselessly. "Throw it! Throw it!"

But the Kid still went on running forward. He was thirty feet from the dome—twenty—ten! Then his arm went back for the throw, and Gordon could see that the lever was already released. The Kid turned to face him, just as the grenade struck.

Where the edge of the dome had been, a clap of thunder seemed to take visible form. The webbing straps broke, and the dome jerked upward, twisting outward and falling into ribbons. The Kid's body seemed to disintegrate, and the shock wave hit Gordon, knocking him backward against the broken side of a ruin. And beyond him, he could see Randolph's guess coming true; some of the releases had failed, and the dome was falling into shreds on all sides.

His men were pouring forward madly now, and from some of the buildings that had been inside the dome men were emerging in their helmets and Mars suits, waving crude weapons as they headed for both Legals and Municipals. The few of either police force still standing broke into a wild run, but they had no chance. The mob had decided that they had mined and exploded the dome, and knives were being forgotten in the frenzy of crazed mob vengeance that shook everyone.

Gordon found the nearest way back to the Coop and stumbled down it, sick with the death of the Kid and the bloody violence still going on. For once, he'd had more than his fill of it. He stumbled along automatically, disregarding the cars and trucks that had brought his men here.

Then he heard the dull rumble of a heavier machine behind him and he moved aside automatically until the armored vehicle came abreast of him. Inside it, he could see Trench. Sheila was driving.

He started to move further away, but Trench opened the door and grabbed his shoulder. He made no protest as the man dragged him up onto the seat.

"Your wife's quite a woman, Gordon," Trench said. "She took a helluva chance on me. And I guess I took a few myself to set up that mess back there so nobody would ever believe you had anything to do with it. Getting the fight with the Legals set up in time, after we spotted you, was the toughest bit of organizing I ever did. But I guess it was rougher on her, not knowing at first where I stood."

Gordon stared at him, not quite believing it, even though it was no crazier than anything else during the last few days. "So your visit to me was legitimate, and you left instructions with Sheila on how to contact you. Why?"

Trench shrugged. "I told you once my grandfather helped set up the air machines. I grew up hearing about the wonders of Mars from him. And I spent a lot of years getting here—and had to join Security to get my pass, finally. You know what I found. Earth was a long ways away, and Wayne was here. Besides, he gave me a hand when I needed it. So eventually, I joined him and stopped trying to beat the system. And every so often, I got a vacation long enough to see the real Mars out there. But after Wayne came gunning for me, nobody owned me. So when I heard you were Security, I came out. I figured I owed you for saving my life, just as you owed me a favor for covering for you about that business with Whaler. Well, here we are."

He indicated the Coop. Gordon got down, followed by Sheila, while Trench moved over behind the wheel. "What happens to you now?" Gordon asked. "They'll be blaming you for the end of the dome."

"Let them. I expected that. Isiah Trench got torn to

pieces by the mob, leaving only parts of a uniform and such to prove it. And a man with another identity goes back to his farm in the boondocks—and his waiting wife and kids. Even Wayne didn't know about that." Trench stuck out a hand. "So-long, Gordon. You're like Security—do all the wrong things but get the right results."

Sheila watched him drive away, smiling faintly. "Men! He'd never put it into words, Bruce, but he thinks a lot of you."

He stared at her, then grinned. "Women!" he said.

Then he stiffened. Coming down through the thin air of Mars was the bright blue exhaust of a rocket. The real Security was arriving!

XVII

Three days later, after the last long-delayed freighter from Deimos had dropped, Gordon finally heard from Security. His name had been on none of the lists previously published and broadcast. But finally, a young man with an official patch and no helmet brought a brief note for him. He scanned it quickly and then swore.

"Dont' call us, we'll call you!" he reported the contents to Sheila. "Some kind of red tape about a man being held up on Phobos who should handle my case! So I'm to hang around where I am until I hear from him! How long am I to twiddle my thumbs?"

She tried to comfort him, but without success. And finally he shouted at her and stalked off to watch men sealing and removing the last of the drug supply from the basement of the Coop.

He wasn't being easy to live with, he knew. And he

knew he would become worse with each passing day. He couldn't stand prolonged silence between himself and Sheila—but conversation inevitably led to speculation that he also found impossible to take. And the fact that she stayed on with him, when she could have joined the others busy moving out into the reunited city of Marsport, made him feel guilty, and he took his guilt out on her.

He was sure that the outcome of his interview with Security would bring disaster, but it was the waiting that was hardest to bear. He wanted to face his penalty and get it over with. If they had wanted to let him go, it would have been simple for them to accept him on his *de facto* work as a Security agent—they could have done that temporarily, even if there was doubt in their minds. They had already begun sweeping in all the other minor agents and using them. But they seemed unimpressed by the fact that, one way or another, he had cracked their problem for them.

Now, however, that the dirty business of killing and fighting was done, Security wanted the meek to run their errands for them. They were taking no blame for the blood and violence that had put them in the saddle here. They had taken over the beginnings of the organization he'd begun under the Security name, but they'd left him outside, to cool his heels.

Most of the others left the Coop for business of their own. Randolph was the last to go, but a week later his equipment was packed onto a truck and hauled away. The little publisher was doing the *Crusader* again on a small press from some printing shop. Even Rusty was gone back to open his bar and try to find liquor to restock it. Only Gordon and Sheila were left in the old wreck.

He heard her coming down the decaying stairs and looked up morosely.

"We're almost out of food," she told him. Her voice was apologetic, and his guilt toward her rekindled his impatience. "I'm going to see what I can find at the stores over beyond Rusty's."

He nodded, not trusting himself to speak. He had

already tried to tell her that she should pack up and join her grandfather. But she was as stubborn as he was, and he wanted no more arguments. He watched her go, suddenly lonely and miserable beyond his previous level of self-pity.

She was hardly gone, however, before the helmetless kid with the official patch began kicking at the front seal of the Coop. This time the note was shorter, but it seemed to settle things. He was to report to a specific room in a specific building at the specific time of three that afternoon.

He could have waited and taken the battered three-wheeler that had been left for him. But he was tired of waiting; he wanted to see what he had wrought. He climbed into his uniform at once, pulled down his helmet, and started out the door. Then he hesitated. He'd never be back, he was sure. And it was probably best not to have to go through the painful goodbyes when Sheila returned. He went up to the little room they had shared. The thread was still down the middle of the mattress. He caught it savagely, ripping it out, and then began stuffing it into an inner pocket.

She'd be better off without him, he told himself as he took the back way and headed toward the place where the dome had been. It might hurt her now, but she was still young. There would be other men for her, probably better than he could ever be.

He saw a man come running across the rubble, shouting. Gordon's hand dropped to where his gun had been, and his legs tensed for a leap. Then he grimaced as the man went on, yelling at a bunch of kids climbing out of an old building. Maybe it was a good thing they were picking him up; he had no place here where peace was beginning to be declared.

Out on the spaceport, the distant noses of the rockets from Deimos were clearly visible, gathered thickly. A long line of trucks went chugging along the road that led to inner Marsport. Credit had been established again, backed by hard Earth money, and some businesses were already open. Here and there, men were coming out of the old ruins, heading toward the game halls and the bars, indicating some credits in their pockets again. A few factories were already starting to hire help.

A group of young punks outside one of the ruins was busy shooting Martian craps, and one was making motions with a knife. Then a man with the armband of the volunteer police came around the corner, yelling at them. Sullenly, they broke up and began heaving the rubble into a truck to be hauled away. Those otherwise unemployed were being put to work cleaning things up. How much good that would do, Bruce Gordon had no idea.

For the time being, the hoods and punks were having a rough time of it, with working papers demanded as constant identification. But while the situation lasted, at least, outer Marsport was having its face lifted. Gordon passed a bunch of men erecting temporary bubbles built like the dome, but opaque for privacy. A lot of those, he'd heard, had already been shipped down in collapsed form.

Hunger still marked the kids playing around them, but it was a taint from the past, with none of the gaunt fear that had been in their eyes before.

As Gordon drew closer to the old foundation of the dome, the feeling around began to clarify into something half-way between what he had felt on the real frontier of Mars and what he had known as a kid in Earth's slums.

Then he passed into the formerly enclosed section. Momentum still carried it along better than the outer part of the city, and conditions were still an improvement over the outer slums. But there was an uncertainty and clumsiness—and sometimes a bitterness— here that was opposed to the rising confidence he had seen further out. People were still adjusting to the lack of an artificially maintained atmosphere around them.

They had been lucky. The dome had exploded upward into shreds, long after the alarm had sent them to shelter. The buildings had come through the explosion of the pressure with little damage. Some of the people showed their good luck, while others moved about with

209

traces of numbed despair that had replaced their brief fury. But generally, there was a realization that the days of the dome were over, and that men still had to go on.

At least, there was now one police force, not two. Gordon grinned wryly. Schulberg's volunteers had been made official. Izzy was acting as chief of police; Schulberg was head of the reconstruction corps, and Mother Corey was temporary mayor of all Marsport, acting for Security. The old charter for Marsport from North America was dead, and the city was now under Security charter, like the rest of the planet. But the agents had left most of the control in the Mother's hands, and the old man was up to his fat jowls in business.

Gordon moved automatically toward the Seventh Ward. There was no use heading toward the Municipal Building. His friends were there, but they were busy, with no time for a man without a planet or a job!

He was only good for fighting and killing—and for the time being, those skills were no longer needed here.

Fats' Place was still open, though the crooked tables had been removed. Dice and cards were still in evidence, but the games now seemed to be penny-ante stuff.

Gordon felt in his pouch to be sure he'd remembered his money; like other former depositors, he'd been issued a hundred of the new credits against his account until the banks could be opened again. He heard the crackle of the bills and dropped to a stool, slipping off his helmet. He reached automatically for the glass of ether-needled beer. This time, it even tasted good to him. Maybe it was time he was getting off the damned planet—even to the mines of Mercury! Then he spat and reached for his purse to order another beer.

"On the house, copper," Fats' voice said. The man dropped to another stool, rolling dice casually between his fingers. "And bring out a steak, Mike! I just got a few in, and you look as if you could stand one. Fats don't forget old friends!"

"Friends and other things," Gordon said, remembering the first visit here. "Maybe you should have got me that first time, Fats."

The other shrugged. "That's Mars." He rolled the dice out, then picked them up again. "Guess I'll have to stick to selling meals, mostly—for a while, at least. Somebody told me you'd joined Security and got banged up trying to keep Trench from blowing up the dome. Thought you'd be running things now."

"That's Mars," Gordon echoed the other's comment. He studied the plate in front of him and fell to, more from politeness than hunger. "Why don't you pull off the planet, Fats? You could go back to Earth, I'd guess."

The man nodded. "Yeah. I went back, about ten years ago. There had been a little trouble back there, but I squared it. Sold out, packed up, and away I went. Spent four weeks down there. I dunno. Guess a man gets used to anything . . . Hell, maybe I won't make as much here now—but if we get a half-way decent government, without all the graft, I'll net more. Figure maybe I can hire some bums to sit around and whoop it up when the ships come in, and bill this as a real old Martian den of sin! Get a barker out at the port, run special buses, charge the suckers a mint for a cheap thrill."

Gordon grinned wryly, remembering the drummer he'd met on the trip here. Fats would probably make more than ever.

He finished the meal, accepted a pack of the Earth cigarettes that sold at a luxury price here to cover air tax, and went out into the thin atmosphere of Mars.

He moved down the street woodenly, almost missing a sudden hail from one of the women's houses. Then a hand was plucking at his arm and he swung around to see Hilda, the girl he'd escorted to the auction.

"Hey, cop! Don't you speak no more?"

"What—?" he began.

But she grinned at him. "Oh, they freed us all from our contracts—first thing they done! So I came down here right off. Duchesses treat me like I was a real swell—caught on just like that! You should come inside. They got rugs on the floor!" Then her face sobered suddenly, almost taking on its old look. "Hey, what ever happened to Sheila? A real queen, she was. She—"

"I married her," he told the girl.

She blinked and then laughed. "Well, whatta ya know? Oh, oh!" A whistle had sounded from the house, and she swung back. "Somebody wants to see me. That's my whistle. So long, cop—and you tell Sheila I was asking for her."

Gordon glanced at his watch and turned toward the building east of the Municipal Building, where Security now had its headquarters.

It had been instructive, at least. He knew now just how important he was. Marsport was rebuilding into its new life, and the old elements were being forgotten, unless they fitted in. Fats would feed him, and a few people would remember his face and talk to him—until the business of living took them away again. But the city was no longer interested in iron cops from its past.

He was on time when he gave his name at a desk, and he hardly had to wait before being ushered quietly into a small office. And there, behind a make-shift desk, sat the man who'd first sent him to Mars.

There was a faint smile on the man's face as he stood up and held out his hand. "Hello, Gordon. I've finally got your record pretty complete and made my decision."

"Mercury?"

At the other's nod, Gordon let himself down carefully onto the second chair in the room. He'd expected it, but . . .

"Yeah," he said at last. "I suppose you know everything. I ruined the damned dome, was supposed to have killed Whaler and pretended I was a Security agent."

"You *were* Security," the man corrected him. "Our top man here from the moment Whaler must have decided to give you that badge. Oh, we know about Whaler. We even located Trench and talked to him, though he seems to be trying to make good-citizen rating now, so we aren't throwing the book at him."

"Just at me," Gordon observed drily.

"Nor at you. Damn it, we sent you here to get results, and you got them. We sent a lot of others the same way—we couldn't operate legally here under the charter—and they failed. Those are the chances we had to take. You acted a little drastically—that I have to admit—but you found the solution we had guessed might work, and you saved us from a lot of nastiness here. So we're one step closer to keeping nationalism off the planets, and that's all we care about."

"I wonder if it's worth it," Gordon said slowly, while his sentence to Mercury slowly settled toward reality in his mind.

The other shook his head. "We can't know in our lifetime. All we can do is hope. We'll probably get your friends Corey and Isaacs elected properly; and for a while, things will improve. But there will be pushers as long as weak men turn to drugs, and graft as long as voters allow the thing to get out of their hands. Let's say you shifted some of the misery around a bit. You've given them a chance to do better. Now it's up to them to take it or lose it. But it was a damned fine job, anyway."

"So I get sent to Mercury?"

"No. You *go* to Mercury. Our Primes—and you're still listed that way with us—don't get sent; they get advised of what would be desirable, then they go. Look, you can't stay here. Right now, Trench is being blamed, but there are little bits of rumors that are going to come together after a while. Those things always come out when enough people are involved. You wouldn't be safe—or you wouldn't stay where we could keep you safe." He sighed. "You can go back to Earth, for a while. But down there you're going to be branded everything from cannibal to murderer—and there'll be some who engineered the Legal grab who'll blame you. They have long memories. Anyhow, you wouldn't like it. You're a fighter. You fit best where there's trouble.

"And right now, hell is brewing on Mercury—worse

213

than here, though we don't know just what kind it is. It will be hell—and the only thing you'll get out of it is a chance to fight for a better chance for others some day—maybe—and a promise that there'll be more dirty jobs until you get old enough to sit with me at some desk on Earth and fight every bickering nation to keep the planets clean. You'll have every card stacked against you, as far as reward or glory go. You'll be shipped out of here with the real rotten eggs we're deporting. You'll be tried on the Moon for every crime we can stack up against you. And when you're proved worse than any other criminal who ever lived, you'll be shipped to Mercury with a yellow ticket—and our hopes. There's a rocket on the field waiting. You don't have to go—but we think you will. We thought you'd earn your Prime, after we'd studied all your charts. We don't make many mistakes that way. Well?"

Gordon sighed. There had to be places where a man could hide out. Mars was his planet now—he'd earned his right here. Then he straightened his shoulders. "You'd better tell my wife that . . . well, that I didn't just run off on her. She's had bad luck with her men."

"She knows," the Security man said. "She got here about an hour ago. And she doesn't agree about her luck, Gordon. She insisted we send her with you. She's gone off to raise hell with her grandfather now, but I'll send her to you when she gets back."

Gordon flinched. He couldn't take that now. It was better for her to have it break clean, too. Let her think him a total bastard; maybe it would help her get over him.

"No," he said harshly. "I won't see her. But if I've got any salary coming—yeah, I figured there must be—well, see that she gets half of it in ways she won't trace."

The agent nodded and held out his hand again. "You'll be held here for a while, before the bus takes you out to the airport, but I won't see you again. Good luck, Gordon!"

There was a bitter humor in that final wish, somehow, Gordon felt as a very polite young man guided him back to an improvised cell and carefully locked him in. Then he was left alone with his thoughts. They were ugly. But little by little, he accepted what had to be ahead of him. Maybe he'd be lucky enough to get killed early on Mercury. But he doubted it. He'd probably live to a ripe old age, with years of memories to haunt his waking hours.

The door opened suddenly, arousing him from his grim reverie. Then he gasped as Mother Corey came in. The old man was almost immaculate, though not much prettier. And the smell of decay was gone, not merely covered by perfume.

"I sent Sheila off to see a lawyer friend," he said. "Got her out of my hair so I could see you. But they don't give me much time." He dropped onto the cot beside Gordon, making it sag alarmingly. "Look, cobber, this joint isn't much. I can get some men and crack it like an eggshell. But I wonder—you want out, just between us? Or do I smell things here that I think I smell?"

Gordon looked at the old man with new respect. Mother Corey had spent a lot of years watching the tangled affairs of men. It seemed that he hadn't missed much. "Let it ride, Mother," he said quietly, dropping one hand onto a pudgy arm and squeezing gently.

"I thought so." Mother Corey's breath was wheezing and there seemed to be a sniffle as he rose ponderously. "I'll—oh, drat it, I'm getting old and soft. Izzy's waiting to see you."

The little man slipped in at once and dropped to a seat where the Mother had been. His face was tense, more weasellike than ever, and his voice was barely above a whisper. "I've been thinking, gov'nor. There's a lawyer on Earth so good you could shoot the judge in front of the jury and he'd get you off. And I know where all the confiscated junk is. That's worth enough—"

"It wouldn't be honest, Izzy," Gordon told him, a touch of amusement cutting through his darker mood.

"Neither is this after what you did for them."

"It is in my book, Izzy."

For a second, the sharp eyes stared at him in surprise. Then his face seemed to crumple, and Izzy nodded. He started to leave, then turned back at the door. "So long, Bruce," he said simply.

The next time the door opened, it was the polite young man, together with two heavy guards in full uniform. Gordon went out and down the hall, heading for the back of the building. There the polite young man waited while Gordon's helmet was sealed, then left. The two guards moved forward, with Gordon following them.

There was an armored bus waiting for them, and the door opened as they drew nearer. Then the inner door of the lock admitted them. The guards escorted Gordon to his seat, nodded to others at the back of the bus, and left him.

Other passengers were being escorted out, he saw. And some of them he could recognize. Gannett was one of the first, and Nick the Croop came later. There were about a dozen of them, the worst that Security had found to keep him company. The men who had almost managed to poison a planet.

Nick the Croop looked across the aisle at him and tried to grin. "Hi, Gordon. Imagine the iron cop with us." But his voice was tense and the skin was gray under its normal swarthiness. Gannett sat huddled in his seat, staring numbly at the hands that were clenched on his lap.

The bus driver was beginning to fidget and glance at his watch. He picked up his short-wave phone and talked into it, then swore again. He was still grumbling when the polite young man—now in suit and helmet—came across the field and through the lock. The man dropped down beside Gordon.

"Your wife's lawyer has issued a paper," he said quietly. "He found an old colonial law that permits a wife to accompany a husband into exile, unless he signs a refusal. I've brought the form, if you want to sign it."

Gordon reached for it and then hesitated as his eye caught a motion through the window. She was on the field; there was no mistaking her uniform, as she stood waiting beside the huge figure of Mother Corey and the smaller one of Izzy. She stood quietly, making no move as his head turned toward her.

He reached for the paper again, then shoved it away. Once a fool, always a fool!

A minute later, the young man was gone and she was settling into the seat beside him. Her voice was soft, almost fearful, as she unfastened her helmet. "Thank you, Bruce. I know you didn't want me, but . . ."

"Did they tell you just what you were getting into? All of it?" At her nod, he dropped his eyes from her face. There was little more to say. "Then you're the biggest damn fool in the Solar System."

She smiled faintly as the bus began moving out again toward the spaceport. Mars began flashing by the window, and he concentrated on that. What would it be like from now on? Would the men here use the opportunity they had been given again—or would they let it all become the old, familiar mess that men so often made of their affairs? And would he ever know the outcome?

"I can't help being a fool," she said quietly, as if she'd been thinking it over. Then she shoved a little package into his hand. "Grandfather sent you this."

He looked down to see a brand-new deck of reader cards, marked exactly as the ones he had first used on Mars. It figured. He was going as he'd come, with a hundred credits, a yellow ticket and a deck of phoney cards. Full circle!

She stirred beside him, breaking the circle.

He reached out for one of her hands, and she tightened her fingers quickly, moving closer to him. They sat quietly, holding hands until the bus stopped beside the rocket that was to take them into whatever lay ahead.